THE CORNER SHOP IN COCKLEBERRY BAY

NICOLA MAY

Lightning Books

Published by
Lightning Books Ltd
Imprint of EyeStorm Media
312 Uxbridge Road
Rickmansworth
Hertfordshire
WD3 8YL

www.lightning-books.com

First published in the UK in 2018 by Nowell Publishing
This edition 2019
Copyright © Nicola May 2018
Cover design by Ifan Bates
Cover illustration by John Meech

British Library Cataloguing in Publication Data
A catalogue record for this book is available from the British Library

Printed and bound in Great Britain by Clays Ltd, Elcograf S.p.A.

ISBN 9780956832351

This edition published in collaboration with Canelo Digital Publishing Limited

For women everywhere:
Who can, who will, and will keep on doing so…

Out of suffering have emerged
the strongest souls;
the most massive characters
are seared with scars
Kahlil Gibran

4

PROLOGUE

'Are you sure you've got the right person?'

Rosa took off her bright blue woolly hat and scratched the back of her head, causing her dark brown curls to become even more unruly.

The tall, pinched-faced solicitor nodded. 'Yes, of course we have. Evans, Donald and Simpson do not make mistakes. You, Miss Larkin, are now the official owner of the Corner Shop in Cockleberry Bay.'

He handed the bewildered twenty-five-year-old a battered leather briefcase and pointed to a small combination padlock on its brass clasp.

'Here. The will stated that you – and only you – can open this, using your date of birth.'

'This is all very strange,' Rosa said. 'And where exactly is this Cockleberry Bay?'

'Devon, dear, Devon.' The solicitor looked under his rimless glasses. 'I take it you know where that is?'

'I may have a cockney accent, Mr Donald, but I'm not stupid.'

'Well, open it then.' The solicitor was shifting from foot to foot in anticipation. He confided, 'We've been wanting to know what's in there for days.'

Showing no emotion, Rosa gazed at him with her striking green eyes and asked coolly: 'Is there anything else I need?'

'Er, no – but are you not going to…?'

'I need to get to work.' Rosa put her hat and scarf back on, zipped up her fur-lined bomber jacket and headed for the door. 'Thank you so much for your help.'

And she was gone.

'Rude!'

The solicitor peered crossly out of the window of the offices in Staple Inn and watched as the young woman, the briefcase in her arms, strode across the frosty cobbled courtyard and out into the bustle of London's ancient legal quarter.

CHAPTER ONE

'You're late again, Rosa. This is a discount store, not a charity shop.'

'Oh, turn that frown upside down, Mr Brown. I'm here now, aren't I?'

But there wasn't even a glint of the usual smile from her now reddening supervisor.

'I'm going to have to let you go, Rosa. I need committed staff, and to be honest, I don't think you know what that word means. You've had all your warnings. I will speak to Head Office, and they will settle your final pay.'

Rosa sighed. 'Really?' When Mr Brown said nothing, she picked up the briefcase from the floor and added: 'Whilst you're at it, maybe you could tell them I've been wanting to stick this shitty, unfulfilling job right up their pound-coin-shaped backsides for weeks anyway.'

Rosa's elderly neighbour was putting a holly wreath on her front door when she arrived at home, mid-morning.

'You're back early, dearie.'

Rosa murmured under her breath, 'And Ethel Beanacre wins the award for the Nosiest Neighbour of the Year.'

'What was that, love?'

'Nothing, Ethel, just talking to myself.'

The sight of the worn briefcase secured further interest.

'Robbed a bank, have you?' Ethel's awful cackle reminded Rosa of Catherine Tate's 'Gran' character.

Rosa scrabbled for her key. 'Don't tell anyone, will you.' She put a finger to her lips and winked.

'So, are you going back to work later?' The old lady pursed her lips. 'Can't be doing with that dog of yours barking until you come back at lunchtime.'

Ignoring her, Rosa shut the front door, put her back against it and slid down to the floor. An excitable mini-dachshund charged up to greet her and began licking her face with gusto.

'It's not a good day, Hot Dog,' Rosa told him. 'Mamma's got the sack again.' She stroked his smooth brown coat. 'However, all is not lost, since I am now apparently the owner of a shop somewhere miles away. What do you think of that, eh?'

'What are you on about?'

'God, Josh, you made me jump! What are you doing here?'

'Well, I do live here.' He yawned. 'Needed a lie-in. Big Christmas drinks last night – you know what us rugby boys are like.' He smiled. 'No rent again this month then, I take it? It's a good job I like you.'

Josh, six years older than Rosa, was rather handsome in a big bear way. He was tall, broad, and this morning, sporting sexy stubble. With his job in the City, she was sure he earned enough not to need a lodger. Rosa reckoned he just liked having the company. She knew his terraced house in a street off the Whitechapel Road in the East End, once a poor area but now a very desirable neighbourhood, must have cost him a pretty penny – and her £400 per month rent was very cheap for London.

Josh took her arm and pulled her up from the floor in one easy movement. 'Come on, let's have a cuppa, and you can tell me what's happened this time.'

Hot started barking again.

'Shut up!' the two of them shouted in unison and walked through the dining room into the kitchen.

Sitting at the table with steaming mugs of tea, they gazed at the unopened case, which stared back at them like some unwanted guest.

'So, you must have some idea who left it to you?' Josh said eventually.

'What – little old Rosa Larkin, with no family to mention? Being brought up in children's and foster homes doesn't give me a lot to go on, really, does it?'

'Sorry, Rosa. I didn't mean…'

'Don't be silly, Josh, it's fine. Even the solicitor doesn't seem to know who's behind this. It's all very odd. The briefcase was simply delivered to his office with a letter containing my details and enough cash to pay their fee for contacting me. Goodness knows how that mystery person tracked me down, being as I am of no fixed abode and most frequently jobless. And I haven't done anything to deserve a legacy like this. In fact, I'm surprised I haven't been struck down already for stealing Hot.'

'But he was being beaten outside the shop! You did exactly the right thing.' Josh lifted the tiny sausage dog onto his lap. 'Poor little fella. I can just imagine you stuffing him in your rucksack and then running like the wind.' He laughed. 'You'd be great at scoring a try. Maybe you should join our team – we could do with someone like you.' He put another sugar in his tea and groaned. 'God, I feel rough, but come on, let's open this case. It's not like you to be holding back.'

'For some reason I'm a bit scared.' Alert to her change of

9

mood, Hot looked at Rosa and gave a little whine.

Josh put his hand on hers. 'Don't be. We're here with you. Now, go on.'

'Whoever left it to me knew my date of birth – that's so weird.' Rosa took a deep breath and turned the rusty dials of the combination lock.

Inside the case were three brown envelopes. Rosa began to rip them open.

The first contained the deeds to the said property in Cockleberry Bay, plus a variety of paperwork to do with the services, council tax, et cetera.

Josh took them from her. 'Here we go. The deeds should give the name of who the registered owner is…mystery solved. Oh.'

'What's wrong?'

'It's blank – the information we want is blank. God, this is so strange and I'm not sure that it's legal, but let's go with it for now. The bills are in the name of a Ned Myers though. Hmm… He could have just been renting it though. Does that name ring any bells?'

Rosa shook her head.

Josh took a slurp of tea. 'Anyway, carry on.'

The second envelope contained a set of keys on a starfish keyring. There was also a note written in a shaky hand.

Dear Rosa

Don't question this gift, for your soul and fortune it will lift.

Allow your angels to guide, then peace will be by your side.

Rub your keyring if unsure; the energy it holds is free and pure.

I will be by your side, however high the tide.

'What a load of bloody crap!' she exclaimed.

'I think it's beautiful, Rosa.'

'Oh Josh, you are such a wuss sometimes.'

'Thanks. There's gratitude for you.'

'Look, to whoever was thinking of me as they shuffled off this mortal coil, I guess I have to be grateful. This place might be a shack though, so let's not get too excited. It could also be some bloody awful joke – who knows? It all seems a bit too good to be true.'

'But it's bricks and mortar, Rosa – you have been given your very own property. It really is amazing.'

'I will probably just sell it anyway. What do I want a shop for? And why would someone want to leave me something good, anyway?'

'I don't understand you sometimes, I really don't. Here, open the last one. It might give us more of a clue.' Josh handed her the last bulky envelope.

'Oh my God – look!' Rosa started tipping bundles of notes out onto the table while Hot barked in excitement. 'I can buy those boots I've wanted for ages now.' When another letter in shaky handwriting flew out, she said, 'Oh, not more sentimental tosh. You read it, Josh. I'm going to start counting.'

'You don't need to. It says it all here.' Josh began to read out loud.

Dear Rosa

This sum of £2,000 will allow you to move down to Devon and help get you started.

One proviso of my gift to you is that you must NEVER sell the Corner Shop in Cockleberry Bay. When you feel the time is right, it can only be passed on to someone you feel really deserves it, and only then.

11

'Oh, that's scuppered that plan then. But how would they know if I sold it anyway?'

As she spoke, the TV in the kitchen suddenly came on. Hot opened one eye, whimpered, then snuggled back into Josh's lap.

'Did you just sit on the remote, Josh?' Rosa said nervously.

'No, it's on the fridge. Maybe "they" are by your side eh, Rosa?'

'Don't you start. It's hard enough being in the real world, so why come back as a ghost? It was probably just an electricity surge.' She counted out £500 from the cash and handed it to Josh. 'Here's this month's rent – and I'm sure I've stolen more than a hundred quid's-worth of food out of the fridge before now.'

Josh put it straight back in the envelope. 'Keep it, with my best wishes. I'm so happy for you, Rosa. However, this doesn't take away the fact that you're going to be leaving me now, does it?'

'You'll manage,' Rosa grinned.

'I'll bloody miss you, you crazy bitch.'

'You'll miss the best drunken BJs you've ever had, you mean.'

'And that.' It was his turn to grin. 'Do you want me to come with you to check everything's legit? The place may not even have running water. And you'll need to find somewhere to live.'

'No, I need to do this on my own,' she told him. 'You've helped me enough, and I'll have Hot to keep me company, of course.'

'But surely you'll wait until after Christmas to go, won't you?'

'No, I hate Christmas. You'll be with your parents anyway and it will take my mind off the usual shit. I'll pack some things and leave tomorrow. I take it trains go down as far as Devon?'

Josh laughed. 'You're amazing.'

'I wish to be.' Rosa smiled.

Josh straightened his tie. 'Look, I'd better get to work. I'll pick

12

up a take-out on the way home and we can look at your route down later.'

'Best be fish and chips, I reckon, seeing as I'm moving to the seaside.'

CHAPTER TWO

Rosa felt butterflies in her stomach as the train pulled into Cockleberry Bay station. Hot had slept nearly the whole way but was now agitated and whining.

She climbed down from the train as quickly as she could with a heavy suitcase and black bin bag in tow, and almost felt the relief herself as the dachshund immediately cocked his tiny leg on the edge of a coffee-seller's stall.

'Oi.' The ginger-bearded bloke manning it was not happy. Looking at him, Rosa likened him to a skinny Viking.

'Oh my God, I'm so sorry,' she said immediately. 'I should have got out at Exeter but wasn't sure if we'd have time to get back on again. Let me buy a bottle of water and I'll wash it down.'

The man took in the dishevelled stranger in front of him. Brown curls stuck out from beneath her bright blue bobble hat, neatly framing her small round face. Well-fitted dark jeans met black Nike trainers which had seen better days. She had a tiny scar on her left cheek which resembled a miniature bolt of lightning. And despite not wearing a scrap of make-up, she was naturally very pretty, he decided.

He smiled. 'Travelled far, then?'

'Yes, from London.'

'Visiting family for Christmas, that it?'

Blimey, Rosa thought. She'd rather hoped she could enjoy the anonymity that a new town might offer.

'Yes – that's right. Now I really must be going. Where is the taxi rank, please?'

The bearded man laughed, revealing a missing tooth. 'Taxi rank? I can give you a number for Ralph Weeks. He lives in the Bay and does the driving around here. But I'm not sure how free he will be, as Wednesday is his busy day – on account of there's no bus running to Ulchester. I'm Seb, by the way.' He held out a gloved hand.

'I'm Rosa, and this is Hot.'

Seb properly belly-laughed. 'Hot…Hot Dog? That is the funniest name for a dog I think I have ever heard.'

'Well, he is a sausage and I did steal him, so he's hot.'

'That makes it even funnier. Here, let me ring Ralph for you, he's already in my phone. You say you stole Hot?'

'Long story, but don't you be phoning the police on me. Or are there none of those in the Bay either?'

'You're learning fast, Rosa.' He held the phone to his ear. 'No answer. Look, I'm freezing and was about to finish up anyway. Maybe I can give you a lift?'

It was already four o' clock and dark, and feeling cold and tired herself, she agreed, saying, 'If you can just drop us at the Ship Inn, that would be lovely.'

With passengers and luggage safely on board, Seb shouted over the obviously blown exhaust of his old white van: 'Not a limo, I'm afraid, but it gets me from A to B.'

With Rosa supporting his little body, Hot craned out into the dark to see what was going on.

'An absence of streetlights here too then?'

15

Seb laughed. 'Yep, a torch is definitely your friend down here. I know every broken paving slab and bump in the road now. Although the council do make the effort with a few Christmas lights, which we'll get to in a minute.'

Rosa tried to locate the Corner Shop as they made their way down a narrow street, but the address was in her bag and she didn't want to make it obvious to Seb that she was looking out for anything. It was her business and she wanted to keep it that way – for the time being anyway.

Turning into another narrow street, she perked up as she saw quirky gift shops, a bakery and a butcher's shop, all decorated beautifully for the festive period. As all she had ever known was the hustle and bustle of city life, it was almost like going back in time to her. She noticed a couple swinging their child by his arms and then bundling into one of the cafés displaying an impressive array of cakes in the half-steamed-up window.

She had never really known normal family life as such. Her birth mum had been an alcoholic and there wasn't a father named on Rosa's birth certificate. The story was that at six months, despite every effort her mum had made to look after her, social services had still taken her away.

And then there were Maureen and Len who, after having no luck bearing children themselves, had fostered her with a view to adoption. Tragically, Maureen was diagnosed with terminal cancer when Rosa was just six years old and Len was unable to cope with a young child and a dying wife. Then began an unstable journey of children's homes and foster carers. There were a couple of 'almost' adoptions along the way, but with Rosa being such a troubled child, nobody had been willing to take her on permanently.

Rosa sighed and nursed Hot into her lap. Being honest, her dysfunctional, blow job (only when drunk) relationship with

Josh had been the nearest feeling to happiness that she had ever felt – and now she had given that up too.

But giving up was a common occurrence for Rosa. She didn't tolerate fools.

Seb looked over to her. 'That was a big sigh. We are nearly there – just around this corner and the Ship will be in front of us.' He slowed down and changed gear, waiting for a motorbike to roar past.

It was then Rosa noticed it. The shop. Lit by the van's headlights, she saw that it had an interesting curved frontage. Turquoise paint was peeling from the front door, where a battered-looking CLOSED sign still hung. In faded letters, above the beautiful curved windows, were the words The Corner Shop. There seemed to be a vacant flat above the shop. Seeing this, Rosa felt a surge of excitement. If accommodation was part of the package, then suddenly the whole thing didn't seem such a bad idea.

'What a shame,' she said softly to herself.

'The Corner Shop, you mean?' Seb asked.

'Yes.'

'It's been shut for about five years now. Used to be a little goldmine.'

'What did it sell?'

'Everything and anything. It was a real favourite with locals and tourists alike. Bit of a mystery actually, as old Mr Myers who ran it literally worked until he couldn't manage the steep steps up to the flat any more.'

'Aw, bless him, but why a mystery?'

'Oh, just that none of us can understand why it hasn't gone up for sale.'

'Did he not have family?'

'Not that he ever mentioned. He died at the age of ninety-eight, in the nursing home up the hill, surrounded by the many friends he had made here.'

'Ah, right.'

'Here we are then. The Ship Inn, me lady.'

'Thanks so much, Seb. Can I give you some money for petrol?' Rosa was suddenly conscious of the wads of cash in her bag and remembered sensible Josh saying she should open a new bank account with it as soon as she could.

'Nah, don't be silly. Buy me a drink in here one night.' He smiled. 'Now you and Hot Dog get settled – and if I don't see you, although I'm sure I will down here, have a lovely break and Happy Christmas to the both of you.' He tickled the tiny dachshund behind his ears then got out to help Rosa down from the passenger seat before lifting her luggage from the rear.

CHAPTER THREE

Rosa was feeding Hot in her room at the Ship when Josh phoned.

'Just checking you made it down to Devon all right.'

'Yes, we got here safe and sound. The shop is in disrepair by the look of it though. I learned that it's been empty for five years and I hate to say it, but I think a few of the locals are going to be a little perturbed by a young upstart from the Smoke taking it on.'

'So, you've been to see it already, have you?'

'Nope, just drove past it on the way here. It is really quaint with the most beautiful bay windows.'

'So, reckon you're up for the challenge then?'

'Well, I don't have much choice, do I? I can't let my mystery benefactor down. Although I'm scared, Josh. I know nothing about running a business.'

'Don't worry. Go in and take a proper look tomorrow and see what you think. I can drive down with my mate Carlton, if you like. He's renovated loads of shops. It may just need a good clean and touch-up.'

'OK, thank you. My room's cosy here at the pub though and I'm glad I've booked it for a few nights. I'm overlooking the bay. Oh Josh, I've only seen it in the dark but it really is quite beautiful with the twinkly Christmas lights reflecting onto the sea. I cannot wait until morning so Hot and I can go and explore. But listen, the main thing is – guess what? There's a flat above the shop.'

'Oh Rosa, what a bonus! How amazing is that?'

'Well, let's see what state it's in, shall we? It belonged to an old man in his nineties and he lived in it for years.'

'Do you think it was him who left it to you then?'

'I don't even want to think about that. I am here now and need to see what's going on.' At that moment, the dachshund stood up on the bed and started slapping her face with his tongue. 'Eeek,' Rosa said, trying not to laugh. 'Hot says hi, by the way.'

'Hi, back.' Josh paused, then added: 'It's bloody lonely without you two.'

'You'll be relishing the freedom soon – and like you say, you can pop down anytime you like. I don't know how big the flat is yet. I will give you a call tomorrow night.'

'OK. Sleep well and just be positive when you go in there tomorrow. I think this is good for you – a fresh new start.'

'I love London though, Josh.'

'I know you do, Rosa, but remember – how many times have you said you wanted to be your own boss?'

'Be careful what you wish for and all that, eh?' Rosa laughed. 'Hot and I will be just fine. I'm trying to make sure he doesn't bark the pub down tonight, but bless him, he seems as knackered as I am. Right – bath and bed. Night, night.'

'Goodnight, madam.'

CHAPTER FOUR

Rosa was awoken from a deep sleep by a knock on the door.

'Morning, dear. Just checking if you would like breakfast? We finish serving in twenty.'

'Oh yes, please.' Rosa realised that in all the excitement of her arrival at the pub last night, she had not had any dinner and was starving. 'Is it OK for my dog to come down to the dining area with me?'

'Of course. I cannot wait to see the little fella, to be honest. I've got some pigs' ears on the bar with his name on.'

Rosa smiled. Everyone did seem super-friendly down here. She would make the most of it before they realised she was now the new owner of their beloved Corner Shop.

Sheila Hannafore had what Rosa could only describe as bright white hair, in a sort of old-fashioned brushed-out perm style. She must have been in her mid-sixties but looked really good for her age. Her ruddy cheeks suited her pleasant face and she had the most perfect teeth Rosa thought she had ever seen.

'Sheila, isn't it? Sorry, I'm terrible with names.'

'Yes, that's me. Owner and manager of the Ship Inn for the past thirty years. Live and breathe it, my love, I do.'

'You run it on your own, do you?'

'Sadly, yes. Brian, my late husband, passed just last year.'

'I'm so sorry.'

'Don't be, he was a miserable old bugger and I had a face-lift and my teeth done with one of his insurances, which helped numb the pain slightly.'

'I almost commented on your teeth, they are amazingly bright.'

'Yes, the sailors say we don't need a lighthouse any more when I start flashing me gnashers.'

'That's funny.'

'Right – full English, is it, girl? Or are you one of those funny Southerners who's frightened of a bit of wheat or meat?'

'As it comes, please.'

'Good, good. I'll bring some water – and help yourself to an ear for your dog. Although in this place it's more hair of the dog that's required. I've only gone and forgotten his name now.'

'Hot.'

'No, not today, love. It's minus one out there.'

'No, that's my dog's name – Hot.'

'Well, I never. You've thrown me a little over the edge with that one.'

Rosa laughed. She liked the Devon accent. On first impression, she liked Sheila Hannafore.

'I'll just take him out for a quick walk whilst you're cooking,' she said.

'You do what you need to do, my lovely. I'll be back out in a jiffy.'

With Hot walked and happy and now under the table chewing on his pig's ear, Rosa felt her tummy rumble loudly. Just in time, Sheila appeared from behind the bar with a huge plate of food.

'Now that's what I call a feast.' Rosa picked up her knife and fork. 'Thank you so much.'

'Enjoy, my love – and can I ask what brings you to these parts?'

'Er…just visiting family.' Rosa dipped a sausage into the bright yellow yolk of one of her eggs.

'Who be that then? I've never seen you down these parts before.'

'Sheila – it's OK if I call you Sheila, is it?'

'Of course, dear.'

'I just needed time out from London. It gets mad there and I heard how lovely Devon was, and well…I'm here now.'

'So you're not spending Christmas with your folks then?'

'No. We're not very close.'

'Aw, that's a shame. My boys never fail to visit. The youngest, he'll drive down later. Shame his excuse for a girlfriend will follow, but you can't tell 'em what to do at your age, can you? My oldest is coming with Martha, that's his wife, and of course all the grandkids, Christmas morning. They just live around the corner, see. Three of the little darlings I've got, and I love 'em to the horizon and back.'

'That's nice.'

'Well, I hope so. They'll have to muck in a bit, it's the hub of activity in here over Christmas. I've got turkeys stuffed out back, ready for the deluge.'

'So, you open Christmas Day, do you?'

'Oh, it's three hundred and sixty-six days a year here, love. I always add on a day for the number of lock-ins we have.'

'Sounds like my kind of place,' Rosa told her.

'Well, you're booked in until Christmas Eve – why don't you stay a couple of days longer? It's one big happy family here.'

'I may well just do that. I'll let you know later, if that's OK?'

'Course it is. I always keep one room spare for waifs and strays. You'll be sharing the bathroom with my lot, but they are

23

all completely house-trained. Right, I'd better get on. I've got cakes to ice. Enjoy your time here, my love.'

Rosa let out a huge burp as she walked up the steep stairs back to her room.

'Better out than in, I always say.'

'Pardon me.' Rosa put her hand to her mouth. 'Sorry, I didn't know anyone else was up here.'

The girl at the top of the landing carried on, 'I'm Titch Whittaker. Five foot nothing with tits to die for, according to Seb Watkins.'

'Ah, right.' Rosa grinned.

'Just been cleaning your room, whilst you scoffed. Nice bomber jacket you have hanging up there.'

'Er…thanks.' Titch must be in her early twenties, Rosa thought.

'Well, enjoy your day – Rose, isn't it?'

'Rosa, and thanks, I will do.'

'Isn't Rosa a gypsy's name?'

'Um, I'm not sure.'

'And that raven hair of yours – it's really lovely. You're like a wild animal, Rosa.' With furniture polish in hand, Titch disappeared back down the stairs.

Rosa opened her case and double-checked how much money she had left. Bless Josh for not taking the £500 rent she owed. He really was quite a special person. With the £100 train fare taken out and if she now paid for five nights here at £60 per night, that made £400: she still had around £1,600 left. A fortune to her, in cold hard cash. It wouldn't hurt to go and look around the shops and have a little spend-up later, she thought, but her first visit must be to the Corner Shop.

She dug out the set of keys on the starfish keyring that had

24

been in the battered case, put Hot on his lead, carried him downstairs and headed out.

Despite it being cold, the air was fresh, and Rosa sighed happily as she took in the beautiful scenery all around her. The pub was situated on the sea front, so she just had to walk down a few steps and was right on the beach. Once off the lead, Hot barked and ran around crazily. He had never felt sand on his paws before and had only ever dipped them in water in a fountain at Battersea Park. Rosa had also never seen a beach quite like it, with rock pools and cliffs to each side, leading up to fields with a well-trodden cliff path that seemed to go on forever.

The sea was still and sending up little wafts of steam in places where it hit the cold air. She threw a piece of driftwood to Hot, then walked down to the edge of the water, wondering at the lacy, rippling effect as it touched the shoreline. Holidays had never really been on the agenda at the children's home; they did go out on day trips now and then, and when they did go on what they called a holiday, they were just shipped down to an equivalent home in Wiltshire, where it was more fields and flowers than sea and sand.

Rosa imagined how glorious it would be here in the summer, but also how busy – which would be good if you were running a business here. Today though, she quite liked the fact that it was just her and one other dog walker braving the winter chill.

She looked back at the Ship Inn. It was an old, white-painted building, weathered by the elements, and with an old-fashioned sailing boat depicted on the sign, and she wondered what stories it could tell. The other dog walker – a tall, skinny figure – was striding towards her and as he got closer she could make out the beard and ponytail of Seb Watkins.

'All right, Rosa? How's it going?'

Rosa had a chance to see his face properly in the daylight. She had trouble guessing his age, as despite having a youthful-looking face, the wrinkles around his eyes were quite evident. Early thirties maybe, she thought. She wondered what he'd look like without a beard. She didn't mind gingers one little bit, but hated beards. They reminded her of a male carer at the children's home, whose greedy eyes for the teenage girls, including herself, had made her feel sick.

'Fine, thanks. You didn't mention you had a dog.' The black Labrador was now sniffing around Hot before they started playing together.

'I don't mention a lot of things,' Seb told her, and smiled.

'What's his name?'

'Jet. Anyway, bet you're stuffed to the gills with a Ship's breakfast?'

'Bloody lovely it was too.'

'Yes, Sheila certainly knows how to keep everyone's stomach happy, at least. So, what are you up to today?'

'Oh, this and that. Going to explore a bit more, I think. Look round the shops, you know.' Fingering the keys in her pocket, she thought she might have to come clean about the shop far sooner than she wanted to. It certainly wasn't like London down here; it would be nigh-on impossible to keep herself to herself.

Hot came running up to her with an old plastic bottle that had been washed up on the shore and dropped it at her feet.

Seb shook his head. 'Ruddy plastic bottles.' He leant down to pick it up. 'We have one planet – people need to realise that.'

'You not working today, Seb?'

'Yep, but not till a bit later. There aren't that many passengers on the earlier trains this time of year, so it's not worth my while.'

Hot barked his annoyance at Seb for confiscating his new toy. Rosa hastily clicked on his lead.

'Well, have a good day,' she said.

'You too. I'll see you around.'

It was a steep walk back up to the shops from the beach and Rosa felt quite puffed when she reached the top. The nearest she did to exercise back in London was just walking to work or to the many bars she used to frequent. And, of course, walking Hot, but with his little legs he was easily pleased with a quick tramp around the block.

It was lovely to smell coffee and baking coming from the various eateries. In fact, it was lovely to feel free. No boring job to have to go to. No rush-hour Underground to negotiate. In fact, she was beginning to realise just how good it felt, simply to have some time. Time to herself. Time to be free.

She looked back down to the bay. Seagulls were now swooping around the front. She would certainly have to get used to the noise of their cries, which were nearly as annoying as Hot in one of his barking episodes.

In trepidation, she arrived at the front of the shop. Luckily it was opposite a bank, which hadn't opened yet, so there were no immediate voyeurs. Turning the key in the old lock, Rosa felt a rush of excitement. Whatever lay waiting for her behind the blue door, the old Corner Shop was, as Josh had said, her very own bricks and mortar. Her very first home. A gift. It was unbelievable really, and she was still unsure if it wasn't all a big mistake. She had never been given anything before – and why her, anyway?

She jumped as a cobweb fell from the door frame. Brushing it from her face, she quickly shut the door behind her, Hot close on her heels. She remembered watching on TV an episode of *Location, Location, Location* where a blind lady had said that her guide dog would know if a house was right for her, so she was going to make sure she watched how Hot reacted.

She pressed the light switch – nothing. But then of course there wouldn't be; the shop had been empty for five years. She shivered with cold. There was a radiator in the corner, so at least when everything was up and running, she would have heat. The plentiful, once-white shelves were thick with dust. Smiling to herself, she lifted a dirty blue teddy bear and an old copper kettle, which sat next to a damp pink scarf and an alarm clock; remnants of the eclectic stock that old Mr Myers had apparently been so successful at selling.

Gingerly lifting a faded green blanket, she revealed an archaic cash register – an exact replica of one she used to love playing with as a child in the Home; when you pressed the keys, the amount pinged up in a glass section.

The whole place smelt damp and musty, but she was relieved that the ceilings and walls appeared to be intact, and short of giving the place a massive scrub and repaint it wasn't in that bad shape at all. Behind the counter was an archway which led to a small kitchen area and toilet, and a flight of stairs up to the flat above. Further on from that, a small storeroom opened onto a cute little courtyard containing an ornate round metal table and two chairs. A tattered parasol leant against a set of metal spiral stairs, presumably going up to the flat above.

Hot seemed very content in his sniffing mission and hadn't barked once, so that was a good sign. Shivering, Rosa lifted him into her arms. 'Come on, boy, let's check our new home out.' They went back inside, and she closed and locked the back door with the key on the starfish keyring.

As she climbed the stairs, she realised why, as an old man, Mr Myers had had to admit defeat. They were the steepest and narrowest steps Rosa had ever been faced with.

'I might have to install a doggy lift for you on these,' she puffed into the dachshund's ears and for a second inhaled his comforting doggie smell.

At the top of the stairs was a small landing, to the left of which was a tiny, but functioning kitchen. An old whistling kettle sat on the hob of a small white oven and amongst the grubby white tiles were several with images of starfishes. The units had seen better days, but nothing that a good clean wouldn't sort out.

Rosa opened the fridge and baulked slightly at the mould that greeted her. She left the door open, vowing to give the interior a going-over with some bleach. There was space for a washing machine, but that was no big deal anyway, as she had spotted a launderette in one of the narrow streets when she was in the taxi the other night. Further along to her right was the bathroom.

'Avocado – nice,' she said aloud and giggled, picturing house-proud Josh's face when he saw the dated suite. A worn-looking plastic shower hose was still in situ on the double taps. The same starfish tiles were dotted around, and Rosa loved the old showbiz dressing-room-style mirror that had bulbs all around the outside.

There was one decent-sized bedroom that housed an old iron-framed bedstead without a mattress and a large mahogany wardrobe that needed a good polish. Net curtains and musty-smelling thick navy curtains hung against original sash windows. She checked the view: the window looked over the street, which was now starting to fill with early-morning shoppers.

Further along, another small room contained a beautiful, green leather-topped desk. The walls were a horrible mustard yellow, the curtains dark brown.

Hot started to whine as he sniffed around the desk.

'Let me just check the lounge, little one, and I'll take you down for a wee.'

But she didn't need to take him downstairs for that. Open-mouthed and clutching both sides of her face with joy, Rosa couldn't believe what was now before her eyes. Yes, the long sitting room's cream paint was tired and there were cobwebs hanging from the ceiling, but the double doors at the end of it, now letting in streams of winter sunshine, opened onto a small roof-terrace area that offered beautiful views towards the bay and surrounding countryside. What's more, the spiral staircase she had noticed in the rear patio led up to this balcony.

'Wow, just wow.' Rosa rarely cried, but right now she could feel tears pricking the back of her eyes. She had wondered what the odd-shaped key on the keyring was for – and here was the answer.

Hot barked loudly as he scampered out to cock a tiny ankle against an old terracotta pot. Rosa stepped out to take in all that was around her. Lifting her head to the sky, she breathed: 'Thank you. Whoever you are, thank you so much.'

A white feather drifted down in front of her…

The magical moment was broken when Hot spotted a seagull on the edge of the metal railing that surrounded the terrace and started to bark again.

'Get in, Hot. Stop it now.'

The last thing Rosa wanted to do was to attract attention. Shooing him back inside and closing the French doors behind her, she phoned Josh and left him a message.

'Oh my God, Josh, you have to see it. The lounge has a roof terrace that looks over the sea. And the shop's got one of those old press cash-tills. There's lots of work to do, but I think it's probably just cosmetic, painting and so on – so it's all manageable. There is no electricity though and I haven't tried the water yet. Maybe you can call me later as I'm not sure what I have to do about all that.'

Coming back to reality, Rosa shivered again. Shame it was bloody winter. She'd have to get the heating organised before she started cleaning everything as it would be too cold to spend long in here without getting hypothermia. She went to get the keys out of the balcony door. Funny, she was sure she had left them in the lock. Suddenly Hot appeared with the starfish key ring in his mouth.

'Ah, there they are, I must have dropped them in all the excitement. Right, come on, Mamma needs a coffee and then we can try to sort out getting some light and heat on the matter.'

Coffee, Tea or Sea was a quaint little coffee shop. It had free internet too, which was always a bonus. There were shelves all around adorned with seaside-themed knick-knacks, plus all kinds of books headed with a sign that said *Read me, Replace me, Replenish Me*.

Rosa loved the fact that dogs seemed welcome everywhere down here. Restrictions had always annoyed her – and what were a few pet hairs between friends anyway?

She secured Hot's lead under the table leg in the corner and went up to the counter where there was a lit-up reindeer sporting a Christmas hat and a ceramic burlesque dancer money box, holding a sign that said *Nice Tips*.

'Oh hi, Rosa.'

'Blimey, you get about.'

Titch smiled. Her blonde cropped haircut suited her pixie features, and noticing her oversized boobs squeezed into a tight jumper, Rosa could understand Seb's un-PC comment about her now.

'That's what they all say,' she winked. 'You have to take what work you can get around here, and I'm not shy of it. Now, what can I get you?'

'Just a normal coffee, please.'

'A normal coffee? That's lucky because we don't do all that fancy London shite in here. I mean, a flat white – why don't people just ask for a white coffee? And as for a skinny lah-di-dah, what's all that about? Full-fat milk all the way, I say. It's much better for you anyway. Want some water for Hot?'

'I hear you – and yes, please, that would be lovely.'

'You're staying down over Christmas now, aren't you?'

'Er…yes, probably. Sheila says there's room.'

'Do it, live a little – and Christmas Day with the Hannafores will be a hoot. Her youngest son's a bit of all right too. He's got a girlfriend now though, which is a shame. Here you go.' She handed Rosa her coffee. 'That'll be two pounds, please, and I'll bring the dog bowl over.'

Two pounds for a coffee wasn't bad, compared to London prices. Living here was becoming more appealing by the minute.

As Rosa was taking her jacket off, Josh called.

'Sorry I missed you,' he said. 'I was in a meeting.'

Rosa was comforted by Josh's familiar tone. 'How dull.'

'I know, but we can't all be beneficiaries of estates by the sea, now can we? So go on – tell me. You were gabbling away so excitedly in your message that I didn't get the chance to take it all in.'

Making sure she spoke quietly enough so that Titch couldn't hear, Rosa had great delight in relaying what she had discovered.

'It has made me realise though, that I haven't got a bloody clue when it comes to normal domesticity. The only bill I've ever had to pay in my life is my phone bill. I've always lived in rented accommodation before, so I've handed over the rent and never had to think further than that.'

'OK, let me help you. So, there's no electric, gas or water?'

'Hmm. I didn't actually check the water.'

'In the circumstances, I doubt if it's on. Did the toilet flush?'

'I haven't used it yet.'

'OK. Now – remember the first envelope you opened?'

'The boring one with all the paperwork in?'

Josh smiled to himself in his office in the City. 'Yes, that's the one,' he said. 'Well, there were bills in there. For example, the ones for gas may say British Gas. The ones for electricity will also be obvious. What you need to do is contact all the suppliers – there will be telephone numbers on the letters – and let them know you've moved in, so they can set an account up in your name. You may need to prove that it is a new ownership, but let's worry about that when we come to it. The electricity may just be turned off at the meter so it's worth checking that first. The water is probably just turned off at the stopcock, so check there. The system may also have been drained down, so it will need refilling.'

'Stopcock? Ha ha. I've used that expression before but nothing to do with water. How will I know where that is?'

'OK, you will need a plumber for that. I'd do it today if I were you though, as it's so near to Christmas when everything closes down for two weeks. The plumber can probably advise you on the electricity meter too.'

'OK, thanks for that. It doesn't sound so hard, after all, and once I've got all that up and running, I can start cleaning and then move in.' She sighed with pleasure.

'Maybe stay at the pub in some comfort and you can get cracking between Christmas and New Year then. I was going to say I can pop down from my parents' house for a couple of days too – if you want me to, that is?'

'That would be amazing, Josh, if you're sure?'

'Course I'm sure. It will be good to see Hot – and you, of course.'

'Ha ha, you're so funny.'

Josh laughed. 'I just need to be back for the New Year's Eve bash at the rugby club. Right, I'd better get on.'

'OK, see you – and thanks again, Josh, you're a star.'

CHAPTER FIVE

All the utilities companies had been amazingly helpful. Despite the closeness of Christmas, they had promised to deal with everything straightaway. Finding a plumber had been more difficult. Rosa had looked for a local firm online, but had come up with a blank. So, taking the risk that any inquiry would get the gossip valve opened, she had gone to Sheila and lied, saying that a tourist in the chip shop had been after one, and that she'd promised to get back to him and pass on the number. The landlady obliged straightaway.

Deciding to skip breakfast to avoid any further conversation with Sheila, Rosa had got up early today and, accompanied by an eager Hot, headed straight to the Corner Shop. Delighted that she now had light, Rosa rooted around and was gratified to find an old cylindrical Hoover in one of the kitchen cupboards. She was just standing on tiptoe, reaching up with the hose and happily clearing cobwebs from the ceiling, when there was a loud knock on the shop door.

For some reason she had expected the plumber to be a lot older. Luke, on the contrary, must have been only in his late twenties. His short brown hair suited his cheeky face, and his hazel eyes were accentuated by long lashes. Lashes to die for, in fact. Although Rosa never wore much make-up, when she did, it would take a good five minutes for the mascara wand to coax hers to even half the length of his. At five feet nine or so he wasn't that tall, but then again, most men were tall against her five foot three.

'Morning. Ruth, isn't it? I'm Luke – plumber Luke.'

'Hi. It's Rosa, actually.'

'Sorry, I never write anything down. And can I just say how nice it is to see a new pretty face down here.'

Rosa felt herself reddening. 'Likewise,' she managed.

'Pretty? I usually answer to chiselled, handsome or mysterious.'

Rosa laughed. 'Right, come in.'

When Luke placed a large tool-bag down on the floor of the shop, Hot immediately trotted over and stuck his nose into it.

'Hello, little fella.' The plumber leant down to stroke him gently. 'Aw. I love animals.'

'That's Hot – he's my boy. He may look cute, but he's a noisy stubborn little bugger sometimes.'

'Take after his owner, does he?'

'How rude – when you've only just met me.' Rosa laughed. 'Anyway, sorry I was not much use on the phone explaining everything, but I've not had to deal with anything like this on my own before.'

'Born with a silver spoon in your mouth, were you, Rosa?'

'With an accent like this? I don't think so.' If only he knew, she thought, but she liked Luke's up-front attitude. She couldn't be dealing with people who weren't honest and straightforward.

She braced herself for a barrage of questions about the shop, but the questions didn't come. Luke was helpful and charming and explained everything that would need to be done in order to get the heating and water safely back on track.

'I can pay you cash if that would help?' Rosa offered, hoping that it would lower the bill.

'It certainly would help – thank you.' Luke scratched his head, then said: 'Look, I'm guessing you are just starting out with this, so I'm going to charge you a hundred pounds all in. How about that?'

'Well, thanks, Luke. That's amazing.' Josh had explained that plumbers didn't come cheap, so this seemed very reasonable.

'There's just one thing,' Rosa went on slowly. 'I know this may sound a bit strange, but would you mind keeping this between you and me for now?'

'It's not strange at all. You've obviously already realised that you can't do a silent fart around here without it being in the *South Cliffs Gazette*.'

'Yes. It's taking some getting used to, after being in London. There you could walk around naked and nobody would bat an eye.'

'I would like to have seen that.'

'Hey! So, when can you start?' Rosa shivered. It was freezing cold in the shop, and to have heating and hot water would make everything so much easier.

'Like, right now? If you want me to, that is.'

'I think that's a yes, Plumber Luke.'

As Luke beavered away at getting the heating system restarted, Rosa continued to Hoover and place all rubbish out on the downstairs courtyard area. The hard work made her forget about the cold. After a while, Luke called her into the kitchen.

'Get ready for this,' he told her. He lit a long taper, and with a massive *whoosh* from the old gas boiler in the downstairs kitchen, a pilot flame ignited.

'I can't believe how quickly you've got it started,' Rosa said, thrilled.

'Amazing, aren't I?' Luke joked. 'Being honest, the radiators didn't need that much bleeding. It'll take a while to warm the place, but you and little Hot will soon be hot, hot, hot.' He grinned at his own wit, then added: 'I can stay and set the timing, if you like, plus I want to make sure that all the radiators are working properly.'

'That would be great, thank you.'

'Make sure you get the boiler serviced soon though, it's quite old. OK.' Luke checked his watch. 'Can't believe the time, already. I'm starving. Going to pop up to the Co-op to grab a sandwich – want one?'

'Yes, please. It will save me having to answer any questions from random strangers. Anything with chicken and a packet of ready salted crisps, please. Get us some drinks too – oh, and a tin of dog food for Hot – would you mind? Also, he likes a bit of cucumber for a treat, so if they've got one at this time of year… That'll be great. Here.' Rosa went to her bag, counted out the £100 and gave him an extra £20 on top. 'Lunch is on me.'

When he'd gone, she ran the kitchen tap. The water was warm and she sighed with relief. She reckoned Josh would be proud of her for sorting all this on her own. In fact, she felt a little bit proud of herself. She also began to feel a little overwhelmed. This was a lot to take on – and what if the money ran out? There were so many things still to purchase. She needed a mattress and a sofa, too. She also had to stock the place before she could open it. Plus, she had to be a grown-up now and pay bills for herself. But she guessed this was the challenge, and whoever it was who had given her the money had been confident that under two grand would do it.

Tonight, Rosa decided, turning off the hot tap and filling the kettle from the cold, she was going to go back to her room at the

Ship Inn and start thinking about what she should stock. Seb had said that old Mr Myers had sold knick-knacks, but she'd have to sell plenty of those to make a profit and pay her way.

Luke knocked lightly, and she let him back in. She liked him – in fact, she fancied him. It had been a year since she had had any kind of a relationship – if you could call it that.

Three years ago, she'd met Greg at one of her many jobs – selling insurance by phone in the evenings for a bank. She had bloody hated that too. Greg was her supervisor, five years older. He'd asked her to stay behind one night and they'd ended up shagging in the gents toilets. Not one of her proudest moments, but Rosa had never been one for holding back. Sex was easier for her than getting involved. Emotions hurt. Casual encounters didn't.

They'd had three months of foreplay really. A few nights out in the pub in Holborn near to where they were working and a few more random shags back at his shared house. The relationship had ended when he had said that her sales figures were so low he couldn't hide it any longer and would have to let her go.

Her longest relationship had been when she was sixteen: she'd met Sam Everett in the local sixth-form college. They were together two years. Rosa didn't really know what love felt like, but she knew that whatever they had had at that time felt nice. Sam had professed his undying love for her, even suggested they get married when he came back from university. But within a month of him being in Cardiff, he texted – yes, texted her – to say sorry, he had met someone else and they were finished.

This, along with her abandonment issues from childhood, hadn't boded well for her trust in men, so between Sam and meeting Greg, Rosa had had a series of one-night stands. Although they seemed like fun when you had had a skinful of vodka, these encounters didn't do much for her sense of self-worth.

Luke handed her some change, saying, 'I managed to get back without being spotted. Could see myself as the next James Bond, actually.'

'I'd love to say I'd be your Moneypenny, but my budget is pretty small to get this started.'

They both laughed, and with Hot barking at their heels, they wandered out to the back kitchen where Rosa put the dachshund's food down for him. She cut a chunk of cucumber to give him later.

'Hope you don't mind but I got us this. Felt you deserved a little moving-in gift, even if you did buy it yourself.' Like a magician, or Mr Bean producing a picnic, Luke pulled a bottle of Prosecco and some plastic glasses from his coat. He did the honours of pouring and he and Rosa did a pretend clink of their glasses.

'Welcome to Cockleberry Bay Corner Shop,' Luke said. 'May you – and not forgetting Mr Sausage – be very happy here.'

'Mr Sausage, I like that. And thanks, Luke, this is lovely.'

Two glasses down and Rosa had begun to feel very relaxed.

'Thanks again for helping me out so near to Christmas.'

'Pleasure.' He refilled Rosa's glass. 'So, I know I promised not to be nosy like all the others, but are you here to stay or are you just sorting the shop for someone else? Don't take offence, but you seem really young to have been able to afford a place like this.'

'I dare say I'll be staying here – who knows? I have to make a success of it.'

'For you or someone else?' Luke persisted. He lit a cigarette without asking and took a deep drag.

'Both.'

'What are you going to sell?'

'That's the thing – I have no idea. I have no plan. I just got given the keys, and here I am.'

'Given? See – I said you had a silver spoon in your mouth.'

'It's not like that. Somebody randomly left me it in their will and…'

'You don't have to tell me any more.'

Luke looked directly into her eyes and Rosa felt herself staring right back into them. For some reason she already trusted him.

'I want to,' she told him. 'You see, I don't even know who left this place to me. I immediately thought I could just sell it, but I'm not allowed to by the terms of the will. When the time is right, I can hand it over to somebody who deserves it. That's the deal.'

'Well, don't forget the plumber who sorted you out on Day One, now will you?'

Rosa annoyingly felt herself blushing as they carried on munching on their sandwiches.

With an empty bottle of Prosecco now in front of them, she hiccupped, 'I can't believe I'm supposed to be working today and now you've got me drunk. It's true what they say about alcohol warming you up though.'

'You've done a lot this morning, why not have a rest? You can do some more tomorrow. And I hate to say this, but the tourist trade doesn't get going until Easter down here, so you do need to think of what the locals might want too.'

'Hmm. Thanks for the advice. But come on, let's go back in the shop and see if the radiators will have warmed it up now.'

Luke wrapped the butt of his cigarette up in a sandwich container and followed Rosa and Hot.

'Maybe you can help me to decide what would be good to sell

here,' she said. 'I haven't been around all the streets yet, but is there anything lacking here?'

'My mum always says it would be nice to have somewhere she can go for fresh flowers and nice cards, if that's any help.'

'OK. I need to do some more research to appeal to the masses, I reckon, but that's worth a thought at least.'

It was lovely to feel some warmth at last. She flicked the light switch on and off three times. Light, shelter and warmth: it was a good start.

'You're a lucky girl. I'd give my right arm to have a place like this. I didn't realise the flat was quite so lovely upstairs either. Thanks for showing me around. Right, what's the time now?'

'Nearly four.'

'Shit, is it already? I'd better get going.' Luke started to pack his tools away. He yawned. 'I shouldn't really be driving after that Prosecco, but as long as you don't run anybody over around here, you can get away with murder.'

CHAPTER SIX

Christmas Eve morning and Rosa awoke to the cries of seagulls circling the bay. Her mouth was dry and Hot was whimpering to be let out. She reached for her phone on the bedside table. Six-thirty.

'Oh, I'm so sorry, boy, you must be desperate. What sort of mother am I?'

She leapt out of bed and gently lifted him down. Then she pulled on a pair of joggers and an old jumper, reached for her jacket and pulled her hat over her mad curls. As it was so early, she didn't bother with a bra or any sort of face wash. Grabbing Hot's lead, they both scampered down the shallow fire-escape stairs, which she could access directly from her room at the end of the pub.

At the bottom, Hot peed for what seemed like ten minutes. It reminded Rosa that she hadn't had time to pop into the ensuite bathroom.

Producing a treat from her coat pocket, she knelt down and rubbed his coat furiously with both hands. 'Here you go, you're a good boy. A very good boy.' He snapped up the treats then rubbed his head against her head and sneezed.

Rosa stood up. She couldn't believe how long she had slept.

On getting back to the pub after her encounter with Luke, she'd felt a bit woozy so thought she'd have a little nap. That nap had turned into a marathon twelve-hour sleep. She must have needed it. But she was terribly thirsty now and poor Hot must be starving.

She had no idea what time any of the shops opened, so she put Hot on the lead and they made their way up the steep slope from the bay to Main Street. If anything was going to be open, it would be the Co-op.

As they walked past the Corner Shop, Rosa smiled to herself. She knew this whole thing wasn't going to be easy, and usually, a challenge like this would make her want to run away – but because it was her challenge and hers alone she felt strangely excited. The shop looked very gloomy still, especially as she had closed the old damp blinds last night so that nobody could stare in when she was in there. But it wouldn't be long before she sorted everything out and made it welcoming again.

She then did a double-take: for just a split second she thought she could see a light on in the kitchen at the back. Strange. She was sure she had turned it off, but then again, she had been a bit tipsy. She didn't have the keys on her to check, but once she had fed and watered herself and her dog, she would come up and have a look. She quickly glanced again, and everything was now in complete darkness, so maybe she had just imagined it.

'Hurrah, Hot, it's open.' She tied him up outside and pushed open the door.

The Co-op was empty apart from the sleepy-looking woman behind the counter who was reading a magazine and didn't even look up when Rosa walked in. Getting herself a milkshake, a sandwich, some dog food and a copy of the *South Cliffs Gazette*, Rosa took her basket to the counter.

'They won't have reported it in there yet,' the woman told her, still without looking up. 'Be in next week's edition now.'

'Sorry, I don't know what you mean.' Rosa screwed up her face.

'The incident last night. Did you not see the police car up at the Ship?'

'Er…no, I didn't.'

'But you're staying there, aren't you?'

How could a complete stranger know who she was already? Rosa thought crossly.

The woman rambled on without her response. 'Yes, terrible doings. Sheila's son's girlfriend decided to walk down from the station 'cos her boyfriend was late collecting her, so I hear. Got clipped by a car, she did. Broke her ankle quite badly. What's more, the car drove off – left her lying in the road, poor soul. If it wasn't for Ralph Weeks doing another pick-up, she'd have been there all night. Thank goodness it's mild down here for this time of year or she could have been a goner.'

'Oh no, that's terrible. The poor girl.'

'I know. Things like that don't happen in Cockleberry. The last time I saw a police car was when old Mrs Perivale slipped on the ice and the ambulance couldn't get up her drive.' The woman coughed loudly. A cough that only a lifetime of smoking could bring.

'I'm Mary, by the way,' she went on. 'I live in Seaspray Cottage with my old gran. Rosa, isn't it? That's right,' she answered herself. 'Rosa Larkin. Such a pretty name.'

Did every single person in this town know who she was? Rosa made a conscious note to be more careful from now on, about whom she confided in. Maybe she shouldn't have trusted in Luke, but the Prosecco had loosened her tongue and he had seemed warm and genuine.

Rosa handed over a fiver, told Mary to put the five-pence

change in the Air Ambulance charity box and quickly exited the shop.

She untied Hot, gave him a treat, then drank her milkshake down in one. Making her way back down to the beach, she thought about Mary. The latter was an interesting-looking character. With her long, dark hair that reached down to her bum and a brown, weather-beaten face, she resembled a stereotypical witch you might see in kids' books. Rosa had no idea how old she might be. A bit like with Seb, maybe her weathered face made her look older than her years. But goodness knows how old her 'old gran' was, as even being kind, Mary must be in her early forties. Maybe the sea air kept you going down here, Rosa told herself. After all, Mr Myers who'd had the shop before her had been ninety-eight when he had passed.

As she reached the bay, she checked the pub car park. No sign of a police car now, just Sheila's ancient white Golf convertible.

Rosa picked a rock to sit on, opened her sandwich and started to devour it. The winter sun was rising in the mist, and waves lapped gently against the shoreline. Although cold, Rosa felt peaceful. It really was a very special place.

She pulled bits of bacon out of her sandwich for Hot to snack on, and promised, 'I'll put your food down as soon as we get back, Mr Sausage.' Doing this obviously wasn't a good idea, as the seagulls thought it was breakfast-time for them too, which caused Hot to start barking loudly and chase around at a hundred miles an hour.

'Ssh, little man, people are still sleeping.'

'I wish.'

Rosa jumped. 'Seb! You made me jump.'

'No fry-up at the pub today then?'

'Not today. Hot needed a walk. Is Jet here?'

'Yes.' Seb pointed down to the sea-edge where Jet was chasing

46

waves. 'The Old Bill were hanging around here last night,' he told Rosa. 'Thought I'd better not drive down today in case they were here now, as I'm probably still over the limit after last night in the pub. Not fancy a drink yourself last night then?'

'I was so tired I fell asleep before seven. I can't believe it, to be honest. I never used to do that at home.'

'Amazing what the sea air can do to you down here.'

'I'm beginning to realise that.'

Seb reached down and threw a stone towards the water. Hot charged off after it.

'Anyway, the Old Bill were here because Sheila's son's girlfriend got hit by a car while walking down from the station. Bloody mad, in these dark streets.' He fixed her with a critical stare. 'You townies are all the same – too impatient. She could've waited for him to pick her up.'

'Oh dear, that's awful.' Rosa couldn't be bothered to tell him that she knew already. 'Is she in hospital then or back here?'

'In hospital. Broke her wrist, evidently.'

Rosa smiled to herself. Chinese whispers could be so dangerous. That poor girl would be in a full body-cast by lunchtime.

'What time did all this kick off then?' she asked. 'Can't believe I didn't hear a thing.'

'Ooh, around six thirty, maybe seven, I think.' She then noticed Seb was staring right at her chest area. 'Bit cold, are we?'

Rosa had undone her coat when she had sat down to eat and her nipples, without the protection of a bra, were sticking right out from her jumper. If Luke had said it she might well have responded with some flirty quip, but coming from Seb, for whom she didn't feel one ounce of attraction, it made her feel a bit sick.

She quickly zipped her jacket back up, thinking, Dirty

bastard. Attempting a weak smile, she whistled for Hot, then said briskly, 'Right, we must go. Have a good day, Seb.'

'Oh, it'll be a busy morning at the station, what with it being Christmas Eve and all. I've got plenty of mince pies at the ready.' He started to roll a cigarette. 'So, will we have the pleasure of seeing you in the pub tonight? I'd hope to think so, seeing as it's one of the highlights of the Ship's calendar.'

'Yes, maybe. It's about time I fraternised with the locals, seeing as I am here for Christmas.' And she managed a smile, despite thinking they probably all bloody knew who *she* was already.

CHAPTER SEVEN

Rosa went back to her room, and while Hot wolfed down his tin of dog food she threw on some old clothes that were suitable for cleaning in. Once they were both done, she grabbed her purse and keys from her bag, put a lead on Hot and headed off down the fire-escape stairs before Sheila could find her and ask her where she was going. Despite it not being very nice news about her son's girlfriend, she didn't fancy a long-drawn-out conversation about it all.

Just as she reached the edge of the car park, she saw Titch walking towards her and whispered, 'Bugger,' under her breath.

'All right, Rose?'

Rosa saw no point in correcting her. 'Yep – all good, thanks, Titch. I'm just off for a walk with Hot. Can you tell Sheila I won't be wanting breakfast today?'

'Will do. Maybe see you later? There's always a good crack in here on Christmas Eve and I can introduce you to the few single cocks of Cockleberry Bay too, if you fancy?' She put her hand over her mouth in faux shock and carried on walking.

Titch was making Rosa feel quite chaste. Sex hadn't been on her mind once since she had got here. Actually, that was a lie. If Luke had asked to check her pipes further, maybe she'd have let him inspect her plumbing, but she was genuinely more concerned about getting the shop – and more importantly the flat – ready as soon as possible.

Rosa now had to make the steep hike back up to the Co-op again. She had forgotten all about needing cleaning stuff this morning, but she was on a mission today. Now she had Hoovered everything, she planned to get the downstairs toilet and little kitchen clean, as well as the upstairs bathroom and kitchen. The priority was to get the shop up and running, but without a place to sleep she would be shelling out £60 a night for bed and breakfast at the Ship Inn and she really didn't want to be doing that after Boxing Day.

There was the slight problem of the lack of a mattress, but she had packed her own bedding and the old sagging sofa would have to do for a few nights if need be. She had certainly slept on worse in the past.

Mary was still there behind the counter, unpacking boxes of cigarettes from a big carton. 'Can't keep you away, can we?' she greeted Rosa.

Fearing the barrage of questions that would be aimed at her when she was caught red-handed with a basket full of cloths, bleach, heavy-duty rubber gloves and cleaning sprays, Rosa knew she would have to have her story ready by the time she reached the checkout.

'Thought I'd help Sheila out a bit and do some shopping for her, what with all she's going through at the moment,' she said.

'Well, she doesn't usually buy own brand.'

'Well, she's having it today, Mary.'

'So, what's the latest news then, young Rosa?'

'I really don't know, and I'm in a hurry – sorry.'

Mary coughed. 'You should come and see my old gran. She'll slow you down. She reads fortunes, you see, but maybe you don't need one of those, eh?' She winked, turned her back and continued to pack the shelf behind her with cigarettes.

Rosa unlocked the front door to the shop. The warmth of the radiators had accentuated the damp smell and she went to the back kitchen and threw open the door to the courtyard.

'Pooh, Hot, let's go with ventilation rather than heat today, shall we? I'd rather be cold for a while and start getting rid of this stench of damp.'

Rosa scrubbed and cleaned the kitchens and bathroom until they were gleaming. Well, as gleaming as an old Belfast kitchen sink and a 1970s avocado bathroom suite could gleam, anyway. The downstairs toilet was now as good as new. You could eat your dinner off it! She loved the fact that it had an old cistern with a pull-chain handle and – yes! – a ceramic starfish on the end of that too.

She wondered why there were so many starfish dotted around and then just assumed it must be a living-by-the-seaside thing. She had seen loads of model boats in people's front windows and had lost count of the cottage names relating to some sort of maritime theme.

She just had the upstairs fridge to clean out when Josh phoned. Peeling off her sweaty rubber gloves, she plonked herself down on the saggy beige sofa.

'Mr Smith,' she greeted him.

'Rosalar. You all right?'

'Don't faint, but I've been cleaning for hours.'

'What, the girl from the "I'll just show the table a duster and it'll be fine" school of cleaning – *that* girl?'

Rosa laughed. 'Yes, *that* girl. And I actually enjoyed it. Very satisfying.'

'Whoa, don't say that or we'll be getting snow on Christmas

Day. But it's good that you are sounding so positive.'

'Yes, all is going well, so far anyway. I also hope you might be proud of me, as – listen to this – the heating and hot water are connected and working, and I have electricity already.'

'Bloody hell, girl. You got hold of a plumber then?'

'Yep. I bit the bullet and asked Sheila from the pub for a recommendation. He was cute too.'

'How much did he charge?'

'Just a hundred pounds cash – I thought that was reasonable.'

'Yes, it was cheap and yes, I am proud of you. I thought it would take a lot longer to get all that sorted, this time of year.'

'So, are you coming down to see us then?'

'If you still want me to. Is there anything you're missing that you need desperately?'

''I don't think what I need will quite fit in your sporty two-seater because I need a mattress and a sofa too. The one here is beyond saving. I'm even too scared to put my hand down the back of it to see if there's any money to find.'

'To buy new will be pricy,' Josh mused. 'Maybe have a look at some ads in the paper or in shop windows down there.'

'I can't be doing with a second-hand mattress.'

'Hark at you, when did you get so posh?'

Rosa went quiet. Josh had obviously forgotten the time she had confided in him that she had had to sleep on so many dirty and sometimes wet mattresses, from her own accidents as a child, she had vowed that when she could afford it, she would never have a second-hand mattress again. But then again, they had been drunk when she told him that. She found it easier telling the truth about private things when she was inebriated.

'OK, I hear you. So just bring yourself, that's fine. It will be so lovely to see you. I'm moving into the upstairs flat on Boxing Day, and will sleep on the sofa with my bedding and pillow – so that will do me until I get sorted. But what about you – where will you sleep? Can you fit a blow-up bed and duvet in the car?'

'Don't worry about me, I'll organise something. So, try and enjoy your Christmas anyway, you hear? What are you going to do?'

'I'm going to have a drink with the locals tonight in the pub, then lunch with Sheila and her family on Christmas Day, although the gossip of the year is her son's girlfriend was involved in a hit-and-run accident last night.'

'Shit.'

'I know. I haven't spoken to Sheila about it yet, wanted to keep out of the way for the moment. You won't believe how nosy everyone is around here.'

'Well, on a positive, you're old news now.'

Rosa laughed. 'I hadn't thought of that.'

'How's Hot doing?'

'He loves it down here. He's addicted to the beach and seagull chasing.'

'Aw, bless him. Right, I'd better go. I'm driving down to the folks later and I haven't packed yet. Get your hand down that sofa, you never know what you might find.'

'Vile. Right, drive carefully. So what day are you going to come?'

'I'll stay Boxing Night with the parentals, then head down.'

'Great, see you then and have a good Christmas.'

Rosa put her rubber gloves on for protection and felt down the back of the sofa. She carried on delving down the right-hand side and was disappointed to only come up with a knitting needle, a large safety pin and two pencils.

'Not even a penny, Hot, that's no good.' The tiny dachshund raised one eye and went back to sleep next to her as she delved in the other side. After a moment, she felt something hard. 'Hey, might even be a two-pound coin.'

But it wasn't a coin. Attached to the round object was some kind of chain. Pulling gently, Rosa revealed the hidden object and gasped. For there, attached to a somewhat tarnished but obviously real gold chain was a huge sapphire, centred within an ornate gold setting. Taking off her gloves, she had a good look at it. Around the edge of the frame were the words *My Darling T*. On turning it over she noticed some more beautiful engraving: *Meet me where the sky touches the sea X*

'That's so romantic,' Rosa murmured. Reverently, she rubbed the exquisite piece of jewellery with her duster. Lucky T, whoever T was. She had no idea how old the necklace was, or how long the sofa had been here. Maybe the necklace had been for sale in the shop and had made its way upstairs somehow?

Rosa decided she would show it to Josh, see what he thought. If it was worth a few quid, maybe she could sell it and use the money for stock.

CHAPTER EIGHT

'Bugger.'

Rosa threw her one and only – and now laddered – pair of tights into the rubbish bin beneath her dressing-table. Even though Christmas was not her favourite time of year, she thought she ought to make a bit of an effort. She had wanted to wear her red woollen mini-dress and her black boots. Trying the outfit on, she looked at herself in the mirror and thought, Sod it, I'll just wear it without tights. Her legs were good enough and she knew Sheila would have the fire blazing as always.

Hot was asleep on the floor and raised one eye as Rosa put a chicken chew next to him and a bowl of fresh water. There was a good chunk of the cucumber left too. Ignoring her, he attacked the cucumber in a very un-cute way.

She stroked his soft ears, promising, 'I won't be long, boy. I'll just show my face and be back in no time.'

She put some cash in her purse and went downstairs. Christmas tunes were already blaring out, and despite it only being seven o'clock, the bar was already rammed.

Seb immediately rushed to her side. 'You brush up all right, don't you?' he said, and squeezed her left bum cheek.

'Hey, get off! It's not Christmas yet, sunshine.'

'Seb Watkins, you keep your hands to yourself.' Sheila smiled her film-star smile from behind the bar. 'Now, what can I get you, my lovely?'

'A large JD and Coke please, with lots of ice.'

'Everything all right?'

'Yes, thank you. Sorry I didn't make it down for breakfast the last couple of days. I thought you had enough going on what with Christmas and…everything.'

'Young Jasmine getting knocked for six, you mean.'

'Yes. I was so sorry to hear that – your son must be very upset.'

'He's with her at the hospital now. She had to have an operation – quite a whack she received.'

Rosa didn't want to prolong the conversation and ask whether it was her arm, leg or any other bodily part that had been affected. She was sure she would find out soon enough.

'You've been busy, haven't you?' the landlady said, changing the subject. 'Who'd have thought there was so much to do in this small town.'

She then started serving her next customer before Rosa had a chance to answer. She took a large swig of her drink, wondering, did everybody know what she was up to? Maybe they had special CCTV that linked back to the pub, or perhaps they'd wired the shop ready for when somebody took it over.

Not even thinking to have asked Luke what he was doing for Christmas, she looked around to see if he was amongst the customers. It did seem like half the town was in here.

Titch suddenly bobbed up from nowhere. Her low-cut black dress made Rosa's dress-without-tights combo seem positively tame. The girl was slightly slurring her words.

'Nice dress, Rose. Here, come with me.' She took Rosa by the hand, dragged her over to the corner of the bar, then said in her ear, 'So, am I assuming you are young, free and single?'

'True, yes, but it just so happens I'm not in the mood to mingle tonight.'

'Like it, like it.' Titch was drinking pints of what looked like cloudy cider. Belching, she put her drink down on the bar and confided, 'There are not many decent blokes in this town, and that's the sad truth.' Her eyes lit up. 'I love it when the tourist season is on and we get the odd stag party on their way through to Ulchester. Those guys are always up for it.'

'What about Seb?'

Titch turned up her nose. 'What about him? He's a pervy bastard, that's all he is.'

'Or Luke?'

'Luke? I don't know of any Lukes round here.'

'Oh.' But it was impossible to talk further. Titch had started singing along to the music. 'So here it is, Merry Christmas,' she bellowed, then raised her drink in the air and shimmied over to chat to some people sitting near the fire.

Rosa took another sip of her drink and looked around her. The Ship Inn really was a lovely old pub. The fire was blazing down one end and the seven-foot Christmas tree in the corner was beautifully decorated with old-fashioned baubles that she imagined Sheila recycled, year after year. A holly garland adorned the whole length of the old wooden bar, with yet more twinkly lights.

More people kept arriving, mostly families, some with kids, some not. Several generations celebrating this special time together. Christmas at the children's homes had been a sad affair, really. They got presents and a Christmas dinner, and although Rosa didn't really know any different, she could sense that she was missing something. More than anything, she craved human touch. She sometimes hugged Ellie her friend so tight that she would have to scream for a staff member to release her. Poor Ellie, she had been lucky enough to be adopted when she was ten, but when Rosa had decided to look her up on Facebook a couple of years ago, she was greeted with a page with RIP messages. The girl had tragically taken her own life.

Rosa started having sex at fourteen. At that age it wasn't an intimacy thing to her, she just wanted to feel wanted. She remembered the contraception chat. Laughed at being shown how to put a condom on a banana. But luckily, she had listened. There was no way she was going to bring a baby into this world and have them go through what she'd had to endure. She was barely able to look after herself, let alone another human being.

Hot had changed her view on this slightly; she had been able to throw all her love into the smooth-coated little hound, and it felt so good when he demonstrated his love for her, licking her face all over, putting his little head on her lap or sleeping at her feet. She smiled, thinking back to when she had first seen him. Hearing him barking on the pavement outside, she had looked, then pointed out his funny little walk to Karl, who she was working with at Poundworld that day. Her laugh quickly turned to anger as she saw his owner, a thin-faced, tattooed woman of about forty, hitting his bony little spine really hard with the end of his lead. All he was doing was barking his indignation at being tied up.

Hearing him yelp in pain, Rosa's first reaction was to run out and rescue him, but something inside prevented her from doing that. She knew this must never be allowed to happen to him again. Forcing herself to remain calm, she waited for the woman to come inside the shop and get distracted with her shopping. She then reached for her rucksack which was under the counter, told Karl to man the fort, darted out and scooped up the little hound. Hiding him in her bag, she jumped on the bus then got off near Stepney Green and ran as fast as she could back to Josh's.

The ever-sensible Josh said that it was a clear case of dognap and that she should return him...but then on seeing the scars and welts on the miniature dachshund's back, he swiftly agreed that: one, Rosa had been right, and that: two, yes, the dear little chap was more than welcome to live happily in the house with them.

Seb appeared again at the bar. He had to shout over the music and the ever-growing crowd of revellers.

'Told you it was the place to be on Christmas Eve, didn't I? Fancy a tequila?'

The JD had begun to take effect on Rosa. 'Why not? But let me buy them. I feel I owe you for the lift.'

Three tequila slammers later and they were creating quite a stir at the bar.

Seb laughed. 'For someone so tiny, you can take your drink well. I need a fag, coming?'

Rosa followed him outside. Although not a smoker as such, after a few drinks she would quite happily have a puff of someone else's cigarette. The benches outside were taken with other smokers, so Seb led her towards the beach.

Taking a large toke on the roll-up he offered her, she began to cough violently.

'Oh my God, you didn't mention there was weed in there.'

'Don't tell me you've never smoked a joint before?'

'Of course I have, but bloody hell, that's strong and you could have warned me.' She staggered slightly and Seb grabbed her arm to steady her. As he did so he pulled her towards him, put his hand up her dress and started to push his bony fingers into her knickers.

'Hey – stop that! Get off!'

'But I thought...'

'You thought what, Seb? "She's drunk, so I'll try it on with her on the beach?" We're not bloody sixteen.'

Rosa ran back towards the pub, shivering and with her teeth chattering. Realising she had forgotten her key to the outside door she edged her way to the bar, where she could get up to her room from inside. A Karaoke set was now in full swing, but even a poor rendition of 'Last Christmas' couldn't get her back into the spirit of things.

'Not putting your name down for a song then?' Sheila called over, pointing to the little stage area that had been set up. 'You could do a duet with my Lucas.'

Rosa glanced at the stage – and then her face fell.

'That's Lucas?'

'Yes, that's my son.' Sheila winked.

Rosa shook her head at Sheila in disbelief. Lucas looked over, clocked Rosa and spoke directly into the microphone. 'Ah, there she is, everybody. The lady in red, also known as the proud new owner of the Corner Shop in Cockleberry Bay!'

With anger burning through every pore, and her head spinning from the mixture of alcohol and weed, Rosa shakily passed a now-smirking Sheila, ran up to her room, packed all her stuff, grabbed Hot and left via the outside staircase.

Scrabbling to get her key in the front door of the shop, she jumped as somebody appeared from around the corner.

'More haste, less speed.' The female voice was calm and soothing. 'Are you OK?'

'Yes, yes, I'm fine, thank you.'

It was pitch black, but she could see a dark headscarf pulled tightly around the lady's wrinkled face. Hot was barking wildly.

The old lady gently took the keys from Rosa's hand. 'Ah, a starfish,' she said. 'That's good.' But Rosa was too upset to even respond. 'You see, the starfish represents the Virgin Mary – also

60

known as Stella Maris, which means Star of the Sea. Stella Maris lovingly creates safe travel over troubled waters and is also seen as an emblem of salvation during trying times.'

Opening the door in one, the old lady then handed Rosa the keys.

'Don't question this gift, Rosa. It was left with love.

Before the girl had a chance to reply, the lady had disappeared in to the darkness as quickly as she had come.

CHAPTER NINE

Rosa woke to Hot licking her nose. Her head was thumping.

'Happy Christmas, darling hound. At least you never let me down.'

She eased herself awkwardly up from the sagging sofa and put one hand on her now aching lower back. She groaned, realising she hadn't put a sheet down to sleep on, so her bare legs had been against the dirty sofa. But that was the least of her problems. It seemed that Sheila Hannafore, the Mamma of the Cockleberry Bay Mafia, wasn't quite as pleasant as she had assumed.

How bloody dare she set her up like that – and in such an elaborate way, too? Her duplicitous son didn't even live around here. And worse, how dare he go along with her devious plan? Rosa realised that she had not been open about the shop, but that was her business. Why should everybody know? After all, they would have found out soon enough. Dear, darling Lucas obviously wasn't that bothered about his girlfriend either. Showing off on the Karaoke – you'd have thought he would have been quiet in reflection of what had happened. She put on a funny voice. 'Oh hi, I'm Luke the plumber.' Lying twat!

She threw the double doors open at the end of the lounge and took in the beautiful vista. It was cold, but bright. Gulls were soaring over the headland and she could see the white specks of boats sailing on the horizon. She checked her phone and saw a missed call from Josh. She vaguely remembered calling him before bed and getting no answer.

Still wearing her clothes from the night before, she made her way down to the shop kitchen. Thank goodness she had tea and milk – but that was about all there was, apart from half a sandwich left from the other day and a packet of crisps. She made herself a cup of tea, undid her case and pulled some joggers up under her dress, then put on her coat and went and sat out on the roof terrace, her loyal hound at her side.

Cockleberry Bay was silent, apart from the insistent cry of the gulls. She took a big slug of her tea, blew a massive plume of steam into the cold air and allowed the sound of the sea to soothe her.

Everything had been far too easy up until now, Rosa thought bitterly. What had she been thinking of, leaving the safety of Josh and the London house? But she didn't have to stay here; she could walk away. Then again, what would she be going back to, really? Aside from Josh, what did she have in London? With no qualifications to her name, she would just find another mindless, badly paid job. She didn't even have any true friends since she'd moved to the East End, and those she had met before hadn't bothered to keep in touch aside from the occasional Facebook quip. Yes, there was the odd person she had met in her many jobs, but there wasn't one she could call 'a 3am friend', someone who would drop everything to see her all right at any time of day or night. Maybe even Josh felt a bit sorry for her, she thought and winced – and that was why he had been so kind.

Shivering, she went back inside and shut the doors. Christmas Day, with no food to mention and not even a television on which to watch a rerun of *The Snowman*. If she had had the capacity to cry, she would have thrown herself down and sobbed her heart out.

As she sat mute on the baggy sofa, her nose buried in Hot's comforting coat, memories of the night before started coming back to her. She cringed, thinking of Seb trying to touch her up on the beach. What on earth was he thinking? Had she led him on? No!

Oh lord, how could she ever hold her head up on the streets of Cockleberry Bay again?

She looked at the floor. Her handbag lay upturned where she'd dumped it last night and its contents were strewn everywhere. The starfish on the key ring lay propped up against the skirting board. Picking it up, she noticed a smudge of dirt on it from dropping it on the pavement last night. As she began rubbing it clean with her fingers, a bright shard of sunlight lit up the whole room, Hot came alert and barked.

Gently shushing him, Rosa stood up with a defiant look on her face.

'Fuck them – fuck the whole pack of them. If a few small-minded people think they are going to knock Rosa Larkin down, they've got another think coming.'

She started to run a bath. Hot got up and joined her, settling down onto the old green rug which was currently doubling as a bath mat. Rosa loved a long bubble bath but for now she would have to make do with just water; she didn't even have any shower gel, since in her haste to get out of the Ship last night, she had left most of her toiletries in her room. But at least the water was hot here and the old bath, deep.

Lying back, she closed her eyes. She had got through worse than this, she told herself, and this was her chance to turn her life around and take control. She swirled the calming water around her body. This was her place – her own place – and whoever had left it to her, well, they must have had faith that she could make it work. How sad that they hadn't been able to tell her that in the 'real world' though.

She was brought back to reality by one of the bulbs in her showbiz-style mirror popping and going out. Only five out of the twelve were working now; she really must go and get some more of those too.

Drying herself with her scratchy cream towel, she thought back again to last night. She couldn't even remember what, if anything, she had said to Sheila. In fact, she couldn't even remember the walk back up the hill. One of her social workers had always said to her, 'When the drink's in, the wit's out.' Rosa had obviously berated her for saying it, but the woman had been so right. She thought back to the many times she'd got into arguments, slept with someone unsuitable or just made ridiculous decisions, all of which she had done when she had been too drunk to think sensibly. But she liked drinking, Rosa sighed. It was an escape. Helped her sleep. Helped her forget.

Once dressed, she walked downstairs, took the half-eaten sandwich out of the shop kitchen fridge, fed Hot with some of the chicken out of it and downed a pint of tap-water. She noticed how lovely and cold and fresh-tasting the water was, and she knew from watching the many survival programmes she loved, that even if she couldn't find food in this godforsaken place for the next two days, with fresh water she wouldn't die. She would just have to make sure she could find some scraps for Hot.

Just as she was about to leave, Josh phoned.

'Happy Christmas to my two favourite dogs.'

'Ha ha. Very funny. Now tell me what's happy about it.'

'Uh oh. I suspect a tequila hangover.'

'Stop pretending you know me so well, but yes, slammers and JD and a toke of weed and the plumber not being who he said he was.'

'You what?'

Minus the bony finger incident, Rosa relayed the whole sorry story.

'I really don't understand why on earth they would go to so much trouble to find out what's going on.'

'Nor me. But I've got to ride the storm. I will just keep myself to myself from now on. There are many more people in this town than those few who have already wanted to make trouble for me. And I don't have any reason to go in that pub again. There's another one up the very top of the hill called the Lobster Pot, and Hot and I are on a mission to check it out – in a minute, in fact. On our search for food.'

'Oh Rosa, don't tell me you haven't got any supplies in?'

'Nada. Well, a packet of crisps. It's Hot I'm more worried about, but you know me. When you've lived on the streets before, this isn't even an obstacle, and I've got water.'

Josh's face was pained at the other end of the phone.

'I could try and come down tomorrow, but Mum's invited Great-Auntie Deirdre and tells me it may be the last time I might ever see her.'

Rosa laughed. 'Ho ho ho. What Christmas cheer in the Smith household.'

'Exactly! Wish I was in the peace and quiet with you. The nieces and nephews have been up since five. Mum's already demented with worry that the turkey won't be cooked before the Queen's speech. I should have gone with Dad. He's been out with the dog for two hours, and I'm sure I saw him sneak a hip-flask into his pocket before he left.'

'Suddenly I feel a whole lot better.'

'Good. Now do you want me to Google and see what's open near you?'

'I may be away from the big city, Josh, but I do have 3G. In fact, you've made me think. I need to sort broadband and a phone for the shop too.' Rosa sighed. 'More bloody expense.'

'Welcome to the real world, girl.'

'On that note, shit off now, please. Me and Hot need to get noses down on our search for food and redemption.'

'Ha! The food bit of that should be easier than the other. Anyway, try and make the best of it and I'll see you in a couple of days. Let me know if you need anything.'

'Thanks a lot, and no cracker-pulling in front of Auntie Deirdre.' Rosa put a lead on a now-whining Hot, saying, 'I know you're a hungry boy, but we are going to sort this.'

She was relieved that, aside from another couple of dog walkers, the streets were quiet. She replied with a polite 'Happy Christmas' as they headed the opposite way down to the beach.

Rosa wasn't surprised to find that the Co-op was closed but pleased to see it was open again on Boxing Day for a few hours in the morning. She jerked Hot's lead to try and stop him from licking up the various unsavoury things he could find on the ground. Heading further up the hill, she could see that the Lobster Pot was another picturesque old white building, with lovely hanging baskets full of winter pansies along the whole front of it. A Christmas tree with coloured lights stood amidst the benches outside. It was a lot classier-looking than the rough and ready Ship, she thought. An OPEN FOR CHRISTMAS DRINKS 12 till 2 sign was perched in one of the windows, plus a NO VACANCIES sign.

It was eleven o'clock, an hour until it opened. She had to find Hot some food before then. She vaguely remembered on her journey from the station, a garage at the very top of the hill as you turned down into the bay – probably around a mile away from where they were now. Quite a walk for the pampered Hot. She went to look for it on the internet but couldn't get a signal. Rather than let Josh know that she should have taken up his offer, she kept walking. With her hangover still causing her grief, she stopped for a second to give Hot a rest and to catch her own breath. It was a bloody steep hill, and despite having a great little figure and youth on her side, so that she could eat whatever she wanted whenever she wanted, Rosa was aware that she could do with toning up in some areas, and all this walking would certainly help that.

It was then she noticed the pretty little cottages either side of the narrow street. One caught her eye as there were two beautiful coloured crystals outside on the windowsill. The sign on the whitewashed wall said *Seaspray Cottage* and she remembered Mary saying it was where she and her gran lived. It amazed her that people could leave things out like that and they didn't get stolen. They'd be gone in seconds anywhere else.

She carried on walking up the hill, wondering where dear Lucas's girlfriend had been clobbered. It could have been anywhere, as the road was so narrow and there was no lighting to speak of.

With her mouth now feeling like a badger's fanny, the sight of two cars filling up with petrol in the forecourt of a garage was the most marvellous mirage Rosa had ever seen. But it wasn't a mirage, it turned out to be real, and the SPAR sign above confirmed that not only was the garage open, it also sold food.

She tied Hot up outside, said Happy Christmas to the young yawning lad behind the counter and began to hunt for supplies. But hunt was the operative word. Obviously, this was the only place around here open on Christmas morning and everyone had had the usual last-minute panics. She arrived at the checkout with a wire basket containing dog food, milk, fruit juice and toilet roll. There was no bread, so in addition she picked up a dozen eggs, two packets of bacon, a quiche with a sell-by date of today, a large tin of baked beans and a big bar of chocolate.

'You wouldn't have a bowl I could borrow, by any chance?'

Looking out at Hot, the young lad shook his head. 'Sorry, love, but there's a water tap around the back he can slurp from.'

Rosa walked around to where he had pointed and squeezed a sachet of dog food out onto the ground. Just as Hot was wolfing the last bit down, a car pulled up by their side. A middle-aged woman opened the passenger window and handed her three-pound coins, saying, 'Here, my dear. Happy Christmas and may God bless you both.'

The car had moved away before Rosa had a chance to react. With her mad, unwashed hair and seeing her having to feed a dog on the ground, she might look like a poor homeless waif, but how far from the truth was that. No, she was Rosa Larkin, proud owner of the Corner Shop of Cockleberry Bay – and after last night's fiasco she was more determined than ever to make it a success.

CHAPTER TEN

A family of five were walking into the Lobster Pot as Rosa walked past. Adorned in new Christmas hats and scarves, they were also no doubt wearing their best dresses or Christmas jumpers underneath. As the door opened, she could see another impressively decorated tree and could hear the chitter chatter of people enjoying themselves.

Or were they?

Rosa had read a tweet by JK Rowling once that had made her nod in acknowledgement. *At this time of year, we're bombarded with images of perfect lives, which bear as little relation to reality as tinsel does to gold.*

She *was* interested to see what it was like in there, but couldn't be bothered to talk to anyone and was now also very hungry for her bacon and eggs and a massive glug of orange juice. Since it was easier by far to hurry downhill than it was to climb up, girl and dog were back at the Corner Shop in no time.

Thankful to be in what she now considered to be home, Rosa went straight upstairs to the flat's kitchen, then swore. Yes, all the cupboards were now immaculate – but empty. Josh had insisted that she took a couple of mugs, glasses, plates and some cutlery with her, but she hadn't even noticed or thought to check about cooking utensils. The oven didn't even have a grill pan.

She opened the quiche and cut herself a big slice; thankfully, the baked beans didn't need a tin opener. She portioned two large spoonfuls onto the plate and went to the lounge to eat.

She texted a picture of the food to Josh with the words *No pans or microwave!* and he responded with a 'head in hands' emoji. She raised her glass of orange juice, saying, 'Happy Christmas, Hot,' as she did so.

She imagined that the quiche was pizza and the beans chips, two of her favourite foods after a big night out. She didn't know if it was because she had a hangover attack of the munchies, or had discovered that she was partial to cold beans, that she enjoyed her little feast so much. Remembering that she still had a packet of ready salted crisps in the downstairs kitchen also caused great excitement, added to the knowledge that she could have hot coffee and the bar of chocolate as dessert. Little things!

Hot was also happy, as not only had she bought his favourite sachets of food, she had also luckily managed to find two packets of doggie treats in the bottom of her case.

It was weird not having a TV, but in a way she was pleased; it would only have reminded her of what day it was, and despite her not really liking Christmas and all that it represented, nobody wanted to be alone. As if Hot knew what she was thinking, he came up to her and licked her hand. He then proceeded to emit a wonderful warm leathery smell – the essence of dog – and snuggled himself down on the sofa next to her, lying in ecstasy on his back, with his tummy in the air.

Thankful that the flat was warm and cosy, Rosa lay back on the duvet, still crumpled on the sofa from earlier. Then, reaching for her bag, she began to count the money she had left once again. Goodness knows how much she had spent last night, flashing her cash to buy creepy Seb tequila slammers.

Two thousand pounds had seemed like a fortune to her at first, but now that she was living in the real world and not handing Josh rent for everything, she began to realise that the sum was just a drop in the ocean. She had paid up until Boxing Day at the Ship, which slightly annoyed her as that meant she was £120 out of pocket for that. Money had been easy come, easy go for her before; counting and budgeting it was alien to her. If she had enough for the rent and phone – which wasn't always the case – and a few drinks, she could make do somehow with everything else.

She opened her phone, thinking she would watch some catch-up on TV or listen to some music, but nothing sat right with her. She went to the kitchen again. Opening Notes on her iPhone she began to make a list. Dessert bowls, frying pan, saucepans, wooden spoon, microwave, dog bowls…and so it went on.

Her next list was food. Pepper, salt, ketchup, butter, bread… she began to realise just how lucky she had been, living at Josh's. Had totally taken for granted that free squirt of ketchup or sprinkle of salt.

By the time she had added towels, sofa, mattress and paint and a guesstimate for the regular bills, she was already skint. This was not even considering the mention in the first envelope of business rates, whatever they were, plus insurances. Josh would need to help her with those tomorrow. She also must change the address for her mobile phone bill and open a bank account as soon as the Christmas break was over.

She would just have to sleep on the sofa and manage without a mattress until she started making some money from the shop, but goodness knows when that would be. If she bought a cheap microwave, she could manage with one saucepan. Paint and brushes were a priority, but it was imperative she saved something for stock, which she would need to quickly turn around or she would be in trouble. The last thing she wanted was to have to take a job locally to make ends meet. Imagine the gossip-mongering then! She usually didn't care what people thought of her, but after what had happened on Christmas Eve, it was extra-important for her to make the shop a success. Then they could all eat their words. She would show them.

After a hot mug of coffee and half of the family-sized chocolate bar, she began to feel sleepy. Just as she was dozing off, Hot started barking. He ran towards the door of the lounge and back, barking loudly. It was then she heard a knock at the door.

Getting up slowly, Rosa rubbed her eyes and ran her hands through her hair. She glanced at her phone – four o'clock on Christmas Day. A strange time to call.

She ran downstairs and hid behind the CLOSED sign, calling, 'Who is it?'

'It's me – Mary from the Co-op.'

Rosa unlocked the door.

'I don't want to come in or anything, it's just, well…my gran saw you walking back with bags from the garage and we sort of heard about last night.'

Rosa immediately felt her hackles rising. Christmas Day, and the Cockleberry Bay gossip train was still in action. But she softened when Mary handed her a tinfoil-covered plate.

'A Christmas dinner for you. We're not the best cooks, me and my old gran, but I guess it will taste better than what you had in your bags earlier.' Mary awkwardly stood there, shuffling from foot to foot. She looked younger than when Rosa had first seen her in the shop. Her long black hair was tied up in a bun and her piercing green eyes were accentuated by the floor-length patchy green velvet coat she was wearing.

73

'I'm glad you're here,' she told Rosa. 'I used to love this shop. And Gran and I both want to wish you well.'

Rosa took the plate from her; it was warm. She was quite touched by this show of human kindness, but still dubious in case it was a ruse to get more information out of her. But no more questions came from Mary's mouth.

'Thanks so much, and please do thank your gran too.'

'Pleasure. Happy Christmas, Rosa, and…' She pointed down to Hot who, smelling the turkey, was whining, pawing at Rosa's legs and trying to jump up towards the plate.

'Hot – that's Hot.'

Mary looked even younger when she laughed.

'Happy Christmas, Hot. We've got a cat. He's called Merlin. Well, he's actually called Merlinite, after the crystal, but that's a bit of a mouthful when he goes walkabouts.'

'Ah.' Rosa realised she knew nothing about crystals and their names. 'I saw crystals outside your house earlier. Pretty.'

'One's a stone, actually. Lavender Jade, stone of the angels. I don't recall what the other one is. Gran changes them around, you see. Depending on what we need.' Mary coughed.

The plate of food was going cold and Rosa was starving. She decided she'd had enough of crystal talk.

'Interesting stuff,' she said briskly. 'I shall have to meet your gran and she can tell me all about it.'

'Queenie.'

'What?' Hot's incessant jumping was now becoming annoying.

'My gran's name is Queenie. Well, that's not her real name, but everyone calls her Queenie.'

'Ah, OK. Right, I must go before he tears the plate out of my hand.'

'She does readings if you're interested. Crystals, Tarot,

74

whatever you want, really.' Rosa felt that Mary was a bit of a loner and that the company of just Queenie probably wasn't enough for her, especially today.

'Er...OK. I shall bear that in mind. Well, thanks again, Mary, and enjoy the rest of your Christmas.'

But still Mary hesitated. She was staring at Rosa's cheek. 'Your scar,' she whispered. Rosa put her hand to it, suddenly feeling self-conscious as Mary added hastily: 'It really suits you.'

'Well, thanks.' Nobody had ever said that about her little lightning-flash defect.

'Goodbye, Rosa. And pop by with the plate anytime, you'd be very welcome.'

'I'll do that. Bye.' But Mary had disappeared into the evening.

Rosa exhaled deeply as she managed to shut the door at last. So kind, but *so* intense at the same time.

Black cat, crystals, fortune-telling. She certainly hadn't come across much of that in the Whitechapel Road, and although sceptical about it, she couldn't help but like Mary. She was another one of life's misfits, a person of layers – and Rosa could relate to that.

CHAPTER ELEVEN

Rosa woke on Boxing Day feeling a lot calmer than she had done twenty-four hours earlier. The meal from the Cockleberry Coven had been delicious and Hot was more than happy to get his share of turkey and chipolatas. She had fallen into a restful sleep whilst listening to Adele on her phone, Hot snuggled at her side, and her back didn't even seem to hurt that much from the saggy sofa.

After her feast from last night, she wasn't very hungry, so sniffing to check the out-of-date quiche was still OK, she had a small slice of that. Hot had plenty of food and was getting far too used to eating off a normal dinner plate. She had forgotten to pack his bowls and since forgotten to remind Josh to bring them.

Her plan today was to get downstairs in the shop and give it another good clean. She was also going to do some research as to what she should sell to tourists and locals alike.

She was down in the back kitchen, running hot water into a bucket she had found out in the back courtyard, when there was a knock at the door. She tutted as she really wasn't in the mood for any interruption.

As she got to the door there was the sound of a fake bugle

being played and then the familiar voice of her former landlord could be heard loud and clear. 'The Cavalry has arrived. Let me in, Rosalar.'

Still in rubber gloves, Rosa hugged him tightly, while Hot raced in and jumped madly up at his legs.

'Joshua Smith, I have to admit I don't think I've ever been so pleased to see you,' Rosa said, and she meant it.

Josh reached down and stroked the quivering dachshund. 'Hello, boy,' he said fondly.

'But what are you doing here today?' Rosa wanted to know. 'We thought you were coming tomorrow.'

'I was, you're right. The truth is, I had to sleep on a metre-wide camp bed – and two nights on it were more than enough.'

'It wasn't that you thought I needed rescuing then?' Rosa smirked. 'How did your mum take that?'

'Mum was fine actually. I just had to promise that I went in and saw Great-Auntie Deirdre on the way home.'

'Let's hope she doesn't snuff it before you get back then.'

'You're so wrong.'

'You love it. Now, where did you park? I meant to tell you I saw a car park up on what they call The Level.'

'I found it, but please don't tell me this is the only entrance?'

'I think so.'

'It can't be. How would they have got everything in here?' Josh shrugged. 'Anyway, show me round. I can't wait to see this place.'

Rosa gave him a whistle-stop tour with Hot accompanying them. When they came back down to the courtyard, Josh walked over to the back fence, prodded about and then pushed open a gate that was hidden within the greenery.

'It just needs a handle, that's all,' he pointed out. 'Your bins are out here too, look. And you have your own parking space, by the look of it. Although...I wonder whose van this is?'

A Transit van, sporting a big green weather cover, was parked up at a funny angle – almost touching her fence.

'Hmm. Maybe, as parking is so limited here, and the place has been empty for so long, somebody's just been using it as their own. Anyway, this is excellent. I can bring my stuff in this way. I'll just go and get it. Right, put your knickers on and make us a cup of tea, love. It's been a long drive.'

Rosa grinned as she put teabags into mugs. She felt so safe with him.

'Rosa, Rosa!' he called loudly from the back door. 'Get your ass down here a sec.'

She went to the back courtyard – to be greeted by the sight of a mattress and Josh's big hands poking over the top of it.

'Oh, Josh. You really are a bloody angel.'

'Ssh, and give me a hand, will you, woman.'

After wrestling the mattress up the stairs, they went back down again, Hot yapping at their heels.

'A sofa too! Josh, I actually think I love you.'

'Oh, and there's more.' He disappeared through the gate and came back with a microwave and a box of second-hand saucepans. 'Luckily whoever owned that van left just enough space down the side of it for me to get through.'

With mug of tea in hand and now sitting on the new blue-and-white striped sofa, which definitely did not sag in any way, they could relax and take a breather.

'I can't believe you've done this for me.' Rosa brushed Josh's knee with her hand.

'None of it is new. You were lucky – Mum was having a clear-out, was about to take the saucepans and microwave to the charity shop. What's more, she'd bought a new bed for the Christmas guests and was going to tip the mattress. There's not a mark on it either. They've got too much money for their own good, my parents.'

'What about the sofa?'

'I went to drop some other stuff off at the charity shop for her and the sofa had just been delivered. I borrowed Carlton's van as he's not working over Christmas and – well, here I am.' Josh looked at her a little anxiously. 'It'll do for now, won't it?'

'Do for now? I love it!' She gave him a smacking kiss on the cheek.

'Blimey, wish I'd brought some more stuff now, I'd be guaranteed of a blow job by lunchtime.'

'Hey! You know you only got one of those when I didn't have any rent.'

'Have you considered prostitution for this place too? Sneaky back entrance for punters to come in and out. A sea view for seagull fetishists?' Josh's expression remained deadpan.

Rosa laughed. 'Can you imagine the gossip then? They'd internally combust with excitement.'

Josh stood up and put his mug in the kitchen.

'Hope you don't mind but I didn't bother finding anywhere to stay. Now you've got a mattress and a decent sofa I figured I could kip here. I brought my own sleeping bag.'

'Of course I don't bloody mind.' She put the milk back in the fridge. 'Do you think there might be anywhere open that sells paint around here?'

Josh made a round shape with his hands. 'Let me look into my crystal ball.'

'Talking of that, there's a right weird couple who live up the hill – a gran and granddaughter. They have crystals on their windowsill and everything – and a black cat called Merlin. Bless the granddaughter though, she brought me a Christmas dinner last night.'

'Blimey, that was nice.'

Rosa then stopped in her tracks. 'Shit, I've just remembered something else from the other night. You know when I was drunk?'

'That could be many a day.'

'Christmas Eve, silly. Well, I was struggling to open the door and an old woman appeared and helped me. She said something really strange about this place being a gift or something and then just wandered off. Didn't one of the notes in the case say that too?'

'Oh, Rosa. You're thinking too much into it – this place is a gift. You told Liar Luke that too. Anyway, I'd better go and move the van, I'm blocking the road.'

Josh walked out of the back gate and greeted a short dark-haired man who was lurking by the white van with an 'All right, mate?'

'Is this your van in the road?' the man asked.

'Yeah, sorry – just moving it.'

'No, it's fine. I just need to get something out of mine.'

'Is this the parking space for the Corner Shop, do you know?' Josh enquired.

'Who's asking?'

'I am – for Rosa, actually.'

Instead of answering, the man turned his back and took off the plastic green cover. Josh clocked the writing on the side of the van: *L. Hannafore, Plumbing and Heating Specialist*, and decided to take a chance.

'Ah, so you must be Luke – Luke the plumber?'

'Look, I'm in a bit of a hurry. Do you need to get in this space or not?'

'Actually, yes I do now.'

Lucas sighed. 'OK, give me a minute.' He reversed out and

shouted back to Josh out of his window, 'She's all right, is she? Rosa, I mean?'

'Why wouldn't she be?'

'Tell her I need to speak to her.'

Mouthing the word 'bastard' Josh restarted his engine and watched the white van speed up the hill.

CHAPTER TWELVE

Rosa was in the shop when Josh reappeared.

'Did I just hear you talking to someone out there?' she asked curiously.

'No. You must be hearing things. The van had gone so I managed to park out the back.'

'Oh, OK, that's good. What do you think about me taking these blinds down now that the world and his wife know I'm here, anyway.'

'I'd leave them up for a bit, if I were you. You don't want everyone gawping in whilst you're painting, do you?'

'No, you're right. Talking of paint, let's see if there is anywhere open. Ulchester is the biggest town from here.'

'Well, why don't we take a drive up there? We could have lunch too – there's bound to be somewhere open. And I'm sure this little fella could do with a walk.'

Hot starting barking at the four-letter magic word.

'Oh, Josh. You know not to say that word until we are ready to go.'

'What – "walk"?'

Hot was now beside himself.

Josh laughed. 'Come on then, let's go. There's no rush to paint today. I can stay for at least three nights – if you'll have me, that is?'

'Darling, I'll always have you, you know that.'

Josh smirked, and mock-swiped at her mop of curls.

They were just getting in the van when Titch wiggled around the corner, wearing a short skirt and high boots.

'Hiya, Rose – and hello to you too.' She ran her eyes up and down all six feet two of Josh.

'Titch, Josh, Josh, Titch.'

'You dark horse, you kept him quiet,' the other girl said.

'I am here, you know,' Josh joked. He climbed in and reached over to open the door for Rosa.

'I must be due for an award of some kind then,' Rosa said to Titch.

Titch screwed her face up and cocked her head to the side. 'Award? I don't get you.'

'To be able to keep something quiet in this place. Have a good day, Titch.' And the van set off down the hill.

'Who's she?' Josh asked with interest. 'Great pair of pins on her. Chest not bad either.'

'Josh!'

'Just saying.'

'Titch is her name. Well, nickname anyway, I think. She cleans up at the Ship Inn and works in one of the coffee shops. She's all right, a bit zany. She was there the other night. She's also a bit obsessed with men, I think.'

'Says the Virgin bloody Mary! I was half-expecting you to tell me you'd already had a Christmas fumble.'

Rosa cringed as she remembered Seb's bony fingers trying to enter her.

'Does your silence mean you did?' Josh enquired, frowning

a little.

'God, no. I did fancy Luke, it's true – until I realised his middle name was Judas.'

'No such thing as an ugly face, just ugly people, Rosa.'

'Whatever. Now come on, let's paint this shop red.'

'Red?'

'Josh, just drive.'

CHAPTER THIRTEEN

Days flew past, mainly spent in a whirlwind of cleaning, painting and generally getting the shop as shipshape as possible. Rosa and Josh had also managed to walk Hot on a few different beautiful beaches and then, completely knackered, their nights had consisted of staying in with beers, wine, easy food and general chit-chat before going to their separate sleeping quarters and snoring until the seagulls broke their deep slumber.

Josh made sure that Rosa didn't go anywhere near the Ship, and remarkably, they hadn't bumped into anyone all week to upset their peace.

Josh had measured the old damp blinds and they managed to find some ready-made ones in a big store in Ulchester that were a perfect fit. Rosa had chosen a duck-egg blue for the front door. Josh advised that she should wait until the weather was better before she considered any outside painting.

By New Year's Eve Rosa felt that she was ready to start putting stock on the shelves, but the big question was – what?

On the morning of that day, a bleary-eyed Josh walked into the kitchen to find her making scrambled eggs.

'Want some?'

'Yes, lovely. I'll have breakfast and better get going, I suppose.'

But he didn't sound enthusiastic at the prospect.

Rosa looked down-hearted.

'It's the rugby club New Year bash, you know I can't miss that. Plus, I did promise to pop in and see my Great-Auntie Deirdre.'

'I know you have to go. But it's been so lovely having you here and I really appreciate just how much you've helped me.' Rosa stirred the eggs to hide her sadness.

'So, you're sorted with all the paperwork I went through with you now?'

'Yes.' Rosa turned and made a face.

'Don't be like that. Insurance is important, and for goodness sake get down the bank today and open a new account. You can set up direct debits for gas, et cetera.'

'I will.'

'You're like a petulant child sometimes, you know that?' Josh said sternly.

'And?'

'Same old Rosa, but I wouldn't change you for the world.' He gently smacked her bum. Then: 'So, that Luke was just down here for Christmas, was he?'

'Er…yes. Although if his girlfriend's still in hospital, he might stay down here, I suppose. The *Gazette* is out today – I'm sure it will tell us everything we need to know. Why do you ask?'

'Oh, just wondered.'

'Look Josh, it's fine. *I* will be fine. Maybe I was being over-sensitive. The more people who know the shop is open, the better really. I need as much custom as I can get.'

They took their breakfast through to the lounge and sat with it on their laps.

'Bugger. We should have got you a TV,' Josh said. 'We didn't notice, did we, as we were too tired to care in the evenings.'

'Doesn't bother me,' Rosa said. 'Not having one will make

me concentrate on this place, and when I'm ready I can look at the ads in the newsagent's window; someone might be selling one. Seems that's the most direct place of barter around here, anyway.'

Hot came running in from the balcony, shivering from the intense cold.

'Poor little sausage, come here.' Josh put his plate down and swept the dog into his arms. 'Now make sure you look after your mummy, you are man of the house now. Aw, I shall miss him.'

'And me too, obviously.'

'That goes without saying, you crazy cat.'

Rosa suddenly stood up. 'That's it! I know what I can start with.'

'Go on.' Josh continued to play with Hot.

'Pets! What have I seen the most of since I've been here? Dogs! The Cockleberry Coven have a cat. There were two pub cats. It's genius.'

'Oh Rosa, you can't sell animals,' Josh tutted. 'You probably have to have a special licence.'

'Not the animals, silly, but everything connected with them. Coats for when it's cold, discounted food, toys, flea spray. The list is endless. Don't they say that sex, food and animals sell?'

'Er…I think it's just sex and food.'

'Well, it's going to be pets too now.' Rosa mused, 'When I was in the Co-op, I noticed how limited the dog-food range was – and how expensive. The buses are not very frequent to Ulchester, where the big supermarkets with the cheap prices are, and so I think there could be a market for more choice locally and at a better price. Plus, when tourists come down with dogs, I can maybe do some doggy knick-knacks too. And nice bowls – yes, every dog lover loves a nice bowl. And how about designer doggy stuff too?' Her eyes had gone all sparkly with inspiration.

'OK, it could be a start. I saw a cash and carry in Ulchester – do you want to pick up some food before I go?'

'No, no. I can do this. Let me work out how much spare money I have, then I can get it delivered.'

'Do you need some extra cash, Rosa?'

'No. I must do this myself, using the money that was left to me. I can start small and build on it. Now, come on – think. What else would be a cheap outlay to get me started?'

'Postcards and greetings cards maybe?' Josh suggested.

'Not postcards, too many shops are selling them down this street. But maybe gifts? I love trinket-like things and they will be great for the kids.'

'Good idea.' Josh grinned. 'Whilst Mummy and Daddy look at stuff for their fur babies, their own babies are kept quiet.'

'Exactly! I have to trial and error these things though, Josh. I'm so excited now!'

Josh smiled at Rosa's enthusiasm. 'Next time I come down, the Corner Shop will be like a mini hyper-market.'

'Let's hope so, eh. Oh my God!'

'What?'

Rosa scurried off, then reappeared a moment later, carrying something.

'Here, look. I forgot all about it. The mention of extra cash reminded me.'

Josh unwrapped the toilet paper from around the object she had handed him.

'Wow, Rosa, that's beautiful. And with the size of that sapphire, I should imagine it's worth quite a bit too.'

'That's what I thought. Look at the engraving.'

'Aw, that's so sweet.'

'I found it down the back of the sofa.'

'I told you,' Josh said triumphantly. 'You just never know what you might find.'

'I see nothing wrong in selling it, do you?' Rosa asked. 'Finders, keepers and all that. It will be just the kick-start I need.'

'Don't do anything rash though, Rosa. I'd get it valued properly first.'

'Yeah, I will.' She wrapped it back up in the toilet roll, then cried: 'Oh, I don't want you to go yet!'

'OK. I'll do you a deal. How about we take Hot for a walk and then have lunch in the Lobster Pot. You need to check it out in there and it will be easier if I'm with you.'

'Cool. Let me go and get ready.'

The Lobster Pot was quiet with the calm before the New Year's Eve storm. A poster inside announced that there was to be a fancy-dress party that night: two free glasses of fizz and a buffet, with £10 as the entry ticket price.

'That would be at least fifty quid in London,' Josh noted between mouthfuls of his fish and chips.

'I know. It's so much cheaper down here. This food is bloody lovely too. Do you reckon they own this place then?' Rosa pointed to the couple of men behind the bar with her fork.

'Maybe. They were both really friendly, weren't they, and their voices didn't sound as if they're from these parts.'

The interior of the Lobster Pot was more gastro-pub than Devon local. Beautifully handwritten blackboards announced the local fayre and there was a big display of fresh flowers on the end of the bar.

They finished their lunch and Josh drained his pint of lager.

'Right. I'd better go, Rosalar. I've got a long drive ahead of me, so no more booze for me.'

But Rosa, feeling a bit tipsy from a large glass of Merlot, wasn't ready for the party to finish. 'Go on, Josh, just one for the road,' she wheedled.

'If I have one more, I shall have to stay.'

Rosa stuck her bottom lip out and faux-fluttered her eyelashes at him. 'Pretty please.'

He immediately gave in. 'Oh, go on then...'

By five o' clock, Rosa and Josh were not only a bottle of wine and three pints down respectively, they had sat at the bar and learned that the managers of the Lobster Pot were Jacob and Raffaele, a married couple who had sold up in London to make a life down in the South-west.

The two men had been able to afford a beautiful cliff-top home in Polhampton Sands, where they spent their time off. Jacob, who had a camp taste in humour, ran the bar, while husband Raffaele was the chef. Jacob's sister Alyson worked behind the bar; she ran the place when they took time out. Her boyfriend Brad helped Raffaele in the kitchen.

'I'm afraid I'm going to have to ask you lovely people to leave now,' Jacob said. He was cleaning down the bar. 'We need to get everything ready for later, plus I've got to put my glad rags on.' He dramatically pushed back his brown fringe. 'One has to be the Belle of the *Balls,* obviously.'

Rosa loved him already. 'Who are you coming as?'

He spun around. 'Looking at this arse, I know you're probably thinking Kylie in her gold hot pants. But me and my hubby have decided on Betty Turpin and Bet Lynch. The best hotpot-maker and landlady in history.'

Rosa looked perplexed and Josh laughed out loud as Jacob explained, 'From *Coronation Street,* darling, characters before your time probably. Right, off you go. Happy New Year, unless of course you are coming back later. And goodbye, little one.' He waved down at Hot, who had been remarkably quiet, sleeping under Rosa's barstool.

As they were putting on their coats, a young good-looking guy appeared in chef's whites. He must have been twenty years Jacob's junior. Jacob introduced them.

'Meet Rosa, a newbie in the village – owns the Corner Shop no less – and this is Josh, her *friend*.' He lingered on the last word.

Raffaele shook their hands. 'Hi, pleased to meet you both, but I've got to dash – sorry. I've run out of gherkins.'

'Not like you to fall short of a gherkin, dear,' Jacob called after him as he opened the door for Josh and Rosa. 'Time to go, people. Happy New Year.'

'I don't think this is a good idea, Rosa.'

'Look, I'll have to face them sometime.'

'But you're drunk,' Josh said nervously, 'and you know how you get when you're drunk.'

'I've stopped you going home to your rugby club New Year's Eve bash, so there's no way we can consider just sitting in the flat with not even a TV to watch Jools Holland's *Hootenanny* on.'

'Well, we could go back to the Lobster Pot – I think it would be a laugh there. We'd get to see the guys in drag.'

Josh half-wished he had left when he wanted to earlier, but Rosa always had a way of cleverly manipulating him. They had got back from lunch, fed Hot and then downed two JD and Cokes – and now here they were, marching down the front to the Ship.

The live music was already blaring when they arrived, and the bar was packed with old and young alike.

Seb was propping up the bar and he smiled lasciviously when he saw her. 'Ravishing Rosa. I've missed you.'

She felt slightly sick. 'Hi Seb, this is my friend Josh. Josh, this is the guy who kindly gave me a lift from the station.'

'Ah. I understand now.' Seb nodded and winked. Rosa cringed inwardly.

'Understand what?' Josh mouthed, moving them away.

'The reason I turned him down the other night.'

'Oh. You hate beards – is that why?'

'No, I hate dickheads, that's why.'

'Singles now, I reckon, Rosa.'

'Josh, don't be bloody ridiculous, it's New Year's Eve.'

'Mustang Sally… Ride, Rosa, ride.' Lucas appeared and began to sing loudly into Rosa's ear. Just then, the band decided to stop – leaving Rosa to shout her drunk reply for all to hear.

'Well, oh well. Here he is, the man whose mouth is obviously bigger than his dick.'

People around sniggered. Sheila walked down to the end of the bar and addressed her.

'Don't be like that, Rosa. It's just our way down here – when a stranger arrives.'

Josh took her arm. 'Come on, let's get out of here.'

'No, Josh, I have something to say.'

At that moment, a girl appeared by her side, hobbling on crutches. She must have been around Rosa's age, immaculately dressed with a perfect shiny brown bob, a tiny pointed nose and a thin top lip. Rosa didn't trust people with a thin top lip.

'Hi, I'm Jas, Lucas's other half. So, you're the reason he was late picking me up the other night. He told me how full-on you were when he did your plumbing. Pleased with yourself, are you?' She pointed to her plastered leg with one of her crutches.

Lucas was already hot-footing his way to the gents.

'Full-on? *Full-on!* How dare you? He didn't even mention he had a girlfriend and I wonder if he told you that his mother had sent him round just to find out exactly what I was up to with my new shop. I hope you realise what sort of family you are getting yourself into.' Rosa was just about to kick one of Jas's crutches away, when Josh lifted her under one arm and negotiated his way out of the pub with her.

He gently put her down by the rocks at the start of the beach. 'That went well then.'

'Why do you always have to be my knight in bloody shining armour, Josh? I can sort things on my own. I don't need you.' She screamed and stamped her foot like a child.

Josh remained calm. 'But sometimes you just need to turn the dial down. It wasn't the right time to take that lot on. You could have sorted it out another day – when you were sober.'

'Sober, shober. I didn't try it on with her bloody boyfriend. I flirted a bit but that was all – and who are you to tell me to turn the dial down? You sound like another bloody social worker.'

'Maybe she's just testing you. A bloke wouldn't tell his girlfriend that another girl was full-on – too much information. To be fair though, if he was late because he was with you and the poor cow got run over, well…'

'Well – what? He didn't mention he was late. In fact, he didn't mention her at all. Anyway, shut up, Josh. Mr bloody Sensible. I wish I'd come here on my own now.'

Josh bit his lip. He knew that when Rosa was like this, there was no reasoning with her.

'Are you coming back to the shop with me?' he asked.

Rosa's back was now to him as she looked out to sea.

'No, I'm not. It's only eleven 'o' clock on New Year's Eve. Boring bastard.'

Josh walked slowly up to the flat, giving her the chance to

follow if she wanted, but there was no stopping her when she was in this sort of mood. He was worried about what she might do, but there was only so much he could take – and short of carrying her the whole way home, what else could he do? She was an adult. But a troubled, misguided adult, and when drunk, all her childhood insecurities rose to the top and sprayed out like an out-of-control firework.

He went in, let Hot out for a pee and sat on the roof terrace. The sound of the music carried in the still air and he could hear all sorts of singing and shouting. He was tempted to go up to the Lobster Pot and see the New Year in there, but then thought better of it. He called Rosa's phone; its familiar ringtone rang out from where she'd forgotten it in the lounge.

At ten to midnight, Josh couldn't bear to think what sort of trouble she was getting herself into and headed back down to the beach. Rosa was no longer on the rock, sitting where he'd left her. He pushed the pub door open and the next thing he knew, he was being forced back outside with Titch's lips pressed full on to his.

'*Nooo!*' At that very moment, Rosa rushed past them both. 'Not her!'

Josh broke free from the man-eater's grasp and started running after Rosa.

'It wasn't what you thought!' he called out breathlessly.

'It never bloody is with men, is it, Josh?'

'And why do you care anyway? You talked to me like a piece of shit earlier.'

Rosa continued to march ahead up the hill. She turned and said nastily, 'Don't think I care, Josh. It's just I can't bear them having something else to talk about.'

'She just grabbed me, Rosa, I swear.'

'Like I said, I don't care.'

Josh caught up with her and swung her around.

'Maybe this will make you.' He held her tightly, so she had no chance to push him away, and kissed her passionately on the lips. He could feel her body melt into his, but the might of her mind enabled her to yank herself free.

Her voice was cracking. 'Like I said, Josh, I really don't care.'

CHAPTER FOURTEEN

Rosa was sitting looking out to sea on the roof terrace when Josh woke from his broken slumber. Hot was on her lap, his little pointed head poking out of the top of the duvet she had wrapped tightly around herself.

Josh pulled a chair round so he was sitting directly in front of her, found her hands and took them in his. She turned her head away so as not to look at him.

'I thought you would come and find me on my rock last night,' she said.

'Oh, Rosa. I did.'

'You left me down there.'

'You said some terrible things to me.'

Rosa bit her lip. Seagulls were swooping and crying overhead.

'I wish I could be a seagull, free from all this shit.' Tears ran down her face.

'It's fine. You weren't that bad – and I very much doubt if anyone will even remember seeing you. Even the landlady seemed three sheets to the wind.'

'I hate it here.'

'No, you don't, you're just hating yourself right now. Everything will be all right, I promise you. Look, come in out of the cold and I'll make us some coffee.'

Hot scrabbled free as Rosa waddled in with the duvet still around her.

'You look like a penguin,' Josh teased, and Rosa managed a tiny smile. 'Ah, there she is – my old Rosalar.'

'I'm not your Rosalar.'

'Well, yes, that's obvious. I'm – what was it? – a boring bastard.'

Rosa put her hand to her head. 'I'm sorry. So sorry.'

Josh wrapped his big arms around her and the duvet. She rested her head on his shoulder.

'Drinking's not good for me when I'm angry, is it?'

'No, Rosa, but we've been here before and I'm sure we will be again. Maybe next time, head up the hill rather than down? At least Jacob at the Lobster Pot will make you laugh.'

'I ruined your New Year's Eve, didn't I?'

'Well, it will certainly be one to remember.'

'Please tell me you didn't make a move on Titch. When I saw you kissing her –

Well...'

'Well – what?'

'Oh, it doesn't matter.'

'I promise you, I had no say in what happened. I pushed the door open to come in and find you, and she literally launched herself at my face like some praying mantis. You're right, she's an odd one. And where were you? I imagined finding you waving that crutch in the injured girl's spiteful face.'

'What kind of bitch was she too?' Rosa put on a voice. '"The reason I'm like this is because you were trying it on with my boyfriend." Stupid cow.'

Josh got up and went to make coffee. When he sat down again, Rosa threw the duvet off her and sat up straight, saying,

'Josh, will you hand me the *Gazette* for a minute, please? They had found a stray copy on the table in the Lobster Pot as they left yesterday; in her drunken state, Rosa had just thrown it down on the lounge floor. The headline read:

HIT AND RUN IN COCKLEBERRY BAY
Jasmine Simmonds, of 9 Chichester Terrace, London W9, was hit by a moving vehicle at around 5.30pm on 23 December near the junction of Main Street and the Ulchester Road. The vehicle drove off and police are continuing with their inquiries.

'Oh my God, Luke or Lucas rather, left here at around that time. Do you think it was he himself who knocked her down – and if so, why would he not stop and help his own girlfriend when she was lying there in the road?' Rosa let out a long, shocked breath. Instinct told her she'd hit upon the truth.

'Didn't you say you had drunk a bottle of Prosecco?' Josh remembered.

'Yes, but only one between us.'

'He'd still have been over the limit, Rosa – and maybe he didn't realise it was her. You know how dark it is around here.'

'It doesn't matter who it was, it's still terrible. Fancy leaving someone lying there, hurt, and likely to get run over.'

'Yes, it is terrible, and I'm actually surprised the police haven't been here to question you, since you would be his chief alibi.'

'But why would they do that? Surely her own boyfriend would be the least likely person they'd suspect.'

'I guess so, but I still think you should voice your concerns.'

'To the police, you mean? No way. I reckon Sheila would have me run out of town like a lone cowboy if I messed with her precious son's life.'

'But it would be the right thing to do,' Josh persisted. 'I mean, what do you owe him? Nothing. He lied to you from the start.'

'No. He's got his own guilt to deal with, and Jazzy Pants didn't die, did she? And let's be honest here – no good would come out of it for me. He'll be back in London before we know it, and with any luck I will never have to come face to face with him again.'

'OK, but promise me you will keep away from him.'

'I promise.'

CHAPTER FIFTEEN

The flat was far too empty and quiet without Josh. Rose had held Hot's paw up and waved him off that morning, and since then had drifted in and out of sleep on her new sofa. Her head was banging. She yawned and looked around her blearily. She had decided to keep the old sofa too. She would give it a proper scrub with some upholstery cleaner and get some coloured throws and cushions for it. But they were luxury items now, until she sold the necklace and got some decent cash behind her, at least.

Hungry, she opened the fridge, but not in the mood for cooking, shut it again. There was half a cold pizza on the side that Josh had not cooked when he got in last night. She must have crashed out straightaway as she had no recollection of anything – well, anything after *the kiss*, that is.

She was so pleased that he hadn't mentioned it. She and Josh *didn't* kiss. She had enjoyed having the occasional bit of action with him, yes, but that didn't constitute a relationship. In her eyes, a kiss did – and anyway, she didn't want a relationship with Josh. He was her friend – her brother, almost. And he was too staid for her.

She poured herself a glass of milk and took the pizza back

through to the lounge, letting a whining Hot out onto the roof terrace as she did so. She sat and stared at the wall, now wishing she had got herself a TV. She felt hungover, she felt empty. Walking back into the kitchen, she spotted the half-full bottle of JD on the side. It was New Year's Day – what else was there to do – and at least it would make her sleep and forget about the awful night before.

A few hours later, a text from Josh woke her.

Home. Great-Auntie Deirdre still alive. I am too – just. Hope all OK?

Rosa felt groggy and cold. She had forgotten to shut the roof-terrace door, which was a good thing for Hot but not for her. Shivering, she made her way to the bathroom. Peeing like a horse, she put her head in her hands.

She had been so positive about the shop yesterday, but today everything seemed kind of dark somehow. Josh's advice to 'turn the dial down' rang in her ears. He was right, of course, and she knew alcohol wasn't the answer, but all these things were easier said than done, and today Mr Jack Daniel was her best friend.

She was just washing her hands when there was a knock at the door and Hot began barking. Checking herself in the fading showbiz mirror, she saw that she looked a fright. Her hair was more mad than usual, and last night's make-up was caked around her eyes.

She was not going to bother to answer the door, she decided – but whoever it was made it plain they were not going away. Wiping the smudges of mascara from under her eyes, and swilling a blob of toothpaste around her mouth, Rosa slowly made her way downstairs to the front shop door.

Squinty-eyed, and still feeling a little squiffy, she opened the door a crack.

'Rosa, it's me, Lucas. Can I come in, please?'

101

CHAPTER SIXTEEN

Josh checked his phone for the third time: no text from Rosa. She'd probably gone back to sleep. He'd give her a quick call before he went to bed. At home in the house off the Whitechapel Road, he walked into her old bedroom and smiled at the picture of the back of a nude man she had insisted he bought from a stall at the Old Shoreditch market.

Rosa was a pain in the arse at times, but he already missed her vibrancy, her energy. She was like an unbroken horse. Beautiful, but wild. Josh knew that taming Rosa Larkin wasn't the answer. She needed to be free, and to work things out for herself. He would just check she was OK later and despite how he felt about her, he would leave her be for a while.

He lay down on the sofa and, flicking on the TV, thought back to kissing Titch. Secretly, he had enjoyed that too. Not the fact it was Titch specifically, but he was a man, he had needs, and they hadn't been met properly for far too long now.

CHAPTER SEVENTEEN

'I'm busy, Luke, Lucas, whoever you are,' Rosa said wearily.

'Busy? Nobody's busy on New Year's Day – and Happy New Year to you too.' Hot was sniffing his shoes. 'And to Mr Sausage, of course. It's just I'm going back to London tomorrow and wanted to say goodbye.'

'There – you said it.' She began to close the door.

He put his foot out to prevent her. 'Rosa, please don't be like that.'

Rosa took in his handsome face and tight jeans. She thought of Jasmine's pinched little mouth spewing out that she had been 'full-on' with her boyfriend. Feeling horny with a hangover, she half-wished she had been now.

'Come in then, but for no more than five minutes – and don't expect any sort of hospitality. I'm minging and not in the best of moods.'

Staring at her pert little bottom as she walked up the stairs, Luke smirked. Her fiery, devil-may-care attitude was a complete turn-on for him.

Rosa poured herself another JD and Coke. 'Drink?'

'Really? No, thanks.' He sat down. 'New sofa – nice. Did your boyfriend buy you that?'

'He's not my boyfriend.'

'Fit guy though. Thought he was going to lump me one when he asked me to move my van on Boxing Day.'

'What?'

'Yeah. I'd parked my van in your parking space. I did tell him I wanted to talk to you. Did he not mention it?'

'Of course he did,' she lied, 'but why would I want to talk to you after the way you treated me?'

Luke put his hand out and rested it on her shoulder. 'Rosa, calm down.'

The fact that Josh hadn't told her he'd seen Luke outside in the back made her far from calm. She didn't need protecting. She shrugged off the hand.

'What do you want? Just spit it out and then make your sorry journey home with your bitch of a girlfriend.'

'Whoa.'

'What do you mean, whoa? You're the one who got me tipsy, wheedled information out of me and then told the whole of the bloody Bay.' She snorted. 'They'll be dribbling with excitement for weeks on this one. That is, if they haven't forgotten about the hit-and-run.'

Luke looked uncomfortable. He stood up.

'I just wanted to say I'm sorry about all that. You've probably realised my mum is not a woman to argue with and – well, she thought she'd be helping you too, as she told me not to charge you a lot.'

'How bloody thoughtful of you both.'

'Nobody got hurt, and on a positive note, everybody will be flocking to your door to see what you are selling now, when you do open.'

'She only had to ask me. I would have told her when I was ready.'

'Sheila Hannafore waits for no man, you need to understand that. My dad certainly is resting in peace now.'

He held out his hand and in doing so, curled his finger under, stroking Rosa's palm. She immediately felt the electric spark of lust.

'Talking of getting hurt, it is a terrible business about your girlfriend,' she said, removing her hand. 'How frightening for her, to be left in the road like that.'

'Er...yes. She's going to be fine though. She had an operation in Ulchester General to fix her ankle with pins. If she's careful, it'll be six weeks in plaster, then physio. Rosa, about that...'

She took a slurp of her drink as Luke continued.

'It's just I left here about the same time as the accident happened. So, if anyone does ever ask, do you mind saying that I didn't leave here until around six? I saw the police cars and as I'd had a glass or two of that Prosecco and didn't want to get breathalysed, I just drove straight back here and parked up out of sight.'

He looked appealingly at Rosa. 'I know it was cowardly, but at the time I didn't even realise it was Jasmine lying there.'

'So why leave the van here the whole time?'

'Because I lied to cover my arse about drink-driving and said that I'd got the train down from Paddington and was going to go in my mum's car to pick Jas up from the station. I realised that the more lies I was telling, the guiltier I was looking. I've actually parked round the back of the park now. I'm going to sneak off after dark tonight as there definitely won't be any police within a twenty-mile radius of here, today of all days.'

It did all sound very plausible and he had been kind to her that day, despite being on his fact-finding mission. However, in Rosa's eyes you couldn't kid a kidder and she would reserve judgement, for now, at least.

Lucas sat back down on the sofa next to her.

'I know it's a big ask, Rosa, and the chances are slim the police will come to you, but just in case, eh? And look how cheaply you got your pipes fixed, remember?' He looked right into her make-up-smudged green eyes and placed his right hand gently on her left thigh.

Rosa removed his hand, then ran hers up the front of his jumper. Gently scratching him as she did so, she whispered, 'I won't tell if you won't.'

He urgently pulled her jumper up over her head, revealing that her nipples were already standing to attention.

She wasn't wearing underwear, hadn't had a bath since yesterday but really didn't care. The last few days had hurt her, she needed touching. And she knew from experience that a lad like Luke would be able to do that in just the right way.

Grabbing a strategic condom she had hidden down the sofa when he walked in, she pulled off her leggings and reached for his flies.

'Mum's the word, eh, Lukey boy,' she murmured, putting a finger to his lips.

CHAPTER EIGHTEEN

The first working day of the year had brought with it rain and wind. In fact, it was howling so loudly around the roof terrace that it had woken Rosa and was making Hot whine nervously. She could see white breakers on the waves way out at sea, and even the seagulls' cries were muffled as they struggled to soar and plane their way through the grey skies.

Surprisingly, despite yet another hangover, Rosa had woken in a positive mood. She didn't have one regret about sleeping with Luke. The sex had been good and there was no way anyone would find out about it. He was the one who was being unfaithful, not her. And no good would come of admitting it to Josh, especially as she had promised him she wouldn't see Lucas again. Rosa put the entire incident to the back of her mind. If she did ever see him again, there would be absolutely no mention of hit-and-runs or random shenanigans.

She fed herself and Hot, then wrapped herself up ready for the elements. The poor sausage dog hadn't had a decent walk for days. Rosa had always thought it was poncey to dress your pooch up in a little coat, but now she was thinking of becoming a pet-shop tycoon, maybe she should have a look and see what would suit him. Anyway, bless his tiny socks, it was bloody freezing outside today.

Rounding the corner to the beach, a big gust of wind almost knocked her sideways and she quickly whisked a whimpering Hot up in her arms.

'It's all right, darling,' she told him. 'Let's get in the bay where it's maybe a little more sheltered.'

The waves were crashing on the shore, bigger than she had seen since she'd come here. Rosa tipped her head back into the pouring rain and soaked up Mother Nature at her fiercest best. She needed to clear her head of everything that had happened over the past few days and this was just the tonic.

She put Hot down and laughed to watch him chase bits of wood and rubbish from the bin; the wind was strewing its contents everywhere. Every time Rosa tried to catch some and put it back, the wind flung it in the air again and away from her.

It was a relief to turn around and walk back up the beach without the wind blowing directly at them. The rain still stung Rosa's eyes though, and she put her arm up to protect her face from what now felt like hailstones. Hot shivered at her feet and she hefted him up and tucked him inside her coat.

Through all this gloom, she could make out someone walking towards her, optimistically holding up an umbrella which promptly blew completely inside out, nearly taking the woman carrying it, Mary Poppins-style, along with it.

As the woman got closer, Rosa recognised the silver-white hair, now dripping like rat's tails, of Sheila Hannafore. The landlady stopped and spoke, but she had to shout above the elements to be heard and even then, it was difficult to understand what she said.

'I didn't expect to see you anytime soon, so I took the chance to come out now. Here, take this.' She handed Rosa an envelope. 'Why don't you come up and get dry by the fire?'

Although she was reluctant to make any sort of conversation with this woman, Rosa was by now so cold and wet, and could feel Hot shuddering against her chest, that she followed Sheila up to the pub. Before she went in, she stood in the porch and opened the envelope. In it was £120 in £10 notes.

'There's coffee on the bar, dear. Help yourself – and take a pig's ear for the little man. There's a drip mat under the coat rack, so get that coat off too or you'll be chilled to the bone. Here's a towel for Hot.'

'Thanks, and thanks for the money back.'

'I may be a nosy cow and do things in my own way, but I'm not a thief, Rosa. And you didn't stay here those two nights you paid for.'

'But I don't expect you resold them, so...'

'I never usually sell rooms over Christmas with the family here.' She started taking her own wet things off, saying, 'It's fine, don't you worry.' Then: 'Right, I'm in the middle of making bread, so I'd better go. Help yourself to more coffee if you want it.'

Rosa knew that was the nearest she would get to an apology from Sheila Hannafore, so she'd better accept it. Maybe it wasn't 'normal', the way she had gone about things – but what was normal anyway?

Once Hot was dry and had finished growling with joy, guarding and demolishing his porky snack, Rosa put her damp coat back on and headed for the door, dreading the walk back home up the hill. Hot too, appeared reluctant to leave and was pulling on the lead, trying to take her in the direction of the fire. Just then, Sheila appeared at the bar.

'What are you going to be selling in there anyway?' she asked outright.

'You'll have to wait and see,' Rosa told her with a smile, 'but

I'm sure whatever it is, you will be the first to know.'

Sheila smiled back – she knew when she'd met her match. 'Have a good day, Rosa. It's Quiz Night on a Tuesday down here, if you're interested. Quite a young crowd too.'

'I'll see.'

With that, Rosa headed back out into the noisy weather and began to struggle up the hill towards home. Like son, like mother, she thought. Sheila Hannafore hadn't really wanted to make amends with her. She knew her son was guilty as hell and that Rosa was his only alibi.

CHAPTER NINETEEN

Rosa had just shut the shop door behind her, when Josh phoned.

'Bloody hell, you are alive then?'

'I'm sorry, I crashed out last night and then have been walking with Hot on the beach. It's blowing a gale down here today.'

'Good. OK. So, are you feeling better about life today then?'

'A few days off the booze and I'll be right as rain. Sheila Hannafore just caught me on the beach, almost apologised and gave me a hundred and twenty quid back for the room I didn't sleep in.'

'It's the least she could do. Has that tosser of a son gone back yet?'

'Er…I didn't ask, but I expect so.' Rosa tried to put the vision of her and Luke going at it like rabbits on her sofa to the back of her mind.

'Good job too. Time to concentrate on you and the shop now.'

'Yes. Broadband should be up this afternoon, so I will dig out the old laptop you gave me and get on a stock-finding mission. I was looking at the most bizarre pet accessories earlier on my phone. How about a Flower Rear-Butt Pup Cover?'

'Do what?'

'Basically, a plastic flower you stick up a dog's bottom to hide

111

its bum-hole.'

Josh laughed. 'Vile.'

'I'm thinking of getting myself one too.'

He laughed louder. 'Even viler. But anyway, it's great that you are on the case. I was thinking, maybe you should organise a little launch event, get the *Gazette* on board.'

'That's a bloody brilliant idea.'

'I do have them from time to time. Right, I'll let you get on. I'm at a conference for the rest of this week so you won't hear from me much.'

Josh hung up and sat back in his home office chair. Rosa probably wouldn't even realise he was trying not to contact her, in order to give her a chance to find her own feet. He had to let her fly on her own for a bit.

Rosa had a hot bath and put on fresh clothes. With Christmas and New Year out of the way, everything seemed very real now. She checked in the fridge and cupboards to see what supplies she had left, then headed up to the Co-op. She was just about to go in when she heard her name being called from up the road.

Jacob was busy tidying up the pansy-filled hanging baskets outside the pub. No doubt they had taken a hammering in the wind. As she got closer she realised he was doing it in a hopping fashion. Hot began to sniff around the legs of the benches outside.

Jacob was very attractive for a man in his early forties. His salt and pepper hair was cut in an immaculate style, and even wearing joggers and a jumper he still emitted a certain style. Even the now-evident plaster on his foot was a trendy black.

'Happy New Year, you two.'

'Happy New Year, Jacob.' She pointed to his foot. 'Don't tell me the phantom hit-and-run driver of Cockleberry Bay has struck again?'

'No.' Jacob laughed out loud, realising how much he loved this colourful character already. 'I twisted right off Betty Turpin's four-inch heels whilst doing the Macarena on New Year's Eve. Raffaele said I should have stuck to the brogues she used to wear, but darling, I really haven't got the calves for a flat. And I was so jealous of his Bet Lynch wig, boobs and heels.'

Rosa couldn't contain herself. 'Sorry,' she choked.

Jacob put his hand on her shoulder. 'Laughter, my dear, is the best medicine. Ooh, hark at Dr Jacob here.' He awkwardly balanced himself to sit down on one of the benches. 'That's better.'

'Let me help you with this. Hold him, will you?'

She handed him Hot's lead and began finishing the job in hand, replanting the uprooted pansies and picking off leaves and other debris.

'Rosa, dear, there's something I wanted to ask you. I didn't think of you until now and I know you're obviously busy setting up the shop, but have you done bar work before?'

'Is the Pope Catholic? Indeed, I have.'

'Excellent. It's just, I can't be standing up for long at the moment and we could do with some help. Alyson, my sister who you met the other day, she can manage without me as January is dead as a dodo down here, but I can't expect her to work on her time off, so how would you feel about covering a couple of evenings for us? Just six until eleven on a Wednesday and Friday. I'll pay you forty pounds cash per shift, plus tips.'

Rosa paused to think. She had vowed not to take on extra work, but since she hadn't sold the necklace yet, it would make sense. Plus, it would give her the chance to meet new people and potentially spread the word about the shop.

'OK, but just temporarily, if that's all right with you?'

'Yes, yes, of course. They said six weeks for this thing to come

113

off, but if I keep doing the exercises, I reckon it won't be any longer than four.'

'So, when do you want me to start?'

'Tomorrow would be amazing if you could manage it. I can sit at the bar and show you the ropes.'

'OK, that's a date.'

'You are a dear, Rosa, that's such a help to us.'

'Can Hot come too?'

Jacob was petting him under the table. 'Of course he can. We've got two boys ourselves, Ugly and Pongo, the most beautiful pugs in the world. Young Hot here can look on it as a play-date.'

'Aw. Thanks so much, Jacob, and I can't wait to meet those fur babies of yours.'

'Ugly, Hot and Pongo – sounds like a boy band.' Jacob reached for one of his crutches and began pretending to sing into it. 'Thanks for helping with the pansies too.' He couldn't help sucking in his cheeks at the words 'pansies'. 'It's mucho appreciated.'

He really was a scream. Rosa walked back down to the Co-op with a slight spring in her step. The extra cash would definitely come in handy, and she had already decided that Ugly and Pongo would be the first on her Open Day guest-list.

Mary was at the counter. She broke into a smile when she saw Rosa.

'Happy New Year, my dear.'

'Same to you, Mary, and I haven't forgotten I still have your plate. The food was delicious, by the way. A real treat. Sorry, my friend Josh has been staying, so I didn't get a chance to pop it back, then I thought I might see you in the pub on New Year's Eve to thank you, before now.'

'Oh, I don't drink, Rosa. In fact, I don't go out that much at

114

all. How about you pop round later? I know my gran would love to meet you.'

'Um.' Rosa had had visions of just chilling on the sofa, surfing for stock, but Mary wasn't going to take no for an answer.

'You don't have to stay long, just have a cuppa with us.'

'OK, then.'

'I finish my Co-op shift at five, so how about five-thirty?'

'Perfect. I will see you then.'

CHAPTER TWENTY

When Rosa tentatively knocked at the Cockleberry Coven's door, she was half-excited, half-terrified to see what was behind it. She had never really been into anything supernatural and thought that fortune-telling was just an easy licence to get money out of innocent, troubled souls.

She noticed that the blue-and-white Seaspray Cottage sign had a little seahorse emblem on it too. The crystals had also changed, she thought, since she last walked past.

But she wasn't here for fortune-telling, she was here for a cup of tea, to give back the ladies' plate and to meet old Queenie Cobb, although goodness knows why Mary seemed so insistent she meet her. Maybe it was just to while away some of her own lonely hours. If she didn't drink, what did they do for light relief, Rosa wondered.

She could hear Mary coughing as she walked towards the door. She opened it and said, 'Hello, Rosa,' then looked down. 'No Hot Dog?'

'He's at home. I wasn't sure how Merlin was with dogs, because Hot's not the best with cats, to be honest. Here's your plate before I forget to give it to you.'

'Thank you. Now come in, come in.'

116

Rosa likened Mary's walk to that of a penguin, shifting the weight of her large frame from left to right.

The front door led straight from the pavement into a cluttered lounge. There was a small TV in the corner and a comfortable-looking green two-seater sofa; a sun-and-moon-patterned black throw adorned the armchair in the corner, which had a threadbare footstool in front of it. The shelf above the fireplace was glowing with the light of around twenty candles. Every wall seemed to hold shelves which overflowed with an assortment of ornaments and lines of old, leather-bound books. Above the old-fashioned lace curtain hung a pretty feathered dream-catcher.

Rosa followed Mary into a larger kitchen, the centrepiece of which was a table, covered with a black tablecloth and with a chair on either side. Despite being very old, with its Formica units and original slate flagstones, the kitchen was immaculately clean.

'The original two-up two-down, this was. They made do with a tin bath and an outside toilet when Gran moved in. When my mum came along, Ned – you know, Ned who had your shop – he fitted a bathroom. So, it's now a two-up, three-down.'

'Does your mum still live around here?' Rosa asked. She was fascinated by the stories.

'She died, Rosa.'

'Oh Mary, I'm so sorry. You must have been so young.'

'I never met her. She died whilst she was having me.' Mary tipped back her head to stop the coming tears. In a faint voice, she said, 'I miss her every day, even though I never met her, if that makes sense.'

'Total sense. And your grandad?'

Mary cleared her throat and said, 'I never met him. Gran brought me up. That's why I'm here now. I thought at ninety-three she might be slowing down a bit and would need me, but…well, you'll see for yourself.' Her chuckle turned into a lengthy cough.

Rosa didn't dare ask any more questions. She couldn't deal with emotions at the best of times and at least she would never have to experience the grief of losing her own mother – in the traditional sense, anyway.

She was saved by the toilet flush, for Queenie Cobb appeared from the bathroom that led straight off the kitchen. She was wearing dark glasses.

'Enough of that maudlin talk now, Mary. Rosa doesn't need to hear this.'

If words could kill, Rosa thought somewhat nervously, Queenie's granddaughter would be fighting for her last breath.

The old lady's face was etched with deep lines, her skin very brown. Her lips were cracked, and her long grey hair was tied back into a bun. Rosa wondered why she was wearing dark glasses in the house.

'Hello. So, it was you I need to thank for letting me into the Corner Shop the other night,' Rosa said.

The old woman shook her head. 'You must be mistaken, dear. The only way I will be leaving this house now is feet first.'

Mary quickly chipped in with, 'Gran's sight is terrible now, she's near-on blind. Tea, Rosa?'

'I can read your leaves, if you like?' The old lady eased herself onto one of the chairs at the kitchen table, letting out a little fart under her layered skirt as she did so.

'Oh no, it's fine,' Rosa said hastily. 'I'm not really into that sort of thing.'

'You don't have to be frightened.' Queenie grabbed hold of Rosa's hand. 'There is nothing to be frightened of but fear itself, you know that.'

Rosa sensed that the old lady wasn't going to take no for an answer. Queenie pointed to the chair opposite her.

'Come on, sit yourself down, lovey.'

Huffing and puffing, Mary put a pot of tea on the table. She pulled a stool out from under it and plonked herself down, her large buttocks spilling out over each side as she did so.

'Let me sit there,' Rosa insisted.

'No, no. You're our guest and I wouldn't dream of it.'

There were no handles on the cups and Queenie guided hers shakily to her mouth with both hands, saying, 'It's refreshing to have a new face down here. The youngsters usually run when they get to a certain age. Find it all a bit boring. But you've got a focus. You can stay.'

'Oh.' This wasn't exactly making Rosa feel uplifted, but she didn't have to stay in Cockleberry Bay for ever, just make the shop into a going concern, get a bit of money out of it, then hand it over to someone who deserved it.

'Dotty was a friend of mine, you know. Well, for a while anyway. Until…' The old lady looked up to the ceiling.

'Dotty?' echoed Rosa.

'Dorothea, from the Corner Shop,' Mary chipped in.

'Ah, right.'

'Ned's wife.' Queenie added.

'Gran, come on, let's talk about something else. Rosa doesn't need to hear about all this.'

It was Mary's turn to try to change the subject. Rosa couldn't understand Mary's agitation. She seemed so nervous. Of course her gran was going to be upset about losing a friend. Rosa was intrigued to be learning more about her predecessor and his life, and she was surprised that nobody had mentioned a Dorothea before.

'Such a lovely woman. Such a shame…'

'Gran!' Mary snapped.

'So, what did they use to sell, Dotty and Ned?' Rosa tried to lift the mood.

'Anything and everything really. It was like a magical shop. If you needed cotton for your sewing machine or a heel for your boot, even a pint of milk at the last minute, Dotty seemed to have it. When she...' Queenie took a deep breath. 'When she died, he kept it going as she would have wished.'

'That's nice.'

Queenie carried on. 'Before that blasted Co-op came along, we had two butchers, a fishmonger and a florist. No doubt you've seen we have just the one butcher now, Alfie Davies. He took over from his old dad Bill – not quite as good in my opinion but we still get our pork chops from there, don't we, Mary?'

Mary nodded.

'I didn't really want her to work in that blessed supermarket, but needs must around here, hey, Rosa? And I mean, who wants to be cooped up with an old woman like me twenty-four seven.' Queenie reached over and put her bony fingers to Rosa's face. Feeling around it, she then touched on her scar. 'I see now,' she murmured to herself, then more loudly, 'You are very beautiful, aren't you?'

'Oh Gran, really.' Mary seemed beside herself with embarrassment. Rosa, not sure of how to react, carried on picking loose tea leaves out of her teeth. Queenie pounced at her empty cup as soon as she had finished.

'Let me have a look for you,' she said. Rosa didn't dare ask how she could do that if she couldn't see properly. Without removing her dark glasses, and as if reading her mind, Queenie snarled, 'I can make out the outlines and feel.'

At that moment, Rosa was completely startled by the cat flap

120

flying open and the appearance of the biggest black cat she had ever seen. He went straight to his bowl of crunchies on the floor, stuffed a few in and then without warning jumped up on her lap, causing her knees to buckle and fur to fly into her mouth.

'Merlin, get down.' Mary tried to shoo him off a slightly agitated Rosa, who was now pulling bits of cat hair as well as tea leaves from her lips.

'He likes you.' Queenie smiled. 'And animals are very good judges of character, you know.'

Merlin made a funny sort of growling sound, then took himself off to his basket in the corner of the kitchen and began to noisily clean himself.

The old lady had started to move her hands over Rosa's cup in a circling motion when, without warning, she emitted a cross between a hiss and a groan, which caused Merlin to emit a deafening meow and Rosa to nearly jump out of her skin.

'It's OK, Rosa,' Mary whispered. 'They both do that every time.'

Realising it would probably be easier to escape from Colditz than here, Rosa sat tight and waited to hear what was said.

Queenie looked down into Rosa's cup. Then reaching across the table, she took hold of Rosa's hand.

'I see paper, a bundle of paper.' Queenie hesitated for a second as if waiting for Rosa to say something. 'Remember always, that love was at fault. The mermaids know that.'

Queenie let go of her hand and started again. 'Dark-haired and smooth; a crooked life. But he isn't to blame this time...' She began to swirl her hands over the top of the cup again. 'I see lots of animals.'

Rosa was now already beginning to switch off. Mary had obviously been told about Luke and it was obvious she liked animals, as everyone could see what Hot meant to her.

'Don't be fooled by the tall one...' the old lady then warned her.

If that was Josh, Rosa thought, then she knew this really was rubbish. Josh would never lie to her. Mind you, he hadn't mentioned that he'd seen Luke the other day and she had forgotten to ask him why. The old lady continued at great speed.

'Be free with your energy, Rosa, and your angels will guide you. Believe in yourself, and happiness you will find. Eat well, but drink less. A lot less.'

Mary was now sat as still as a stone; even Merlin had settled down to a one-eye-open nap. But old Mrs Cobb hadn't finished yet, and on hearing Rosa move restlessly in her seat, she shouted, 'WAIT!' Even Mary jumped this time. 'Don't jump to conclusions.'

She suddenly opened her eyes and stared straight at Rosa. Her voice was now soft again.

'You have a good future ahead of you, my dear. Don't waste it.'

'If I keep away from all these men, obviously,' Rosa said lamely.

'Did I mention any men, Rosa?'

Although not sure if it was the right thing to do, Rosa thanked Queenie and tentatively asked if she owed her anything.

'Rosa, please, of course not. I invited you to do this. But when you're ready, Merlin could do with a new lead.'

'I er...a lead?'

'Yes, our Mary takes him for a walk sometimes. He loves it, he does.'

Mary nodded furiously.

'Well then, Merlin shall have the finest cat lead on the market. How did you know I was thinking of selling pet products?'

'Did I say that? I don't think I did. No more questions now, my dear girl. Please, just tell me you're leaving soon, as I really could do with a sleep.'

'Gran!'

'Oh, ssh now, Mary. You know how tired this makes me feel.'

Rosa stood up. 'It's fine, honestly. I need to get back to Hot anyway.'

Queenie Cobb slowly got out of her chair. Resting both hands in front of her on the table to steady herself, she said quietly, 'If you find it, don't sell the necklace, Rosa.'

Rosa was now open-mouthed. 'But… How…'

The old lady shook her finger at her. 'Keep it in a very safe place and tell no one about it. No one.'

Relieved to be back in the peace of the Corner Shop upstairs flat, Rosa quickly cooked herself a cheese omelette, put on her pyjamas and snuggled up on the sofa with Hot and her laptop.

She thought back to the tea-leaves incident and had to admit that her disbelief in fortune-telling had been slightly blown out of the water. How on earth could Queenie Cobb have known about the necklace – and why couldn't she sell it, or the shop for that matter?

Tired from thinking too much, she typed the words 'cat' and 'leads' into Google and gaped in disbelief at the sheer number of options that came up. She wouldn't think any more about what old Queenie Cobb had said, she decided. She, little Rosa Larkin, was quite capable of creating her own destiny and that was that.

CHAPTER TWENTY ONE

There was not one person drinking in the pub when Rosa got there for her first shift. Raffaele came out to greet her. If he hadn't been gay Rosa would definitely have been hot on his very expensive-looking Gucci heels. He was dark-haired and about the same height as Luke, with the sort of face that was so cute you just wanted to squeeze it.

When he spoke, Rosa noticed that he had a slight Italian accent. It then all came flooding back from the New Year's Eve drunken afternoon at the bar. Jacob told her that he had interviewed Raffaele for a chef's position and had asked if he wanted to live in. Raffaele had said yes, not realising he was moving straight into Jacob's flat. Luckily Jacob's ruse worked. They had hit it off and had been together five years, married for one.

'Ciao, Rosa. How are you?'

'Good, thanks, Raffaele.'

'Jacob will be down in a minute – and don't worry, it won't be quiet like this all night. We've got a table of four and a table of two in for dinner later. Why don't you familiarise yourself behind the bar, and do help yourself to a drink.'

'Great, thanks, I'll do that.'

When Raffaele had made his way back to the kitchen, Rosa

looked around her. It really was a lovely space, with stained-glass windows at the front and a smart wooden bar stocked with every drink you could imagine lined up along it, cleverly lit to create a relaxing ambience.

'Hiya, kidder, you all right?' Jacob hobbled towards her.

'Yes, good, thanks. I left Hot at home tonight, by the way. Thought I'd better concentrate without having to worry about him.'

'Oh, the boys will be disappointed. I'd already told them there's a new sausage in town.'

Rosa laughed out loud as Jacob limped towards her.

'How's the foot?' she asked.

'Bloody painful, but hey, I've got another one.'

'So, I'm slightly confused, do you live above here then?'

'Yes and no. Like I told you, we have a beach house in the next town, but we also have a room here, for when we have late nights, et cetera. My sister and her boyfriend live above full-time. The dogs always come with us, wherever we go. We get to our other house as much as we can, which is quite a lot since Alyson and Brad are more than capable of running the joint. I like to keep a hand in though.'

'What a nice position to be in.'

'Yes. I'm very lucky. Now, to business. So, you've had a look at the beers on pump. Here are the menus for drinks and food. White wines are in the bucket.' He pointed to a shelf to the side of the bar. 'Reds under there. If you can be waitress too tonight, that would be great. Any cash tips you get, you can keep them all.'

'OK, great.'

'Let me just show you the till.'

Rosa watched carefully as Jacob showed her all the buttons.

'It's a bit more modern than mine in the Corner Shop,' she

said, 'but I'm tempted to keep that one anyway, as it's so old-school.'

'I don't want to sound like an old dog teaching you new tricks, Rosa, but watch the pennies and the pounds will take care of themselves. It's handy having a till that does all the sums for you. Helps with your accounts. Have you run any sort of business before?'

'No. To be perfectly honest, I haven't got a clue. Like I said the other night, I was left the shop. Before that I've literally been doing bar work, shop work and the occasional telesales job. But I figured it can't be that hard. Buy stock, sell stock, buy more stock, make a profit, spend the profit on nice things.'

'And also, you need to add to your list: pay bills, buy food, pay accountant, upkeep property, have time for a life...this lark is harder than you think, Rosa.'

'You sound just like Josh.'

'Just keeping it real, honey. Plus, you need to deal with being the new girl on the block. It took us at least six months before we were accepted here. This place used to be a rundown boozer; every local had their specific stool at the bar. They didn't like it when the townies came in, took away their seats and turned it into a gastro-pub. It was when I started taking business from Madame Hannafore that it got really interesting though. I had a fire in my stockroom last summer. Yes, it was an incredibly hot day and the smoking area is adjacent, but I still have questions.'

'Really?' Rosa was wide-eyed.

'I'm not saying anything like that will happen to you, but make sure you get your insurance sorted pronto. And don't get me wrong, there are some great people down here – the majority, in fact – and when the tourists start coming, it is good fun and that's when the money begins to flow. But just watch your back, Rosa.'

'Josh kept on about insurance on too. I will sort it tomorrow.'

'He's cute, your Josh.'

'He's not "my" Josh – he's not my type. We're friends because he used to be my landlord. OK, he's more of a friend with the very odd benefit, but more benefit for him really.'

'Aw. I thought you went well together. Tell him though, if he wants to teach us how to rugby tackle next time he's down, send him our way.' Jacob grinned saucily at her. 'Any idea what you are going to sell yet, anyway?'

'Actually yes. I was thinking of pet products. Leads, bowls, food, gifts, maybe even little doggy coats.'

'I like it – and of course you have your first customers here. I'm not sure if I can see the locals putting their hounds in a pink tutu, but you never know. However, the general pet stuff, yes, I see a definite market for it. There are loads of dog-friendly B&Bs and holiday cottages around here too, as it's such a good walking area.'

'That's what I thought.' Rosa felt cheered by his enthusiasm.

Jacob put his hand to his head in thought, then said: 'Actually, there's a guy I know in London who set up an online business selling similar stuff. Would you like me to check out his supplier for you?'

'Oh Jacob, that would be amazing, thank you!'

Just then, the door to the pub opened.

'Here we go, girl. It's over to you.'

Jacob watched on as Rosa ably poured a pint of Guinness and located the requested wine at quick speed. His gut had been right; she was very capable. The customers would love her too.

The girl reminded him a bit of how he was at her age. In his twenties, the nearest he got to looking to the future was booking his next holiday, and relationships just ebbed and flowed with no sense of settling down. It wasn't until his thirties that he had bucked up his ideas and started making a success of himself. He had wished he had had some guidance earlier on, but hindsight is a wonderful thing and he certainly had created his own path in a good way. He had also been very lucky to meet Raffaele, who was not only extremely fit, but was also loyal and a hard worker, with a close family who had similar values to his own.

The evening moved along swiftly, with Rosa taking both food and drink orders without incident and chatting amiably to the clientele. Both tables were renting cottages in the bay and had taken an extra week off work after the New Year. Jacob had gone upstairs once he was sure Rosa was happy to be left alone, with the instruction that she was to ring the bell at the bottom of the stairs if she needed him.

By ten o'clock the place was empty. Rosa was just thinking that on a cold Wednesday night in January it was unlikely they would get any more business and maybe she would ask Jacob if she could go, when the door was pushed open.

'Hey.' She greeted the lone punter with a smile. 'What can I get you?'

The fellow was attractive in a geeky sort of way. Tall and skinny, the top of his nose had a little bump on it and he was wearing horn-rimmed glasses. His blond hair was cut short in a Tin-Tin style, with a trendy little quiff. His lips were full and his eyes light blue and almond-shaped. Clad in a grey woollen hoody and well-fitted jeans, Rosa likened him to a younger-looking Leonardo DiCaprio.

They both stared a little too long at each other and Rosa felt that strong connection that only eyes can make.

'Rocking in here tonight, then?' the newcomer said.

'We've had a few in earlier, but to be fair it is January.'

'I'll just have a half of the local ale, please, to get me back up the hill.' The man took off his hoody to reveal a tight black T-shirt then sat at the bar. 'I'm Joe, by the way.'

Rosa handed him his drink. 'Rosa.'

'Ah, proud new owner of the Corner Shop. As announced by the landlady's son the other night at the Ship.'

'I didn't see you there.'

'Because the last I saw of you was with a big rugby lad carrying you out under one arm, that's probably why.'

'Oh God. Ways To Make an Impression, Part One.'

'It's fine. I doubt anyone really took any notice. Most people were pretty drunk. I guess you've forgiven the landlady's son though, as I saw him skulking out of your place on New Year's Day.'

Oh bugger. 'He was just adjusting my pipes before he left.'

'That's what they call it these days, is it?' Joe winked at her.

'How rude. No way! He has a girlfriend.' Rosa was indignant but fuming inside that someone had spotted Lucas leaving.

'Anyway, what brings a young – and can I detect from that accent, a Mancunian – man to an empty pub in the middle of nowhere on a Wednesday night in January?'

'Boredom. Knowing there was a new pretty barmaid in town. Top marks on the accent, by the way.'

Rosa smiled. 'Flattery will get you everywhere.'

'Good that he sorted the plumbing for you, anyway.'

But Rosa didn't want to be talking any more about Lucas Hannafore.

'I paid him,' she said tightly.

'Same night as his girlfriend got hit up the road, wasn't it? He must have been frantic when he took the call at yours.'

'What did you say your name was again – Monsieur Poirot?' Rosa was beginning to feel uncomfortable.

Joe cocked his head to the side. 'Rumour has it, it was Lucas himself who ran her over, you know.'

'If you live here I'm surprised you believe anything you hear. This place seems to be one big rumour.'

'Ha! You learn quickly. So, how's it going with the shop anyway?'

'Fine, fine. I'm ready to start stocking it up now. Want to make sure it's right though, before I open.'

'People can't wait to see what you are going to be selling.'

'I have a few ideas,' was all Rosa would say. 'Anyway, it's refreshing to see another younger person down here. Old Queenie Cobb was telling me that when kids get to a certain age, they try and escape the boredom.'

'Oh, I don't herald from here, as you've gathered already.'

Rosa felt a surge of disappointment as she clocked his wedding ring.

'So, when do you think you might open?' Joe asked.

'Depends on how quickly I can get hold of stock. I'm thinking of selling pet products, as it goes: food, bowls, accessories, flowery doggy butt-plugs. What do you reckon?'

Joe laughed out loud. 'Interesting – and a fine start to shocking the locals, but the rest sounds like a good idea. There would definitely be a market for most of those things because the nearest decent pet place is around forty miles away.'

'I was actually thinking of doing an Open Day.'

'Great idea.' He downed his drink.

'Maybe you could help drum up some business and then come along. Bring your wife and kids.'

Joe pulled on his hoody and stared right into her eyes again.

'Soon-to-be ex-wife and no, I have no kids of my own. Here, take this. I'd be happy to help.' He pulled a business card out of his pocket, closed his hand around hers as he passed it to her, then left.

Putting his glass in the washer, she whispered out loud, 'Ooh, Joe Fox, Editor, *South Cliffs Gazette*, you can cover my opening any time you like.'

CHAPTER TWENTY TWO

True to his word, Jacob had given her the supplier contact details he had mentioned and the next day, Rosa was up early and on the case.

She had opened a bank account in her name for now, with a view to opening a business account once things got going. Beavis Pet Supplies were happy to take a PayPal payment for her first order, and then if satisfied, they said they would set up an account for her. In just a few days she would be receiving her first order.

Also listening to Jacob's advice, she had managed to find a second-hand till on eBay, and that was on its way too. She had even set up a spreadsheet and worked out her mark-up on goods, whilst ensuring that the prices were still very reasonable.

As a child, Rosa had loved the kind of shop that sold little ornaments, decorated boxes, animals made of shells, bead necklaces, and joke tricks. She had taken a look up and down the main street here in Cockleberry Bay and noticed that nobody was selling old-fashioned sweets – the kind that were shaken out of big glass jars onto a set of scales. For a moment, her mind was full of pear drops, toffee pincushions, lemon bonbons and black jacks. It felt so right! She would cater for the adults with the pet products, and their kids with sweets and holiday trinkets and gifts. She could then see how it went and go from there.

Rosa had always had an artistic flair. She wanted the window and shelves of the Corner Shop to look pretty and unique, so had bought a selection of wicker baskets for display and some flowered fabrics with which to line each one.

On this Monday morning, feeling pleased with her progress, she made a cup of tea and sat down on the sofa upstairs to do some sums. After paying for her stock, she only had £200 left, but with no rent to pay and her little bit of money coming in from the Lobster Pot, she would just have to manage. With dog food on order at least, Hot would be OK. She had lived on beans on toast before, so she could do it again.

On walking into the bedroom and being faced with the pile of dirty clothes in the corner, Rosa accepted that what she really needed was a washing machine. The launderette would be fine for a short while, but carrying heavy bags up the hill, then back up the steep stairs of the flat would soon become a chore. Bless Ned and Dotty, they must have managed somehow. Strange – Queenie had not seemed at all keen to talk much about them, and in fact she had gone a bit funny when the subject of Dotty's passing came up.

Rosa passionately wanted her business to be a success; she felt she owed it to Ned and Dotty, who had obviously worked hard to keep the shop going all their lives. She had an urge to find out more about them. Seb had said that Ned hadn't had any family when he died, so they couldn't have had any children. This snippet of information made the whole inheritance thing all the weirder. Rosa sighed. Why on earth *had* the Corner Shop ended up in her hands?

She opened the desk drawer and reached under some

paperwork for the necklace. How could Queenie possibly have known about it? She had warned Rosa to keep it in a safe place – but why? It had obviously been stuffed down that sofa for years and nobody had known about it. She would just put it on the top of the wardrobe, in a box – it would be fine there.

Rosa climbed on the bed to get a look – and on seeing the amount of dust up there, she immediately got down again and went to fetch a damp cloth. As she cleaned and started to see the grain of the wood through the dirt, she noticed a little brass catch. Intrigued, she pulled it up and it came away in her hands, along with a small square of wood. It was a lid.

Tentatively, not knowing what she would find, she put her hand inside the man-made box underneath and felt around.

Feeling nothing at first, she delved deeper along the small tunnel that had been created beneath the false top of the wardrobe, and flinched slightly as her fingers touched something. Coughing as more dust flew up, she took the object out and placed it on top of the wardrobe.

The tight bundle of paper had yellowed, the blue ribbon that it was tied with was frayed. Rosa sat down on the bed, gently untied the ribbon, pulled a letter from the pile, unfolded it and started to read. She had only got to the words *Dear T* when her phone rang and jumped her back into reality.

With Hot yapping downstairs, she hopped down off the bed and answered it, leaving the letters where they were.

'All right, Rosalar?' came Josh's familiar voice. 'Made your millions yet?'

'Not yet, but I have ordered some stock, plus opened a bank account like you said. How's it going – still missing me?'

'No, but I'm missing Hot though.'

'You're such a liar. Anyway, news on the bay is that I've had my fortune told – and listen to this: old Queenie Cobb told me not to sell the necklace. I mean, how did she know I even had a necklace anyway?'

'Maybe because we chatted about it in front of her granddaughter in the Co-op.'

'Did we?'

'I don't know, but use your brain, Rosa. She's probably just on a fact-finding mission like everyone else. I thought you were savvier than that.'

'I am, but…she was so specific. Anyway, I'm not going to sell it yet. I've paid for some stock up-front – the shelves aren't going to be packed, but I want to see how I go first.'

'When did you ever get so sensible?'

'Since I realised that if I don't pay my bills, I won't have hot water or light.'

'Any more been said about the hit-and-run?'

'No, it's gone all quiet…oh, apart from a guy called Joe who I met in the Lobster Pot. He's a journalist stroke editor on the *Gazette*, and he was actually asking me questions about Luke and his timings. Ruddy cheek. I just acted dumb. Talking of Luke…'

'What about him?'

Rosa suddenly realised that if she asked Josh why he hadn't told her he'd seen Luke, he'd know that she'd seen the plumber. Oh God, it was all too complicated. He would go mad if he knew she'd spoken to Luke again, let alone shagged him!

'Have you been in the Ship again?' Josh asked suspiciously.

'God, no, but Jacob asked if I could do a couple of shifts for him at the Lobster Pot as he's broken his ankle. He fell off his four-inch heels when dancing as the Rover's Return's Betty Driver at the fancy-dress party.'

'That's bloody hilarious.' Josh snorted with mirth.

'I know. He's a decent bloke though. Gave me details of the

supplier for pet stuff.'

'Good. Good. I suppose I'll have to think about when I can come down to see you again.'

'You've only just left. See? You are missing me, really. How about you come down for the opening? I could do with rent-a-crowd, especially if the *Gazette* is covering it.'

'When were you thinking of doing it?'

'Two weeks' time maybe. That'll give me a chance to get the shop looking good and to promote it. The sooner I start making some money the better.'

'OK, just keep me posted – and make it a Saturday, yeah?'

'You're so bloody demanding,' Rosa teased.

Josh got off the phone and sighed. Despite her being a nightmare most of the time, he missed Rosa more than she would ever know. Even after getting drunk at his work's conference and sleeping with Lucy from PR, all he could think of was the quirky ways and pretty face of his errant ex-housemate. But, he had to be realistic, they were worlds apart. He was doing really well in his job too. But the more he tried to pull away from her, the more he seemed to want to see her.

What was wrong with him? Lucy was a pretty girl, not natural like Rosa, but she was a similar age to him, had a great personality and shared the same values, but she didn't have that special something. That special something you just can't put your finger on when you try to explain to yourself why you want to be with someone.

CHAPTER TWENTY THREE

Rosa had finished her Friday shift at the Lobster Pot and was walking home with Hot trotting jauntily beside her. He had been delighted to meet his new friends Ugly and Pongo, and had had a whale of a time running up and down the bar and being petted by the punters. Rosa was feeling happy too: it was nice to have some cash in her pocket.

She noticed a light still on at the Cockleberry Coven and wondered what Mary and Queenie did to fill their evening hours. There was now a beautiful pink crystal placed on the windowsill at one end and a window box of winter pansies on the other.

Hot was still full of energy, so flashing her torch as she did so, she carried on walking past the shop and headed down towards the beach. Rosa loved the feeling of peace and freedom that this quaint little town brought, and felt safe walking about, even in the dark. And despite being on her own a lot of the time, she discovered that she rarely felt lonely. Mind you, she'd always been a bit of a loner. She found it hard to trust – almost expected to be let down. Yes, Luke and Sheila had betrayed her trust, but Jacob, Raffaele, Mary and Joe, to date, had shown kindness.

Rosa acknowledged to herself that she did miss the

familiarity – and the safety too, of living with Josh, as she knew he would always bail her out, whatever kind of trouble she got herself into. However, it was time to stand on her own two feet: also, she wanted to make him proud. She had never known any different, but not having a mother or father to look up to was hard. She had no yardstick of how she should behave. Had never really had any restrictions placed on her, and when they were, she had rebelled against them with an 'it's not fair' attitude.

Being honest, she admitted to herself that she had never, ever felt truly happy. Wasn't even sure what she was looking for to make her so. Money really held no value to her. Men ditto: the only use for men was to satisfy her need for being held and for sex. But, at the moment, Rosa told herself with some surprise, she was all right. She loved the beach and the elements. Loved her new little home and the excitement of running her own business.

Once on the beach, she wound her scarf up around her mouth: it hadn't seemed so cold with the shelter of the terraced houses along the narrow streets. The stars lit the midnight sky and the waves crashed hypnotically on the shore. Apart from that, the night air was still and silent; even the gulls had gone to their clifftop beds until morning.

Letting Hot off his lead for a quick run-around, she looked back to the Ship. It was in complete darkness, aside from a front-bedroom light. Quite early for a Friday night for it to be shut, she thought. But then again it was mid-January and freezing cold. She would go back in there one day, she decided, but not just yet. She hadn't heard a word from Luke, but then why would she? They had both got what they wanted – an hour of no-strings-attached, pure unadulterated lust. However, Rosa did have flashbacks to that moment, as it had been bloody good – and despite what he had done, she did fancy the pants off of him.

It had all gone very quiet about the hit-and-run too – well, apart from Joe seemingly making his own inquiries. Luke *had* to be guilty, although his drink-driving story had seemed plausible. Her supervisor at the pound shop had always used to say, in his rich, northern accent, 'The truth will out.' Only time would tell, Rosa thought, as she certainly wasn't going to say a word. Just recalling her awful time working at that shop made her realise again how lucky she was. To be able to choose to work part-time at the moment was like a dream come true.

She suddenly realised that she hadn't heard from Josh in a while. She looked at her phone. It had been a whole week. So unlike him not to send her a text every other day at least. It was late on a Friday, but she guessed he would still be up. Smiling as she prepared a cheeky opening gambit, her face fell on being met with the empty sound of his answerphone.

She was just about to call Hot and go home, when she noticed a lone figure slumped on the bench at the top of the beach. Strange, at this time of night. With Hot by her side, she started to walk back towards it. Flashing her torch towards the bench, she saw that the figure was sitting knees to chest with head in hands. And as she got closer she could hear muffled sobs.

The tiny figure was wearing just a skirt, thick tights and a jumper. No coat or scarf.

'Titch? Is that you?'

The girl made an opening between her fingers to see who it was as Hot began to jump up at her, barking.

'Ssh, Hot, come now.' Rosa put him on his lead and shortened it.

'Rose? What are you doing down here at this time of night?'

'I could ask the same thing of you. What's the matter – what's happened?'

'I'm a bit drunk.'

'Well, that's not a crime, is it, nor is it a reason to be sitting out here sobbing and freezing to death. Look, how about you borrow my coat for a bit and I walk you home.'

On saying that, Rosa realised she actually had no idea where Titch lived. In fact, she knew nothing about her apart from the fact that she worked in the pub and the coffee shop, and Seb Watkins thought she had great tits.

Titch started to cry again. 'That's the whole point. I have nowhere to go and Sheila Hannafore has fired me as I was drinking on duty.'

Rosa clumsily held her in her arms. She was no good at showing or giving emotion. In a situation like this, her practicality kicked in instead.

'Right, get this on you.' She took off her bomber-jacket. 'Come up to mine, I've got either hot coffee or cold JD – either one will sort you out.'

'Who's that, calling you this late on a Friday night?'

'Er…just one of the lads, pissed up at his brother's stag do,' Josh called through from the bathroom. Lucy propped herself up provocatively on a pillow and arranged her long, blonde hair so that it flowed all over it.

'Well, turn it off now and get back in bed, big boy. I've got a surprise for you.'

Josh appeared in the doorway and smiled. 'Have you now?'

Lucy looked hot, Lucy *was* hot, but as he made love to her all he could think about was Rosa's missed call and whether she was OK.

CHAPTER TWENTY FOUR

Rosa could deal with most things, but vomit wasn't one of them. As Titch threw up the contents of the Ship Inn's bar, the best she could do was take in a pint of fresh water and a towel. She recalled how Josh would always hold her hair away from her face and rub her back when she had been sick before, but there was no way she could get within ten feet of Titch. At least her elfin crop was a saving grace.

She turned the heating back on and checked to see what Hot was up to. He had crashed out on the bed, where she'd put him, and was whiffling softly in his sleep, worn out after his play-date. She dug out the spare duvet and pillow that Josh had brought and put them on the old sofa. If Titch was sick again in the night, it probably wouldn't even show.

Titch appeared looking very white and a little sheepish.

'That's better,' she said weakly.

'Good.' Rosa handed her more water. 'Here. Now drink this and wrap that duvet around you.'

'I'm sorry, Rose.'

'Rosa.'

'I don't know why, but I can't stop calling you Rose. It's stuck in my head.'

Rosa laughed. 'It's fine. I've been called a lot worse, I can assure you. And don't say sorry – we've all been there.'

'But I hardly know you.'

'I've just seen the inside of your stomach, so we're doing OK.'

Titch smiled with trembling lips and took a gulp of water. She then started to talk.

'I'm probably not as old as you think I am.'

'OK.' Rosa had learnt that sometimes it was best to stay silent and let somebody talk rather than butt in. As it happened, she was quite keen to find out more about Titch, since she secretly saw a lot of herself in the girl.

'I'm eighteen, which makes the whole thing a lot, lot worse.'

'Makes what worse?'

'I'm bloody pregnant.' Titch closed her eyes. 'And now I've told *you*. So that's two people apart from me who know.'

'And that's how it will stay, unless you tell me otherwise.'

'Do you mean that, Rosa?'

'Look, Titch, I've had a lot of shit happen to me too. I see no point in bloody gossip. I've got better things to do with my life.'

Titch began to cry again. Rosa brought her some soft loo paper and sat back down next to her, as the young girl blew her nose noisily.

'Promise me, Rosa, you won't say a word?'

'Look, Titch, either trust me or fuck off – and I mean that.'

'OK, I'm going.' Titch shakily stood up, then promptly sat down again. 'I don't even know who the father is.'

'Shit.'

'It could be one of two blokes I slept with on the same night.'

'And do you know them?'

'Of course I bloody know them,' she reared up. 'I'm not that much of a slut.'

'Do I know them?'

Titch laid her head back on the sofa. 'I don't want to say.'

'OK, OK, but bloody hell, Titch, who is the other person you have told already?'

'Just my mum. She went crazy, has chucked me out – said I was a complete disgrace and that she didn't want me anywhere near her. That I'd ruined my life and she didn't think that she could bear the gossip that would ensue. So, I just left the house, went to the pub and got drunk, and the rest is history.'

'Titch, you really should be on the Pill.'

'Hark at Mother Teresa here. I am on the ruddy Pill.'

'Well, have you done more than one test, then? Maybe you're wrong. The Pill rarely fails.'

'Hmm. I sometimes forget to take it.'

'Oh, Titch.'

'I know. Tell me about it.'

'You have options, and the fact you just got so drunk makes me wonder: do you really want this baby?'

'That's harsh, Rosa.'

'That's reality, Titch. My mum was a drinker who couldn't cope, so I was brought up in care. It wasn't much fun, I can tell you.'

'Bloody hell.'

'Would your dad be easier to talk to?'

'He's dead. It's just Mum and me.'

'OK. I can see why she had that reaction then.'

'Can you really, Rosa? I don't think so. You see, Ronnie – that was my younger brother – he died too. Fell off a cliff. Mum's convinced it was an accident – that he slid off his bike. I know different. You see, I found the suicide note he wrote, and hid it from her.' Titch's eyes filled with tears. 'I couldn't keep it to myself. Stupidly, I showed Dad – and the next day he was found hanging in the garage. Now, the only child Mum has left is not only responsible for her father's death, but she's also pregnant with a bastard child.'

'Fuck me. You've trumped my sorry tale.' Rosa managed a weak smile. 'You poor cow – and as for your mum, that's terrible. But you can't blame yourself for your dad taking his own life. How could you have kept that all to yourself? You can only have been a kid.'

'He would still be here now if I'd kept my mouth shut.' Titch gave a howl of grief.

'You don't know that.' Rosa put her hand uncomfortably on Titch's heaving back.

'You have to get on though, don't you?' Titch choked. 'You get one shot at this thing called life. And at least Mum can die still believing that her son died of an accident and doesn't hold the guilt of him committing suicide and thinking she could have helped him.'

'But you've had to hold all of that big secret – and that's hard, Titch.'

'What doesn't kill you makes you stronger, and all that.' The girl blew her nose.

'I hear you, but it's still shit. The pair of us need to stop putting on brave faces, I reckon.'

The youngster rubbed her eyes and yawned. 'I don't want to talk about it any more. You sure you're OK for me to stay here?'

'Of course. And maybe go and see Sheila tomorrow, apologise and say it won't happen again.'

'No, she can piss off, the miserable old cow.'

Rosa sighed. 'Look, things never seem as bad in the morning. Let's have another chat then. And Titch?'

Titch nodded as Rosa got up and turned out the light. 'I will help you as much as I can.'

CHAPTER TWENTY FIVE

Rosa was awoken on Saturday morning by her mobile ringing next to her. Without even looking to see who it was, she said a very sleepy, 'Hello.'

'Blimey, you sound rough, girl.'

'What bloody time do you call this to ring me?'

'Rosa, it's ten-thirty. I'm up and ready for rugby practice.'

'Well, bully for you. I didn't go to bed until around three.'

'Ah, thought you must have been drunk when you called me.'

'Actually, I wasn't. I'd been working in the pub and...' Just then, Titch appeared in the bedroom doorway. 'Hang on a minute, Josh.' Rosa put the phone against her chest. 'Put the kettle on, I won't be a sec.' Titch nodded and made her way to the kitchen.

'Sorry about that,' Rosa apologised.

'Rosa, have you got a man in? You have, haven't you?'

'I wish. No, it's Titch from the Ship. She popped in last night and we had a drink and a chat, and she ended up crashing.'

'That's good. You need to make some friends. Was she wearing just a few clothes like before?' Josh said in a leering voice.

'I refuse to answer that on the grounds of sexual

discrimination.'

Josh laughed.

'Anyway, you all right?' Rosa wanted to know. 'You haven't been bugging me like usual.'

'Yes, all good. Work's been busy. Rugby in full swing.'

'No ladies floating your boat then?'

'How's Hot?'

'I take that as a yes then. Well, good, it's about time someone made an honest man out of you. However, I doubt if they have the Rosalar Larkin BJ skills. '

'I…er…'

'Anyway, whatever, if you don't want to tell me, that's fine.' Rosa became animated. 'Things are good this end. I am down to my last bunch of cash, but the pub money will see me through until I open.'

'That all sounds brilliant. See – you can do things when you put your mind to them. Have you set a date yet for the grand opening?'

'No. I need to suss out how much room all the stuff I've ordered takes up and go from there, I reckon.'

'OK. Well, keep me posted and I'll come down, like I said. Right, I've got to get to rugby. Give Hot a tummy tickle from me.'

'And give your new bird a tummy tickle from me.'

'Rosa, really. Catch up soon, eh?'

Rosa found Titch in the kitchen pouring boiling water into two mugs.

'Sexy Josh, right?'

'He's just a mate.'

'Really? Well, I would.'

'I hear you nearly did, New Year's Eve.'

'Oh, God. I'm sorry, Rosa, I was out of it. Kissed half the bay,

146

I reckon. Maybe this will slow me down now.'

'I don't know why you are apologising. Anyway, how are you feeling?'

'Like shit, been sick again already. I don't know if it's the baby or the alcohol. Anyway, I've got to go, I'm working at the café. And Rose?'

'Yep.'

'I know it's a big ask, but could I stay here again tonight, just until I sort out what I am going to do?'

'Yes, that's fine, but maybe call your mum later – she may have calmed down by now.'

'Hmm. I doubt it. She makes Mount Vesuvius out of a mole hill.'

Once Titch had gone, Rosa did a few chores to get the flat back in order, then sat on the sofa. Titch's story really put life into perspective. There was always somebody worse off than yourself. That's why it was important never to judge a book by its cover.

Rosa glanced down at her phone. Josh had sent her a *Have a good day text*. She couldn't quite understand the niggling feeling she had, thinking of him with another woman. Surely it couldn't be jealousy?

CHAPTER TWENTY SIX

Having missed the first bus out of Cockleberry to Polhampton, Rosa was late, and not in the best of moods. Titch's one-night stay had turned into five, and there had been no mention of buying any food or offering to do any chores. She really would have to talk to her when she got back as it wasn't ideal, her sleeping on the sofa either.

Saying no would have to move higher on the agenda if this business was to be a success. When Joe had called out of the blue that morning, common-sense had nagged that she didn't really have time to go over to Polhampton and meet him today. However, with his contacts, she knew that he would be a great help. And she did need a kick-start with regards to the launch day.

But why could Joe not just have met her at the Corner Shop? He'd surely have a car and it would have been so much easier for him. All the same, she felt strangely excited at the thought of seeing him again. She looked up to double-check she was at the right pub, and then taking a deep breath, she straightened her skirt over her knees and pushed open the glass door.

Joe was at the bar, talking to a couple of surf-type dudes as she approached him. He immediately said his goodbyes and greeted her with a kiss on both cheeks.

'How very PR, sweetie,' Rosa grinned.

He looked her up and down. 'Look at you, dressing up for me,' he teased her back.

'When you get to know me, you'll realise I dress up for no man, Joe. Anyway, how are you doing?' She loved his horn-rimmed glasses and trendy blond quiff.

'Needing a drink, that's how I'm doing. Here.' He put his hand on the small of her back and guided her to a booth which overlooked the magnificent bay.

Rosa took off her coat and placed it along the back of the seat, noting, 'It's quite busy in here for a January lunchtime.'

'Yes, Polhampton is full of the have-and-have-yachts crowd. There are lots of weekend homes for posh City types, plus many have retired down here. This place has got it spot-on for brunches, lunches and an esteemed dinner menu, all year round. They pride themselves on local produce too, which always helps. But enough of that. What can I get you, missy?'

'I know it's lunchtime, but sod it, a glass of red, please.'

Rosa was faced with a breathtaking view. Cockleberry had a beautiful beach, but this bay was something else, with its endless stretch of sand and crashing breakers. She could see why Jacob and Raffaele had bought a place here.

She noticed the gulls gliding between the imposing cliffs, using their wings to balance themselves on the winter winds. A couple of dog walkers braved the elements. She noticed their furry friends were coatless, which was encouraging.

Test one passed as Joe came back with a large glass of wine, without prompting. Rosa couldn't abide meanness. He placed it on the table with his pint of local ale.

'Thank you, and I'm sorry for being late,' she told him. 'I didn't realise the bus would stop at every village it drove through.'

'This is Devon, my dear, not Dulwich. Anyway, it's good to see you.' Joe took a sip of his beer. 'So, are you any nearer to naming the big day?'

'That's a bit forward, isn't it? I've only just met you.'

'Ha! Quite the little comedienne. But once bitten, twice shy on that front, lady – when you're going through the sort of divorce I am.'

'Oh dear.'

'The thing is,' he fingered his wedding ring, 'despite what she did, I can't take this off.'

'Was it really that bad? Sometimes I think people just need to chill out a bit.'

Joe laughed. 'Blimey, where were you when the compassion gene was passed around? And to me, yes, it was. She slept with someone else.'

'A proper affair or a one-off?'

'She says a one-off, but I just can't trust anything she says any more.'

'I hear you on the trust. I don't give people second chances. Saying that, I do see sex as just sex. Life isn't black and white, Joe. There is no rule book – well, apart from the one bloody society throws at us.'

'You're right there. That's why I like being down in the sticks. I do feel I can be more myself here. Away from all the stress.'

'Look, I'm no love guru,' Rosa told him. 'In fact, I haven't managed to combine the sex thing with whatever that love thing is yet. No man has ever made me cry and I've never really hankered after anyone when I've split with them in the past. They say you haven't experienced love until you get your heart broken, don't they?'

'I think you're more likely to get an answer out of that seagull that just pooped on the window than from me about love.

150

Right, let's order some food. My treat.'

The two of them tucked into house burgers and chips.

'Heard from that Lucas again?'

'Er…no, why should I?'

'Just wondered. Was he really just sorting out your plumbing when he came out of your house looking sheepish on New Year's Day?'

'Joe – what is your obsession with Lucas?'

'I'm a reporter, Rosa.'

'And how did you get my number?' Rosa suddenly felt suspicious. 'You gave your card to me, remember, not the other way around.'

'Must be a good reporter then, eh?' Joe smiled and took a slug of his beer. 'Going back to Lucas, I think there were too many dodgy inconsistencies with his hit-and-run story. He's a wily little shit, as well. Needs taking down a peg or two.'

Joe then looked at Rosa, right in the eyes, as before. 'And…I know I don't know you that well yet, but I like you, Rosa. You're different from anyone I've met recently down here, and I wouldn't want to see you getting hurt by someone like him.'

Butterflies did a little dance around Rosa's stomach. 'Aren't we here to talk about my opening?'

Joe nearly choked on his chip. 'I'd love to talk about your opening, madam.'

Test two already passed, Rosa relaxed. She loved a bit of innuendo. 'Now, where shall we start?'

CHAPTER TWENTY SEVEN

Rosa got in, threw her keys on the side in the kitchen and made a fuss of a very animated Hot. She had enjoyed her flirtatious lunch with Joe and it was nice to be treated. However, despite the frisson she had felt between them, he was obviously affected by what was happening in his marriage.

She was relieved that Titch was out as she so needed a night in with some peace. On entering her bedroom, she noticed a piece of paper poking out from under her untidy bed. With everything that had been going on, she had completely forgotten about the bundle of letters she had found in the top of the wardrobe. She stood on the bed, reached for the letters, closed the secret hideaway and picked the stray letter up from the floor. Then kicking off her boots, she lay on her bed and began to read.

2 June 1954

My Darling T
    It breaks my heart to know you are so unhappy. We've made it through a terrible world war. In fact, thinking on it, I've made it through two! So, this is just a mere blip in the

ocean. It's you who I love. We can do this our way.
Do not forsake me. I need you and only you.
Meet me where the sky touches the sea.
Your loving Ned X

Rosa felt her eyes well up. She sniffed and quickly swung her legs over the side of the bed. She had begun to realise what real love sounded like at last, and felt sad that she could never imagine anyone saying those words to her.

So, who was T? Rosa's mind was working overtime. Dotty and Ned had evidently been here for years, well before Dotty's sad demise that Queenie had been so touched by. But then again, that was a long time ago. She reread the last sentence then hurried to get the necklace which she had moved to the desk in the spare room. She was sure that the engraving on it had said something like *meet me where the sky touches the sea*.

So…the necklace had belonged to T, and whoever she was, Queenie must know – or why on earth would she have said not to sell it? It had to be Dorothea's: maybe he had a pet nickname for her?

She pushed her hand to the back of the drawer, which was also now full of bits and pieces she had ordered to sell, but the necklace wasn't there. She tried the drawer on the other side; nothing. Thinking she might have forgotten and put it in the safety of the cubby-hole in the top of the wardrobe, she stood on the bed and scrabbled around in there; still nothing. It was late and Rosa, both tired and worried now, put the letter back in with the others for another day and got down off the bed.

In the kerfuffle of Titch arriving and bits of new stock being delivered every day, maybe the necklace had just got misplaced. She would have a good look tomorrow when she was cleaning the flat.

Rosa was just about to drift off when she could hear knocking at the door. She was sure she had left the key under the stone frog round the back for Titch. Pulling on joggers and a T-shirt, she made her way downstairs, shivering in the night chill. Titch was making a face at her through the window.

'I need your help, look.' She pointed to a bicycle with a single mattress tied haphazardly over the seat. Rosa opened the door. 'My boss at the cafe was chucking it out, and it looks perfectly clean. I can sleep on this in the other bedroom now. '

'OK, great. But do you know what – I'm knackered. Let's leave it down here indoors for now and we'll sort it in the morning.'

'Really? You'll let a woman in my condition sleep on a sofa for another night?' Titch insisted.

Rosa huffed. 'Oh, come on then, let me take the weight, you just guide it. And we need to talk in the morning, please.'

'What, about getting a TV?'

Rose was just about to blurt out everything she had been building up to throw at Titch, when the teenager handed her some £10 notes.

'Take this, Rose. Put it towards food, et cetera, yeah?'

Rosa kept her mouth shut. Maybe she had judged her a little too quickly and after all, the poor girl was in an unenviable pickle.

She placed the mattress on the floor in the corner of the small bedroom and shifted the desk so that it was right at the end of the room and not in the way. She hadn't noticed before, but from its little porthole window you could see right down the street towards the beach. Titch appeared with bedding from the sofa in the lounge and immediately got herself cosy.

'Thanks for having me, Rose,' she said sleepily.

And before Rosa had a chance to reply, Titch was already curled on her side, snoring gently.

CHAPTER TWENTY EIGHT

'What do you mean, you can't find it?' Josh said.

Rosa balanced her mobile under her chin whilst she emptied her washing bin into a holdall. 'Honestly, Josh. I've searched high and low and it's nowhere to be seen.'

'Have you tried down the sofa again?'

'I've tried everywhere.'

'Well, you weren't going to sell it anyway, so it's no loss.'

'I know that, but it's just weird. It can't have disappeared into thin air, and what's more, now I've read that letter I told you about, I feel a strange connection with the necklace. It's as if I need to look after it.'

'Bloody hell, that sea air really has gone to your head, hasn't it?' Josh paused, then went on: 'I hate to say this out loud, but you don't think Titch has taken it, do you? I mean, you said her mum had chucked her out and that she's lost her job at the pub, so she must be feeling the pinch.'

'Hmm. I did think of that, but no – for all her faults, I don't see her as a thief. And to give her her due, she did hand over some money for food and is going to pay me forty pounds a week rent, moving forward.'

'Forty pounds! Are you going mad, Rosa?'

'Oh, Josh, stop it. I'm not in London and she's currently on a single mattress in a room with nothing but that and an old desk. That's plenty for now and the money is really handy.'

'And did you speak to her this morning like you said you were going to?' Josh bit his lip – he sounded just like one of his old teachers.

'Josh, what is this, Twenty Questions? But, no I didn't, as she must be on an early shift at the café.'

'Why did you say she lost her job at the Ship again?'

Rosa huffed. 'Right, I'm busy. I've got to go.'

'So, have you started setting the shop up yet? It will be February before you know it.'

'I know, I know. Stop nagging me! I realise I've been procrastinating slightly, but lovely Joe has suggested a Valentine's Day opening. I'm going to get some heart-shaped doggie chocolates to give away, plus I'll be handing out a ten per cent discount voucher for anyone's next visit. I plan to make the window display look really colourful. In fact, I have some fun ideas for the window in the summer that the kids will love.'

'Remind me who Joe is again?'

'He's the reporter stroke editor guy from the *Gazette*.'

'Ah, yep.'

'He's going to put an editorial in the paper the week before with another voucher that can be spent on Valentine's Day in the shop.'

'Great. So, is Valentine's Day a Saturday this year then?'

'Yes, and it also falls in half-term, so I think it's perfect timing as there may be a few tourists down here then too. I just hope it won't be too cold.'

'So, do I get an official invite?'

'Yes, here is a verbal one. Are you going to come?'

'Of course I bloody am, with bells on. Carlton said he may

come too, as one of his old uni mates plays for Falmouth RFC. So the plan is that he will drive down here with me on the Friday and stay with his friend on the Saturday night.'

'Ah, the elusive Carlton – it'll be good to meet him at last. You're welcome on the sofas, both of you, but you might want to get a B&B.'

'Yeah. Can you see if Jacob has got anything at the Lobster Pot, please?'

'I expect he'll offer you *his* bed when I tell him it's you and another rugger bugger.'

Josh laughed. 'This man ain't for turning.'

'How's your new chick anyway?'

'I take her out for dinner occasionally, it's nothing serious.' He waited for just an incey wincey hint of jealousy, but Rosa remained silent. 'Like I said, it's nothing serious. Anyway, more importantly, do you have any men to mention? I don't recall there ever being much of a man drought when you lived with me.'

'Tragically, Cockleberry Bay is not exactly a hotbed of talent, like London town used to be.'

'What about this *lovely* Joe?'

'He's going through a divorce.'

'Rebound chances then.'

'Ha! Let's hope so.'

'So, the necklace, what are you going to do about it? Report it to the police?'

'God, no. It will turn up. There is no sign of a break-in. Maybe the Cockleberry Coven have magicked it somewhere safe, so I can't sell it.' She replicated a witchy laugh.

'Can't wait to meet all these new friends of yours.'

'Don't lie. But it will be lovely to see you.' At that moment Hot came bounding into the kitchen, barking.

'Aw, there's my boy,' Josh said fondly. 'Can't wait to give him a big smoochy kiss.'

Rosa giggled. 'Right, Mr Smith, me and the hound are off to the launderette. If your mum happens to be chucking out a washing machine, let us know.'

'You cheeky monkey.'

'You love me really.' With that she hung up.

CHAPTER TWENTY NINE

Titch took a deep breath and let herself into the Ship. Sporting a face like thunder, Sheila Hannafore was polishing tables in the bar.

'Hi, Sheila.'

The landlady jumped. 'Whatever do you think you're doing, creeping up on me like that! And what do you want?'

'I've actually come to see if I can have my cleaning job back. I won't be drinking on duty from now on, I promise.'

'You, not drinking?' The woman snorted. 'The only way I might believe that from you is if you were pregnant.' She threw her head back and laughed.

Titch's face twitched, and she looked up to stop tears from falling.

Seeing this, Sheila Hannafore clutched at her chest. 'Oh my God. You *are* bloody pregnant!'

'No, no, I'm not.'

Sheila looked her up and down. 'You can't fool me, dear. You may be only a few weeks gone, but you've got that look,' she said contemptuously. 'It was bound to happen, the number of men you throw yourself at.'

Titch's face went pink. She said tightly, 'I've worked hard

for you, Sheila, and maybe drinking on duty isn't right, but I always put the money back in the till. I'm certainly no thief.' She slammed the door key onto the nearest table. 'I don't deserve for you to speak to me that way either. It's my business what I do.'

'What – be a filthy slut?' Sheila said under her breath and started dusting furiously again.

'Maybe not so filthy, Sheila, when it's highly likely it's your grandson in here.' The girl pointed to her stomach and went to storm out. Sheila grabbed her arm with force.

'You wouldn't dare stoop that low, to lie about something like that.'

'Ask him then – ask your precious Lucas. I'm surprised he hasn't used me as an alibi, in fact. I bumped into him, you see, as he was leaving the Corner Shop on the night of the accident. He did more than fix my pipes in the back of his van, I can tell you.'

Sheila was breathing heavily with outrage as she demanded: 'I take it you haven't told your mother?'

'Yes, and she stands fully by me.' Titch hoped she sounded convincing. To be fair, her mum had started sending olive-branch kind of signals via text messages, and she was going round to see her later on.

'What – you've told her you think it's my boy's?'

'Not yet.'

'I don't believe Lucas would behave like that, especially with Jasmine coming down the same day too.'

'At least it discounts him from running her over, I suppose.'

Sheila ignored that. Instead she said, 'You have options, Titch. You are just eighteen years old. Don't ruin your life.' Titch snatched herself away as a now-softened Sheila went to put her arm around the girl's shoulders.

'Yes, I know I have options, but like I said, it's my business what I do.'

With that, she walked out through the pub door, head held high. Taking a deep breath in of the chilly sea breeze, she threw a little fist bump into the air and mouthed, '*Yes!*'

CHAPTER THIRTY

Rosa was surprised to see how busy the Lobster Pot was when she pushed the door open, all set for her Friday-night shift. Both Jacob and Raffaele were sitting on the wrong side of the bar.

'Did I miss the memo?' Rosa asked, and lifted Hot up for a stroke from the men.

Jacob leant forward on his stool and kissed her on both cheeks, explaining, 'Raffa's brother is staying with us this week. In fact, here he is now. He's a singer. Said he'd do a night for us. I put one post on our Facebook page today and you know what it's like down here.'

Raffaele chipped in. 'Yes, news spread like a wildfire. Live music in the bay, and I think the photo helped. But he's not as handsome as me.'

Jacob put his young husband's hand to his lips. 'Of course not, my darling. I do fear a woman-fest in here tonight though. Mary Cobb might even take her slippers off for this one.'

'I doubt that,' spoke up an old woman, with deep-set wrinkles and wearing a black headscarf. She looked directly at Rosa and said: 'She doesn't touch the drink any more, that one, not after what happened to her.'

Thinking that the old lady might be the same one who had

helped her open the door on Christmas Eve, Rosa was about to question her, when the microphone Alyson was testing let out a deafening screech, setting Hot off barking. Amidst the kerfuffle and noise, the old woman downed her drink and quietly walked out of the bar.

When Rosa had settled Hot in with the pugs upstairs, she came down and asked Jacob, 'Who was that?'

'Who was who?' Jacob was distracted by further punters coming in.

'The old lady with the scarf.'

'I've not seen her in here before. Can't help, sorry. Right, where is Enrique Iglesias when you need him?'

Rosa laughed. 'He's Spanish, isn't he?'

'Who is Spanish?' said a new voice. And with pretend indignation: '*Sono italiano, io.*'

Jacob greeted his brother-in-law, saying, 'Angelo, meet Rosa. Rosa, Angelo.'

Angelo took Rosa's hand. '*Ciao, principessa.*' He was a lot louder than Raffaele, with a trimmed goatee beard and cheekbones to die for. He put a finger to her scar. '*Ecco*, a perfect little lightning flash. *Bellissima.*' He lowered his voice. 'You have been touched by angels – and now by an Angelo.'

Rosa smirked. Rosa *never* smirked.

'Gorgeous, isn't he?' Jacob winked and whispered at the same time.

'So, where you do want me?' Rosa sprang into work mode.

'In a completely different place from where you want Angelo,' Jacob said smuttily and Rosa mock-tutted. 'Start behind the bar, please. Looks like we are going to be busy, so you can help with serving food too, if that's OK?'

'It's fine.' The more tips the better, Rosa thought to herself, sticking her chest out and putting on a big smile for the punters.

By the time Rosa got back to the flat it was midnight. On quietly pushing open the door to Titch's room, she could hear her snoring peacefully. She made herself a hot chocolate and gave Hot a snack then went into the lounge, needing to wind down after such a busy night. Thinking how nice it would be to watch some inane television, she made a note to look for one to buy second-hand tomorrow.

Rosa flicked through her phone. There were no messages and she wondered what Josh was up to. Too tired to be bothered to phone him and talk, she took herself to her room and started to undress. Putting her watch into her bedside table drawer, she stood on the bed and took out a couple more of the faded light blue envelopes and began to read.

10 June 1954

Dearest Ned

How can I possibly be happy when I cannot be with the man I love? But this is how it has to be. I cannot betray a friend. I can't even recall how we got to this stage of affection. So, I am going to stay with my sister Kathleen in London, hoping that the less I look into your beautiful kind eyes, the more the fire in my heart will subside.

I read this quote today from Kahlil Gibran:

'When love beckons to you, follow him, though his ways are hard and steep. And when his wings enfold you, yield to him, though the sword hidden among his pinions may wound you.'

This will not only wound us, but dear Dotty too.

Meet me where the sky touches the sea.

Your T XX

Rosa was open-mouthed. Oh my God, Ned was having some sort of an affair. She was desperate to keep reading, but sleep was overtaking her.

Hot stirred, wagged his tail and made his way over to the bed to lick Rosa's face. 'Hello, baby.' She lifted him into bed with her, settled down, then drifted off into a restful slumber with his clean, leathery smell in her nostrils.

CHAPTER THIRTY ONE

Rosa woke to the sound of Titch being sick in the bathroom.

She rubbed her eyes, pulled on her dressing gown, and with Hot trotting at her heels went to the kitchen to put the kettle on and feed him. Titch appeared at the door, looking pale.

'Oh, poor you. Can you face a cup of tea?'

'Ew, no. Just some water, please.'

Rosa handed her a pint glass of cold water. 'Come on, let's go and sit in the lounge.' She opened the balcony door, letting in the sound of gulls and a rush of cold air. Hot ran out barking, did a wee on his favourite plant pot then came scampering back in.

'I promise I'll take you out in a bit, Mr Sausage.' Saying this suddenly reminded Rosa of Luke.

'So, have you thought any more about what you are going to do?' she asked Titch.

'Yes, I have. I told Sheila Hannafore it's Lucas's baby.'

'*What*?' Rosa spurted a bit of tea from her mouth. 'And is it?'

'Of course it's not. I'm on the Pill, but after getting chlamydia from a cute Scots bloke at a stag do last summer, I also use condoms too.' Titch looked visibly upset. 'But when I slept with the baby's father, I didn't.'

Rosa touched Titch's shoulder. 'It will be all right. So, when did all this happen, anyway?'

'The day Lucas came here before Christmas to help you with your plumbing. I only live up the back of yours, was walking past as he came out. Seemed a bit tipsy, I thought. We chatted then I started flirting and we ended up in the back of his van… and the rest is history.'

'But you told me you didn't know who the father was?'

'I was mixed-up and drunk when you found me that night.'

'So, who *is* the father?' By now, Rosa was thoroughly confused.

'It doesn't help anyone divulging that information, 'cos he's never going to find out. The fewer people who know, the better.'

Rosa actually felt a bit sick about the whole Luke scenario herself now. New Year's Day had been what it was, just consenting sex, a physical act, nothing less, nothing more. She had felt no guilt about her actions, but now on hearing this, she did feel suddenly cheap. Lucas Hannafore was more of a snake than even she had reckoned with.

Titch clocked Rosa's expression. 'Don't tell me you fancy him, after what he did to you in the Ship?' Not trusting her own face, Rosa got up to shut the balcony door. 'Oh my God!' the girl exclaimed. 'Something *did* happen between you.'

Rosa gave a sigh. 'And there was me, thinking I was special in his infidelity. Probably something else that is best left unsaid.'

'Give me some credit, please. And to be fair, you do hold a bigger secret over me. But all the more reason I'm glad I told Madame Hannafore now.'

'But that doesn't answer the question as to what you are going to do, Titch. You must be quite a few weeks' gone by now. If you are going to have an abortion, then the sooner the better.'

'I know exactly what I'm going to do, Rose. I'm going to do absolutely nothing for now, but wait. Just wait.'

CHAPTER THIRTY TWO

Rosa tied up Hot outside the Co-op and pushed open the door. Mary clumsily got up from the stool she was resting her large buttocks on.

'Hello, Rosa, lovely to see you, dear. How are you?' She coughed loudly.

'You really should take something for that cough, Mary.'

'Gran has me on her own ginger, lemon and honey drink recipe, don't you worry about me. Aw, just look at him.' Mary craned her head towards the glass window to get a look at Hot. 'Now, what are you after?'

'I just wondered if I can put this card on the noticeboard, please. Is there a cost?'

'As it's you, of course not. You need every penny to get that shop off the ground. Have you got an opening date yet?'

'Yes, two weeks today, actually. Valentine's Day.'

'That's fantastic. You'd better save me that cat lead for Merlin.' She took the handwritten card from Rosa and read aloud. '"Wanted, a medium-sized TV." Oh, OK, I'll make sure everyone who comes in is aware you are looking. Did you check yourself to see if anyone was selling? Collins the newsagent's have a board too. And you will just make the deadline for the

Gazette if you're quick, but you'll have to pay for that one.'

'Great, thanks, Mary.' Rosa pushed her hand through her hair. 'Right – better get on. I'm having some voucher invites printed up for the opening so will pop one in to you. Should be fun. I've got music, and a face-painter for the children sorted.'

'Cockleberry Bay won't know what's hit it.' Mary's laugh turned into another hacking cough.

'Give my love to your Gran,' Rosa said when she'd come out of it.

'Will do. Have a good day, dear. And – well, I think you should be really proud of yourself.'

Rosa felt a weird tingle go through her body, the like of which she had never experienced before. Maybe it was because nobody in her whole life had said that before. And, yes, it was true: in just a few short weeks, she had achieved more than she had ever dreamt she could be capable of.

'Um. Thanks, Mary,' she said, feeling almost tearful. 'Thank you very much.'

Rosa was just pushing open the door to leave when Mary called her back. 'Maybe I could take your number? Then if somebody does say they have a TV for sale I can let you know straight away, in case they forget to call you.'

'OK, good idea, let me take yours and I will text it to you. Thanks again, Mary.'

Mary's chubby face lit up with a smile.

As Rosa was untying Hot's lead from the post outside the Co-op she remembered what the old lady in the Lobster Pot had said the other night. What an earth could have happened to Mary that had caused her to never drink again? Whatever it was must have been pretty serious for her to have mentioned it. If the time was ever right, Rosa decided she would ask her.

Rosa wasn't sure why, but she felt a bit sorry for Mary in

general. Stuck living with her ancient grandmother and mad cat Merlin, and she obviously didn't make the best of herself. With a good haircut, an eyebrow tidy and a smudge of lipstick and mascara, she would look so much better. But that was Mary's business, and Rosa could empathise as she herself had never been one for beauty treatments or too much make-up either. It had always been too much of an effort for her. She'd never had a problem pulling men, but maybe that was because she was so easy in giving herself away. When she looked in the mirror, she didn't see anyone particularly beautiful, and despite it being small, her lightning-shaped zigzag scar always caught her eye.

'Penny for them?'

Rosa nearly jumped out of her skin as Seb pulled up in a red van right next to her. Hot barked in sympathy.

'Seb! You scared me. New wheels?'

'Yep, the older banger had to go to the crusher. I found this little beauty on eBay. Only two hundred quid, too. You OK?'

Hot whimpered his disapproval of being made to stand still, and of red vans and skinny bearded men.

'Yes, yes, all is well, thanks.' Rosa couldn't bear the way the ginger-bearded one looked her up and down.

'Seen Titch lately?' he asked. 'Been no sign of her at the Ship for a while.'

Rosa didn't know what she should or shouldn't divulge to anyone about her wayward lodger. She didn't even know if the girl had told anyone where she was living. And because of the back entrance to the Corner Shop, Titch could bomb in and out without detection quite easily. It seemed the Cockleberry grapevine was none the wiser – yet, anyway.

'Rosa? What's the matter?' Seb prompted.

'Nothing. I saw her at the café earlier, and she mentioned she was going into Polhampton to try and find some more work.

170

Should I give her a message if I see her?'

'Yes, please. Can you say for her to give me a call as soon as possible?'

'That's it?'

'Yes, that's it. Thank you.'

As Seb went into the Co-op, Rosa received a text. The word PLUMBER flashed up on her phone. *Just checking you don't need anything plunged next time I'm down?* Followed by a winky face. Rosa deleted it immediately.

If she hadn't known that Luscious Luke had also slept with Titch – and in the back of his van to boot – she might have considered a reply, but as it stood, even with her own current alley cat morals, he had overstepped the Rosa Larkin line. There was a one-off cheat on your girlfriend, but just dipping your wick into anything that moved wasn't acceptable in any shape or form.

She was surprised he was even thinking of coming down, considering the *Gazette* was still going to town on the unsolved mystery of the Cockleberry Bay Christmas hit-and-run affair.

She guessed she had to believe Luke now that he hadn't been involved, as Titch was living proof that he had been *hitting on* and *running* in a very different way.

Rosa and Hot walked round the block and she pushed open the rear gate to the shop, only to find that the back door was unlocked. Cross that Titch must have been back and not locked it, she went inside and turned the back-kitchen light off, tutting. That girl really had no idea about saving money. Then she had to smile at herself at her thoughts. Just a couple of months ago she would have been doing exactly the same at Josh's place, with no regard for him having to pay the bills.

'Hiya!' she called out as she walked up the stairs – but there was no answer. Titch wasn't there. Maybe she'd found some more work. Hot flopped down on the floor in front of the sofa and Rosa headed to the bedroom to get her laptop. Ever the sensible one, Josh had insisted that despite her thinking that she had mislaid the necklace, she should lock her valuables away if she was out, so she had just bought a mini-suitcase padlock and put stuff in her small case. She let out an 'Ah' as she saw the letters she'd taken down from the wardrobe sitting in there. She wasn't sure why, but for some reason she had felt obliged to lock these away safely too.

Now though, she couldn't wait to read more. It was all very intriguing, discovering what old Ned had been up to. She could allow herself a little free time to do so, as she had put some of her pub earnings back in the bank so that she had some money to transfer for the launch activities. Rosa had just made herself a coffee and was logging in to read her emails when THE FOX flashed up on her phone screen.

'Joe Fox, reporter, Corner Shop launch organiser and quite frankly the loveliest man in the South Cliffs area, full stop,' he announced himself.

Rosa laughed. 'Blimey, you're in a good mood.'

'Ha. Yes, I am actually. Helped by the fact I'm coming to meet you for lunch today.'

'Bugger!'

'Don't tell me you'd forgotten. I feel mortally wounded.'

'Not really forgotten, just had it on my calendar for tomorrow. What time had we arranged?'

'Eleven-thirty, but I can come for one o'clock instead if that gives you some time? Tomorrow is too tight as we go to press the day after.'

'Yes, yes, that's fine. I literally am just transferring deposits for the face-painter and I've found a little portable Bose speaker

172

on sale for the music.'

'Great. Let's meet in Coffee, Tea or Sea. I can't be getting on the beer today, too much to do.'

'Perfect. See you there at one.'

CHAPTER THIRTY THREE

Josh phoned as Rosa was running out of the door.

'Rosalar?'

'Aw, Mr Smith. Where have you been? I've missed you.'

'Of course you haven't,' Josh laughed. 'I'm dashing into a meeting so can't chat, just checking you've booked a room for me and Carlton at the pub?'

'Shit, shit. No, not yet, sorry. I'm off to meet Joe from the *Gazette* now, I'll pop in on my way. Two nights you wanted, wasn't it?'

'Yes, please.'

'Cool. You OK?'

'Fine, fine, gotta dash, let's catch up properly later in the week.'

Joe smiled widely as Rosa pushed the door open to the café. She took off her coat to reveal a green mini-pinafore and pink roll-neck jumper, with green and pink stripy tights. Her brown curls were all over the place. He loved her quirkiness.

She sat down next to him and clapped her hands together really fast.

'Bloody freezing today.'

Joe stood up. 'Let me get you a coffee.'

'Actually, can I have a mug of tea instead, please, and one of the lemon muffins they do? Here, I'll get the cakes.' She went to hand him a five-pound note, but he pushed it back to her.

'My treat. Anything to get some good news into the paper, especially in January when there's not much going on down here.'

As Joe was at the counter, Rosa took in his well-fitted jeans and trendy hoody. She liked the fact he was a bit geeky too.

'Your mate Titch not working today, I see.'

'No, she's off job-hunting in Polhampton, I think.'

'Oh. My neck of the woods. Not working at the Ship any more, is she?'

'God, you're nosy.' Rosa grinned at him and started to pull off the top of her muffin. Her favourite way of eating them.

'It's my job to be nosy. Talking of that, there has been a development in the hit-and-run case. Part of the bumper had fallen off whatever vehicle it was and there was a trace of white paint on it.'

'That narrows it down – not,' Rosa joked. 'What are the police going to do, check every bumper of every white car in the neighbourhood to see if a bit has fallen off? If it was me I'd have got it repaired sharpish.'

'So, tell me, where are you at with the opening?'

'Basically, just waiting on one more box of stock I ordered today and then I can start dressing the front window and shelves. I'm going to keep a black-out blind down to maintain the intrigue, but I've got a big poster up in the front window announcing it.'

'Good, good. Did you put discount flyers in the pubs, cafés and shops yet?'

'No. I just got them made on one of those quick internet sites and they are due today, hopefully. The plan is for me and Hot to deliver tomorrow.'

'Great teamwork. Don't forget South Cliffs Cottages too; they can put one in every rental, as half-term week is usually quite busy down here. It'll be somewhere for the mums and dads to bring the kids, especially as you've got a face-painter. Louise is great too, really gets everyone involved.'

'Good. The music is sorted, I shall just run it from my phone to the new speaker – and are you still OK to run me to the cash and carry to get a few bottles of fizz and snacks, sometime this week?'

'Will do. Also, how about some jugs of squash and paper cups for the kids – and did you order the doggie-treat hearts?'

'Yep all done, and there's also a couple of heart-shaped balloons with photos of Hot on them.'

'Brilliant! I love that.'

'Yes, fame at last. I thought I could put one either side of the door. It's going to be rather cramped inside, but let's hope it's not too cold and we can spill out slightly into the street.'

Joe cleared his throat. 'I've also managed to seal another amazing PR gig, but I'm not sure how you'll feel about it.'

'Oh God, go on.'

'A morning slot on the South Cliffs Today radio show, the day before the opening.'

'Me? Little old me on the radio?' She put down her piece of cake.

'Rosa, I know you can do it. What's the worst that can happen, other than you swearing, that is? You'll come across great, I know you will.'

'You reckon?'

Joe nodded. 'I will write a script, so you can take chunks from that; you will have plenty to say.'

Rosa put both her hands to her face and jiggled her feet on

the floor, making a funny noise as she did so. 'This is all so surreal, but all so exciting. Thanks, Joe.'

'All is I can say is, phew, as I'd already confirmed the interview. I just know it will be so good for you. I'll come and pick you up, take you there and will wait with you until it's over. You'll be fine.'

'That's so kind of you.'

'I am writing some editorial for it this week too, but what I do need is a name for your business. Oh, and a photo of you and Hot, if that's all right?'

'We will be mini-celebrities! But Joe, can't I just call it the Corner Shop for now? I can't afford to get the sign repainted anyway. I can also then change my mind on what I sell if it doesn't work out.'

'But if you're selling pet stuff, surely you need some sort of pet name?'

'Like Doggie Style or Cat's Cradles.' She laughed. 'Actually, I quite like Doggie Style.'

'Do you now?' Joe raised his eyebrows meaningfully.

Rosa blushed. 'I can't believe I just said that.'

Joe couldn't stop laughing. 'Doggie Style! That is brilliant.'

'Or maybe just plain and simple "Rosa's". I'd be proud of myself if we called it that.'

'Great to hear the positive thinking. I watched a programme last night about recruiting for the SAS and you saying that made me think back to it.'

'Joe, I'm opening a village shop, not saving a nation.'

'Hear me out. You've got no parents, right?'

Rosa liked his northern twang. But she was startled at what he'd said. 'How do you know that?' she asked. She might have mentioned it to Jacob when she was drunk one night, but she never made a big thing about it.

Joe brushed her question aside, saying, 'Anyway, this was the quote from the show and it brought me to tears. Some of the guys doing the training have such sad life-stories but despite it, have so much spirit. I actually wrote it down.' Joe flicked through his notebook. '"When you succeed, there's no one to be proud of you, when you fail or do something wrong, there's no one to be disappointed in you. It's down to you to put that pressure on yourself, to make *yourself* proud – and that's when you find out who you truly are."'

Joe put his hand on Rosa's which caused the alien feeling of tears pricking her eyes.

'You're going soft on me, Joe Fox,' she said, and blinked the tears away.

'It must be hard, growing up without knowing where to turn.'

'You know nothing about me.'

'Well, maybe I'd like to know more.'

Rendering Rosa mute with this comment, Joe picked up his mug and raised it. 'Cheers to the Grand Opening of the Corner Shop.'

CHAPTER THIRTY FOUR

Titch came bounding up the stairs two by two, nearly knocking into Rosa who was holding a tray with her dinner on it.

'Whoa, lady, that wouldn't have been very clever.'

'Sorry, sorry. I'm desperate for the loo.' She eyed Rosa's macaroni cheese hungrily. 'Ooh, any more of that left?'

'No, it's a ready meal. I've had a busy day – and where have you been anyway? No – tell me when you've been to the loo.'

When Titch re-emerged, looking a lot calmer, she told Rosa: 'I've done really well today. I got myself cleaning jobs at two pubs in Polhampton – early starts, but not on café days, so I'll be raking it in. But that's not all I've managed to do today.' The young girl looked triumphant.

'Look!' She pulled a cheque from her bag and started waving it around. 'Three grand! I knew it was just a matter of time.'

'What – did you win the lottery or something?'

'In a way.'

'Titch, stop being annoying and tell me.'

'It really is an "If I tell you, I have to kill you" scenario though, Rose.'

Rosa couldn't even imagine what was going to come out of the wayward girl's mouth this time. She shook her head. 'What have you done now?'

'Well, you know I told Sheila that the baby was Lucas's.'

'Yes. Oh God, Titch. I think I know what's coming.'

'She called me to go and see her, said she had spoken to Lucas and that he had admitted he'd had sex with me.'

'But he would have known you'd used a condom.'

'I told her it had split. He drove off so fast he wouldn't have known that – bastard. Anyway, she believed me and then offered to pay for a private abortion out of the area. But I wasn't happy with that. You see, I need more than that.'

'Oh Titch, what else did you say?'

'That if she wanted an alibi for the hit-and-run she could pay me more.'

'But he was adamant it wasn't him when we spoke about it,' Rosa objected.

'Don't be too gullible, Rose. He asked if you could cover for him too, remember. His drink-drive story could be a complete ruse – and Madame Hannafore knows exactly what happened that night, I can feel it.'

'Titch, isn't that blackmail?'

'I see it as a constructive deal.'

'So, on a serious note, when are you having the abortion? You should arrange it soon.'

'I'm not.'

'OK.' Rosa took a big slurp of her Diet Coke. Hot scratched at the balcony door to be let out.

'Don't worry. I don't expect you to support me and a titchy Titch.' The girl picked up Rosa's can and took a swig. 'I've got three grand here. I've now got two jobs. I am going to save and save so I can afford to rent a little place somewhere. This baby is going to have a blessed life. Well, as good as I can possibly make it anyway.'

'But what happens when Sheila realises you haven't had the abortion?'

'I'll worry about that when it comes to it. By that time, I will have paid a deposit and up-front rent on a place – and what is that saying? "You can't sue a straw man" or something like that.'

'You've got balls, I'll give you that.'

'Also, as I'm so tiny I'm hoping I won't start properly showing for months.'

'It will be hard, Titch. Bringing up a child alone.'

'Life *is* hard, Rosa, and after losing my brother and my dad I can't even think about letting this little life go. I saw Mum today too. She's calmed right down and believe it or not is quite excited about me having the baby.'

'Does she know whose it is?'

'Only that it was a random tourist who had come down at Christmas. I don't want the father to be involved.'

'Ah, so why couldn't you tell me that?' Rosa was glad finally to have some kind of an answer. But she could sense Titch's agitation. 'It's a relief, that your mum has come round and is OK about it anyway. I'd love to meet her.'

'She doesn't go out much as she's in a wheelchair, you see – has got MS. We have a bungalow up the top of the hill now, which helps, but even with a carer who pops in daily, I know she has missed me around the house.'

'Your family certainly have had more than their fair share of lemons thrown their way, haven't they?'

'Yes. I should be face down on the ground with flailing arms banging on the floor screaming, "Why me!" But you and I are survivors, Rose. That's why I love you. We get each other. But Rose...'

Rosa felt the strange tingling feeling again.

'Titch, it's fine. If you want to go back home, then you must

181

go. Your mum needs you and you need to save the money now.'

'If you're sure?'

'Of course I'm bloody sure. The peace will be nice, in fact,' Rosa teased.

Titch poked her in the ribs. 'Oi.'

'We need to get the Titchy Titch Fund up and running, don't we? So, once the shop is open, I'd love you to help out – if you want to, that is – and also at the launch on Valentine's Day. I will pay you the going rate.'

'That would be amazing. Thanks, Rose. Let me give you some extra money for rent before I go. Forty pounds was peanuts.'

Rosa thought back to Josh's kindness when she was about to move down to Devon.

'I wouldn't think of it,' she said. 'It's so important for you to get the best start for this little lad or lady.' It was her turn to bite her lip.

Titch put her hand on Rosa's arm. 'I'm sure she loved you, Rose.'

Rosa got up hastily and walked out onto the balcony, allowing the crashing waves and cries of the gulls to drown out her full-blown sobs.

CHAPTER THIRTY FIVE

Just as Rosa was getting worried that her Open Day flyers weren't going to arrive on time, there was the sound of some post being forced through the letterbox, to land heavily on the front door mat.

She ran downstairs and was delighted to see a thick brown envelope lying there. The flyers! Without hesitation, she ripped open the Jiffy bag and felt quite chuffed. Even though it was one of those 'design your own' quick-print companies that she'd used, the flyers did look really professional.

'Come on, boy, I need to saddle you up,' she told her trusty hound. 'We are going on a long walk up and down the street.'

Jacob was watering his plants outside as they marched their way to the top of the hill.

'Hello, you two.' He got down to make a fuss of Hot. 'Notice something different about me?' he asked Rosa when he stood up again.

Rosa squinted at his face. He pointed to his foot. 'Plaster off. Game on.'

She laughed. 'Aw, that's fab news. Now don't be camping it up in stilettos for a while, eh?'

'Alas, I fear my Louboutin days may be numbered, darling.

Well, for a few months anyway. The young physio they've given me at the hospital is quite cute though, which is always a bonus.'

'What are you like! So, the flyers have come through for my grand opening.'

'Your grand opening, dear? Wouldn't miss it for the world.' He pursed his lips and winked. 'Hand some of them over and I shall get touting for you – and of course we will be there to support you. We being me, Raff, and Ugly and Pongo, of course. I will get Alyson to pop down too. Rent a crowd is necessary, especially if the *Gazette* photographer is coming.'

Jacob gave Hot a treat from his pocket and continued, 'Rosa dear, I was going to ask if you'd like Raff to make some snacks for you? I'm thinking a few canapés and he does a mean homemade scotch egg. On me, of course, as it's a special day.'

Rosa was overcome by his kindness. 'Jacob, that is so bloody sweet of you and the answer is yes, please. I'm down to my last pennies, until I start selling stock that is, so that will be a great help. I'm getting a few bottles of fizz in, and squash for the kids.'

'It will be fun, and I can't wait to see the flower power doggy butt-plugs.' He winked.

After an hour or so, Rosa had got rid of nearly all the leaflets, and was heartened by how friendly everyone in the shops and eateries appeared to be. As she approached Seaspray Cottage, she noticed Mary cleaning her front windows. The woman halted her work the moment she spotted Rosa and Hot. Merlin must have got wind of a pooch on his manor and tore out of the wedged-open front door, screeching his indignation and disappearing down the street.

'Off goes Merlinite mad cat.' Mary tucked her duster and window cleaner into the pocket of her waist apron.

'Don't you worry about him on the road?' Rosa couldn't bear

to think of Hot running free anywhere that might be dangerous.

Mary coughed. 'Gosh no, he's got more than nine lives, that one. Anyway, how are you today, Rosa? You two look like you're up to mischief.' She bent down and stroked the dachshund's smooth, quivering body.

Rosa smiled. 'No, we've just been delivering leaflets to promote the shop opening on Valentine's Day. I would love you to come, and Queenie – if she's up to it, of course. You can join me for a glass of fizz.'

'Oh, I don't know, and you know Gran doesn't leave the house.'

'We have soft drinks too, that's fine. I'd love you to come. Actually, I saw an old lady in the pub the other night who...'

Suddenly, the slightly hunched, deeply wrinkled, dark-glasses-wearing figure of Queenie Cobb was standing at the door. Her long, grey hair was neatly tied in a grey plait that reached down to her bottom.

'Tittle-tattle is futile, Rosa. Always listen to your heart and your gut. Sometimes things aren't always as they seem.' She picked a purple crystal up from the windowsill and cupped both hands right around it, murmuring, 'Even dolphins get caught when they swim upstream, you know.'

With that, the old lady disappeared inside as quickly as she had appeared.

Mary started to rub her ear and shift uncomfortably from foot to foot.

'It's fine, Mary, your gran is a wonderful character and the world would be a better place with more of her kind in it.'

Mary looked directly into Rosa's green eyes with her own of the same colour. 'I will be there on the fourteenth, just briefly. I'm not one for crowds, me. And I know there will be one.'

'Thanks, Mary. The more the merrier.'

Back home, Rosa opened the front door to the shop and let out a sigh of relief. 'Nearly there, Hot. This promoting business is a little more time-consuming than I thought.'

She went upstairs and threw her keys on the kitchen worktop. Queenie was a strange old thing. And what was all that about dolphins? It was as if she'd been listening to their conversation and had interrupted because she didn't want Rosa to mention what the old woman had said in the pub. Poor Mary; her gran was protecting her from whatever had happened to her. But Queenie had a point: tittle-tattle did have no use. She would let it lie.

CHAPTER THIRTY SIX

On approaching the South Cliffs Today radio station, Rosa was experiencing nerves like she'd never experienced them before.

'Did you not get this nervous when you did your exams at school?' Joe asked, reverse-parking into a visitor's space.

'I didn't do any exams at school.'

'Oh. Well, honestly, don't worry. You will be in a room with Barry Savage and his producer, so just pretend you are chatting to them and no one else. Are you prepped with what you want to say?'

'Yes, so I should be all right.'

'I did give him a background brief to what was happening.'

'Good. I will be fine then. I know what I'm selling, I know all about the launch – so what could he possibly ask me that I can't answer?'

Rosa jumped down from Joe's smart Jeep and brushed at her coat. Joe's Great Dane, Suggs, whom she had just met today, was sitting upright, like a human passenger, in the back seat. She was quite glad she hadn't brought Hot along, as she wasn't sure how he'd have reacted to such a big dog.

'Let me come in with you and then I will go and take Suggs for a walk and listen to you through my phone. Have you got anyone else you know listening?'

'Oh yes. Mary, Queenie, Titch and the Lobster Pot are all tuning in. And my mate Josh will be listening on his way down here.'

'And in the *Gazette* article, I mentioned you'd be speaking today too, so fingers crossed we should get some more Opening Day punters from it.'

'Rosa Larkin?' A smart, bespectacled woman appeared in reception with a clipboard. Rosa nodded. 'Great, follow me.'

Joe put his right thumb up as she followed the woman through to the studio.

'Ssh!' Jacob waved at Raffaele to turn off the Hoover. 'Come here, let's listen to Rosa.'

The two of them got cosy on the sofa in the lounge of their huge sea-facing house in Polhampton.

The news came to an end. 'Here's our girl now,' Jacob said. Ugly and Pongo scrabbled up on the sofa and snuggled between them. 'Ssh too, boys.'

The DJ started to talk, and Jacob groaned. 'Oh, it's that awful Barry Savage, standing in for Terry Logan. Remember when we had the fire?' Raffaele nodded. 'Rather than promote the fact that we were open again, all he wanted to do was talk about who might have caused it, almost insinuating that it had been an insurance job on our part.'

'*Si, si*, yes. He is a nasty man. Oh shit, but Rosa is strong. She will be fine.'

'So, I'm here with Rosa Larkin, who is the new owner of the Corner Shop in Cockleberry Bay. Welcome, Rosa.'

Barry Savage was the image of Mr Toad of Toad Hall, Rosa thought, with his beige-and-white checked three-piece suit which was stretched to capacity over his large stomach.

A unified 'Hurrah!' came from all those who knew her and were listening.

'Oh, hi.' Rosa took a swig of water from the white plastic cup she had been given. She never said hi! Remembering Joe's pre-radio pep talk, she took a deep breath and straightened her shoulders.

'How amazing it must have been to find out you'd inherited the shop,' Barry began, smiling at her over his rimless glasses, and suddenly reminding her of the equally smarmy solicitor who had handed over the battered case to her, just eight weeks ago.

'Yes, amazing, surprising, slightly scary – all of those things.' The last thing she wanted to do was to open a can of worms about who had left it to her. Surely Joe wouldn't have briefed him to that effect?

'Is it right that you don't know who left it to you?'

'That's right, yes, but I'm sure your listeners don't want to hear about that. It's the grand opening tomorrow, and I have lots of fun things planned for all ages.'

'Oh, I'm sure they *do* want to hear about it. A mystery benefactor leaving a shop to a young girl who hasn't a clue how to run one. Especially as the shop has been closed for five years and all the locals have wanted a chance to buy it.'

Joe stopped walking along the cliff and clapped a hand to his head in dismay. Of course he'd meant to seed that nugget of information in; it made great radio and would also be an interesting hook to follow up in the *Gazette*. He hadn't, however, anticipated quite how full-on Barry Savage would be. Like Suggs with a bone, in fact.

'Well, Barry,' Rosa said firmly, taking control, 'they are not going to hear about it right now. However, if they would like to come along to the shop – anytime from ten am tomorrow –

189

maybe I can tell them then.'

'*Boom!*' Jacob shouted from the sofa. 'You go, girl. What a complete and utter bastard.'

Joe smiled. Rosa might have no exams, but she was sharper than even he had realised.

Josh, listening in Carlton's car, cared only that Rosa would come out with her confidence still intact. It was a massive day for the shop tomorrow and he was glad that he had managed to get away earlier than expected from work, to share it with her.

'And as for not having a clue about knowing how to run a shop, Mr *Savage*,' she went on, emphasising his last name, 'that's partially true. However, considering I only arrived in Cockleberry Bay a few weeks ago – just before Christmas, in fact – I am patting myself on the back for what I have achieved to date. Tomorrow, I have some great pet products for sale, there will be trinkets and gifts for the children, plus a face-painter. I've even got some heart-shaped doggie treats.'

'Oh, a Valentine's Day theme for pets. I see what you've done there.'

'Exactly. I have a mini-dachshund called Hot and he can be my Valentine anytime.'

'Hot Dog, ha ha ha, that's great. But do you have a real love in your life to mention then, Rosa?'

'Not to mention – no, Barry.'

Josh laughed out loud.

'OK, so everyone, looks like it's going to be a cold but fine day tomorrow, so head on down to the Corner Shop in Cockleberry Bay. Fore Street, isn't it?'

'Yes. You can park on The Level if you are driving, or get the number 48 bus from Polhampton, which leaves at ten-thirty. Oh, and I forgot to mention, there will be free glasses of fizz and snacks on arrival too. Plus a discount voucher for your first purchase at the shop.'

'Sounds amazing – and I wish you all the luck down here in our close community, Rosa.'

The girl felt nauseous at the insincerity coming from his thin-lipped, podgy red face. Thank God the interview was over, since she knew she had made an enemy of Mr Toad.

'Thank you so much, Barry.'

She went to remove her headphones, but he gestured to her to keep them on, intent on moving in for the kill.

'Oh, and just before you go, Rosa. Any ideas about who the Christmas Cockleberry Bay hit-and-run driver might be?'

She put her hands out in a questioning manner, screwed up her face and mouthed, '*What the fuck?*'

'You look surprised, but they would have taken a fast drive up or down from behind your shop, wouldn't they?'

'I really don't want to comment on this, thank you. It is a police matter.'

'A straight yes or no would have sufficed, Rosa.'

'No, then. Thank you – and goodbye.'

The Beatles' 'Can't Buy Me Love' started to blare across the airwaves. Rosa pulled her headphones off indignantly.

Barry stood up to shake her hand, saying, 'Welcome to the world of media, dear. You didn't expect this to be straightforward, did you?'

Ignoring his hand, Rosa snapped, 'To be honest, yes, I did, from a local radio station. It's not exactly Radio Four, is it?'

'You need to tell that Joe not to give me so many good leads in future then.'

Rosa felt sick to her stomach. 'Have no doubt, I shall make very sure of that.'

Joe was waiting right outside in his Jeep. Suggs lay flat out in the back, legs everywhere.

191

Joe held the passenger door open for her; Rosa got in silently and slammed it.

'Who the hell do you think you are, setting me up like that, Joe Fox?' Her voice was two octaves higher than usual. '"Nice and fluffy," you said. "Tell them about all the great things happening at the opening", you said. And then he not only hits me with the mystery benefactor story, but also asks me if I know anything about the hit-and-run.'

Joe let out a big sigh. 'You've got to understand, I'm a reporter by nature, and knew maybe just the opening of the shop wouldn't get you the slot.'

'Fair enough, but bloody warn me in future. I wouldn't have gone on there if I'd have known that part would be dragged up.'

'Exactly.'

'Exactly? Joe, didn't you think that might upset me or make me say something I didn't want to? I trusted you.'

'So, is there something that you do know about the hit-and-run?'

She replied with a quiet, 'No.'

'I'm sorry, really I am.' Joe put his hand on hers. 'I just want you to succeed – and sometimes to do that you have to talk about things you don't want to.'

'Do you mean that?' Rosa asked, looking into his light blue almond-shaped eyes. On close inspection, they reminded her of a dolphin's.

'I mean it, and I'm sorry.' He leant across and kissed her gently on the lips.

'Did you mean that too?'

Joe smiled and squeezed her leg. 'Come on you, we've got balloons to collect.'

With the helium balloons in hand, Joe and Rosa walked into the back of the shop. She guided him through to the front and turned the lights on.

'*Voilà*!'

'Wow, it looks amazing. You've set out the window just beautifully – and look at all the baskets with the kids' stuff. I'm blown away. It looks like a proper shop.'

'Well, what did you expect it to look like?' Rosa bent down to pet Hot, who had missed her during the morning.

When she stood up, Joe put both his hands on her shoulders. 'I can see why you are proud of yourself.' He pulled her towards him and just as he was about to kiss her – properly, this time – there was a loud knock at the front shop door.

Seeing the silhouette of a tall, broad figure, Rosa pulled away immediately, muttering: 'Shit, I forgot Josh was coming today.'

'Josh?'

'You know – my friend from London. I'm sure I've mentioned him.'

Rosa opened the door, but instead of her lovely Josh, it was two very stern-looking policemen.

'Rosa Larkin?' asked the taller one of the pair.

'Um, yes, that's me.'

'We'd like to talk to you about the hit-and-run incident that happened on December the twenty-third last year at the top of this road.'

'What – now?'

'If possible?'

'OK.'

'I was just leaving.' Joe rattled his keys in his pocket. 'Suggs is in the Jeep and I need to get back to the office.'

Hot was now tearing around all of them barking furiously, when Rosa heard the familiar and comforting voice of Josh shouting outside, 'Rosalar! Hot! Rugger buggers alert.'

Joe gave a short 'Hi' as the imposing and very handsome

figures of Josh and Carlton now entered through the small doorway into the shop. With the whole scenario resembling a farce, the smaller policeman let out a huge sigh.

'Shit, Rosa. Everything all right?' Josh kissed her on the cheek. 'Meet Carlton.'

All six feet three of him, with smooth ebony skin and chestnut eyes, leant down and kissed her on the other cheek. 'Pleasure to meet you, Rosa. So that's sorted then, Josh lad. We won't need the hotel room if missy here's in the clink.' He winked at her.

Rosa grinned, then said, 'Why don't you go and check in up the road. I'll join you for a drink as soon as I'm done.'

'If you're sure?'

'I'm fine. Honestly.'

With the boys off the premises, Rosa picked up Hot and hurriedly led the two police officers upstairs. Relieved that Titch was out at the café, she just hoped that she had left the lounge in decent order that morning.

The boys in blue perched uncomfortably on the edge of each sofa. The shorter one piped up, 'Good, now we have your full attention, Miss Larkin, we need to have a serious chat with you. You see, we have reason to believe you were involved in the hit-and-run incident in which Miss Jasmine Simmonds was hurt.'

Rosa opened her eyes and mouth in disbelief. Even Hot stopped barking for a second. After a tricky start to the day, it looked as if things were about to get a whole lot worse.

CHAPTER THIRTY SEVEN

Josh kept half an eye on the pub door, and the moment he saw Rosa push it open, he immediately went to her side. Putting his arm around her, he guided her to the bar, where Carlton greeted her and asked what she wanted to drink.

'I can't drink, I'm working and a bit late already,' she explained. At that moment, Jacob appeared from upstairs. 'So sorry I'm late,' she apologised, and then burst out: 'Jacob, I've only had the local plod round, insinuating I was involved in the hit-and-run.'

'Oh, lovey, surely not. What did they accuse you of? You don't even drive!'

'I know, tell me about it. I thought I was going to be taken down to the station at one stage.'

'You poor poppet.' Then Jacob perked up. 'At least you've got these two gorgeous creatures to look after you this weekend. Look, I tell you what, I can jump behind the bar tonight while you catch up with your friends. You've got a big day tomorrow, what with the opening and everything.'

Rosa kissed him on the cheek. 'That is such a relief, thank you. I've still got loads to do and I'm opening at ten.'

'Raff will have the canapés and sausage rolls ready tonight, you will just need to warm them through in the oven in the morning.'

'Perfect,' Josh chipped in. 'One of us can bring them down for you. You wouldn't want Hot getting hold of them before then.'

'That would be cannibalism, wouldn't it? Sausage – dog – get it?'

'As you were, Carlton.' They all laughed.

'It's all going to be fine,' Josh promised. 'We can help you do anything that's necessary. Carlton doesn't need to leave until ten-thirty for the rugby match, so we can make use of those muscles of his too.'

Jacob let out a camp 'Oof!' then went off to serve a customer.

'Thank you so much, but are you sure you don't want to go to Falmouth with him?'

'No, of course not. I've come down to see you.'

Rosa sipped on a glass of wine. 'I'm literally just having one and going to get back and start laying out glasses et cetera.' After what she had just been through, she could have drunk a bottle down in one, but no, the show must go on.

Once seated at a table in the corner, Rosa relayed the tale about the police incident to Josh and Carlton. The officers explained the reason why they were there: somebody had phoned the incident number they had given out and described a young woman of Rosa's description running away from the scene when the ambulance arrived.

'I told them that I was definitely at home, as I'd just had my heating fixed and was up to my ears in cleaning since I'd only recently moved in. They said if nobody could confirm my alibi, then I might have to take part in an identity parade. When I said I didn't drive – so how could I be involved – they made out I could have been an accessory, and if I was covering anything up, then I could be in serious trouble.' She took a large sip of her drink.

'Bloody hell.' Josh's face looked pained. 'But you're not guilty, so you have nothing to worry about. And wasn't Wanker Boy Plumber round that day, getting the heating sorted for you?'

'He was, but he left around five.'

'And I thought he was going to pick her up, that woman Jasmine?'

'Oh Josh, let's not discuss that in here. I'm sure nothing will come of it. I was in the flat and that's a fact.'

Rosa suddenly felt uncomfortable talking about it, especially as everywhere in this town seemed to have ears and eyes. She had contemplated lying on behalf of that complete charlatan and philanderer Lucas Hannafore, as he had asked her to, but that was before he had shown his true colours. If he really needed to, he could turn to Titch for his alibi now. The last thing she wanted to do was get herself in trouble, to be associated with anything that could jeopardise the success of the Corner Shop.

Thankfully they hadn't asked her anything about his van and whether she knew if it had been parked behind the shop. With no CCTV in this area, maybe his story would stand. Then again, if they were really going to town on the investigation they would certainly be able to pick him up by checking the signals on his mobile phone. It was all very messy – and he might just have to fess up the same drink-driving story he had told her. He couldn't be done for drink driving after the event and if he was innocent of the hit-and-run, then he would be fine. She could see though, how people did get themselves into trouble telling lies on top of more lies.

Rosa finished up her wine. 'Right, I just need to do a final check on everything for tomorrow. You two stay and have a fun night.'

Just as she was putting her coat on, there was a mighty rush of air as the door sprang open and Titch came tearing into the pub. She was carrying a whimpering Hot wrapped up in a bloodied blanket. In floods of tears, she ran to the bar.

'Where's Rosa?' she cried. 'We need to get Hot to a vet as soon as possible.'

CHAPTER THIRTY EIGHT

'Excuse me. Is this the incident line for the hit-and-run incident?' the caller asked, then coughed.

'Yes, madam.' A deep Devonian accent greeted her. 'How can I help you?'

'Do I have to give my name?'

'Not if you don't want to, right now, but if it is a line of questioning we need to follow up, then we may need to contact you again.'

'OK, OK. Well, I heard that somebody answering the description of Rosa Larkin was seen running from the scene?'

'I can't confirm or deny that allegation at this stage of the investigation, madam.' The desk sergeant grabbed his notepad and pen for fear of the message not recording.

'I understand.' The lady at the end of the phone coughed again. 'I just wanted to say that, well, it couldn't have been her.'

'OK. Go on.'

'Because I walked past her shop at the time the said incident was supposed to have happened and I saw her cleaning her front windows, from top to bottom. Giving them a right old going-over, she was. She weren't involved, I can assure you. You need to be looking a little closer to home, you do. A little closer to home.' And with that, the anonymous caller hung up.

Queenie took off her scarf and ran her finger across the engraving on the gold necklace she was now holding. When she reached the words *Meet Me*, she sighed deeply.

'Have you done it, Mary, duck?'

'Yes, Gran. It's all done and dusted.'

CHAPTER THIRTY NINE

'Oh my God!' Rosa leapt up, closely followed by Josh, and took her beloved hound in her arms. Jacob came running out from behind the bar.

'Here.' He pulled car keys from his pocket. 'I'll ring Helen, she's our vet and a friend of mine in Polhampton. She'll open her practice up for us. Josh, can you drive?'

'I've had two pints and don't want to risk it.'

Raff appeared from the kitchen, wiping his hands on his apron. 'It's fine, I can do the bar – you go, Jacob. Brad can hold the fort.'

Titch was inconsolable as she sat in the back of the car with Rosa and a now-shivering Hot.

'I had just got home and had unlocked the front door,' Titch blubbered, 'and Hot came bounding up to greet me as he does usually. I bent down to stroke him when all of a sudden there was a loud noise like a firework or something – maybe a car backfiring – and he bounded out onto the street. Just as he did so, a motorbike came charging up the street and…and…'

'You couldn't help it, Titch, it was an accident.'

'He only grazed him with a pedal, I think, but the bastard didn't even look back and I was in too much shock to get his

201

number-plate. I think his helmet was black and silver.'

Josh was sitting next to Jacob in the front passenger seat. 'He probably didn't even realise what had happened, at least I hope not. Hot is such a little low-down fellow, and if he just clipped him, then phew. It could have been so much worse if it had been a car.'

Nearly two hours later and Jacob and Josh dropped off Rosa, Titch and a very sleepy Hot back at the Corner Shop.

'Jacob, I can't thank you enough.' Rosa hugged him with all her heart.

'It's fine, my darling. I know our pets are like babies to us. Now go and put that little sausage in his basket.'

Josh rubbed one of Hot's ears gently. 'I'd better go back and see if Carlton's OK.'

'Right. I'll see you in the morning then.' The enormity of what could have happened suddenly took hold, and Rosa felt a bit queasy.

'Don't be daft. I'll pop down and have a nightcap with you before I go to bed.'

'I'd like that. See you later.'

Titch linked her right arm through Rosa's left, making sure not to disturb the poor injured pooch.

'Come on, the pair of you. I can't believe that nothing was broken. He's just bruised and has some slight cuts, didn't the vet say?'

'Yes, he will be very sore for a couple of days. Helen has given him an antibiotic for the wounds, and something for him to sleep tonight, which has obviously kicked in already. Bless my little boy.'

'I know – and I'm so sorry again, Rosa.'

'Weird for someone to have fireworks this time of year?'

'Well, whatever it was spooked Hot and caused him to flee –

and you know he never usually runs out of the front as we give him such a telling-off when he does.'

'Oh well, let's just thank God he's all right.'

Rosa gently laid a now flat-out Hot on his own cosy new dog-bed in her bedroom where she could keep an eye on him. Josh had insisted on paying the vet bill up-front, telling her that when she was earning enough from the shop she could pay him back.

As Titch got ready for bed, Rosa laid out two mugs and put the kettle on.

'Did you want a hot drink?' she called out.

'No, thanks.' The girl appeared from the bathroom with toothbrush in mouth. 'I'm going to help you tomorrow, Rose, then I'll move back in with Mum in the evening, if that's OK?'

'Of course, it's OK. Did you catch up with Seb, by the way?'

'Yep.'

'What was so urgent he needed to speak to you about?'

'Oh, nothing of significance. And he can keep out of my way from now on. It makes my skin creep, just looking at him.' She rubbed her little belly. 'It's just me and Titchy Titch from now on. Well, for a while, anyway. Goodnight, Rose.'

Rosa was so tired she couldn't even face going down to check on all the stock. She would just have to set her alarm for six and deal with everything in the morning. The weather report had said cold but sunny, so that was good at least. And to be fair she was pretty organised, so it was just the finishing touches that needed to be addressed.

She had another quick peek at Hot, then went to the lounge, turned on the lamps and shut the curtains. In all of the commotion, she hadn't thought once about Joe. She didn't even know what time he was due to arrive in the morning. She sent off a quick text to him, then went back to the kitchen.

She'd left the back door unlocked for Josh and he whispered a 'Hello, it's only me,' as he came up the stairs. He then gave her one of his massive bear hugs that had always made her feel so safe, even when things weren't going so well for her in London.

They pulled away and he gestured to Titch's bedroom and mouthed to ask if she was in bed. Rosa nodded, then did the universal pregnancy sign of her hand going over a bump on her stomach. Josh's eyes and mouth widened fully. Josh was the only one Rosa could tell and know it would go no further. He whispered, 'Oh my God, whose is it?' and Rosa whispered back that she didn't know.

In the kitchen, Rosa shut the door and spoke quietly. 'It's mad, I know, about Titch. She's only eighteen.'

'And definitely having the baby?'

'Yes.'

'How far gone is she?'

'Josh! So many questions. Why are you so bothered anyway?'

Josh held his hands up in the air. 'Sorry, madam, I was just asking.' He then squeezed her to him again. 'My poor Rosalar and Hot, so stressful, but at least the little fella is safe and sound.'

A text pinged on her phone. Josh reached to pass her the handset. 'Ooh, THE FOX, eh, who's he? Ah, he was the one saying goodbye to you when we arrived. Tell me more.'

He craned over Rosa's shoulder as she read. *Damn Mr Plod getting in the way of our first proper snog. Hope it all went well with them anyway. Let's talk tomorrow. See you around 11 XX*

'Oi! My phone, my text.'

'Proper snog? Ooh – how childish. And two kisses… Have you got a boyfriend, Rosa Larkin? You kept that quiet. You don't do "proper snogs" either. I thought you were a one-night-stand or nothing kind of girl?'

Annoyingly, Rosa could feel herself reddening. 'OK, I like

him. He's quirky, funny, helped me get the gig on the radio and is covering the shop opening tomorrow.'

'Oh, the *Gazette* guy. So, you haven't slept with him yet then?' Josh asked, trying to sound casual.

'No. Anyway, you're seeing someone too – and don't deny it. I can always tell. What's her name?'

'Well, I wouldn't say "seeing" exactly.'

'I know you, Josh: dinner and staying over equates to seeing and you've done that.'

'Why are you so sure?'

'Well, I wasn't, but you've just confirmed it, you div.'

'Oi. All right, her name is Lucy, she works in PR for my company. She's a good girl.'

'A good girl, what's that supposed to mean? I can feel a "but" coming on though.' Rosa poured boiling water onto the Nescafé and milk she'd already put in the mugs.

'She is lovely, we have a laugh and the sex is good, but she's not…' Josh seemed a bit agitated. 'I don't want to talk about her any more. But how cool that you have a real-life fox on the go. Is he as handsome as me?'

Josh preened out his chest.

'Obviously as, if not more.' Rosa laughed out loud. 'Come on, come and see Hot, he looks so sweet.'

Josh followed her to the bedroom to find Hot completely wrapped in a clean blanket, with his little head to the side poking out of the top. His breathing was regular. Hand on chest, Josh went 'Ooh,' as he looked on. Rosa ushered him back out in case they woke the tiny patient from his well-needed rest.

'Bloody hell, it's midnight. I've got to be up at six.' Rosa jumped up from the sofa, nearly spilling her coffee as she did so.

'Is it? In which case I'd better go before I turn into a pumpkin.' They both laughed. 'And Carlton's been on his own all night.'

'I'm sure Jacob and Raff have been amusing him.'

'Ha, yes, I bet they have. Do you want me here at six too? I really don't mind. Unless lover boy is coming to help, of course?'

'Ha, very funny. He can't get here until eleven-ish, as he's bringing the photographer with him, and she's covering some other Valentine's story beforehand, evidently.' Rosa fixed Josh with a beady eye. 'Talking of the Day of Lurve, how's Juicy Lucy coping without having you around on your first Valentine's together?'

'Hmm. I just used the old Joshua Smith charm and got away with it. Said I will make it up to her. She knows how important rugby is to me.'

'So, you didn't tell her you were with me, then? All right, is she, about you having a female friend?'

'God, you women think too much.'

Rosa shut up and handed Josh his coat. 'Honestly, don't worry to get up silly early. Get here when you can. If one of you can bring the food down, that would be useful. I can get it all set up before ten then.'

'OK, cool.' Josh pulled her towards him for another cuddle. 'Bloody proud of you I am, girl. Tomorrow will be amazing, I know it.'

'OK, enough cuddling already.' Rosa pulled away.

She walked in front of him down the steep stairs and closed the front door behind him. Lifting up the black cloth she had put to hide the stock, she waved madly. And, with a childish stick-out of tongue, Josh waved back and turned to walk briskly up the hill.

CHAPTER FORTY

Rosa felt like throwing her alarm across the room when it went off at five-thirty, but remembering her poorly pooch and what a big day it was, she immediately turned on the bedside light, and with hair everywhere and squinty eyes, jumped out of bed.

Hot was still in the same position as last night. He looked into her eyes and whimpered. She knelt down and stroked his ears, murmuring, 'It's all right, boy.' Gently, she unwrapped him to reveal a white bandage all the way around his tummy area, covering the cuts and protecting the bruising. Making soothing noises, she carefully carried him to the balcony in case he wanted a pee. Leaving him to have a sniff around, she put some food down for him in the kitchen, and was glad to see him gobble it up, as well as drinking nearly a whole bowl of fresh water.

The vet had suggested she didn't walk him for a couple of days, and Titch had kindly promised to keep an eye on him throughout the day whilst the commotion of the opening was going on.

Rosa had a quick shower, and was just pulling on joggers and a hoody, when there was a knock on the front door. Smiling to herself, she ran downstairs.

'I said you didn't need to be here at six.'

'What you say and what you mean, Rosa Larkin, are sometimes completely different things.' Josh kissed her on the cheek.

'Right, let's do this.'

By eight o'clock, they'd pulled all the blackout covers down, rearranged the window stock and made sure all price tickets were visible. Rosa charged the till with change and laid out plastic glasses and plates while Josh filled a bucket out the back with cold water and placed the bottles of Prosecco inside. It was cold enough to keep them at a good temperature as there was no way they could all fit in the fridge. They set the Bose speaker up and tested it and placed the balloons either side of the door. Rosa had also put pink ribbon garlands across the front bay window and made a feature of the heart doggie chocolates on a table right at the front of the shop.

The supplier of the dog food had also sent some cute posters for her to display, plus a special hook-type thing on which to hang a selection of leads. She had ordered just a few designer doggie outfits to test the market, but already knew that when Jacob saw the Barbour raincoats and cashmere sweaters, Ugly and Pongo's wardrobes would be set.

'Quick, come out here.' Josh took Rosa by the hand and led her across to the opposite side of the narrow street. He pointed to the shop. 'How amazing does that look!'

Rosa made a funny noise and jumped up and down on the spot. 'That's my shop, Josh. I did that.'

'Yes, you did – and now it's time to start making it a success.'

At that moment Mary penguin-walked towards them.

'Oh Rosa, that looks a right treat, that does,' she said, and coughed before explaining, 'I'm so disappointed. My shift was changed at the last minute at the Co-op, and so I have to work this morning, worst luck. But I was determined to come and say hello and give you this.' She placed something in Rosa's hand and closed her fingers around it. 'It's from me and Gran. I'll come back in and look at leads for Merlin when there's no crowds, if you don't mind.'

'Of course not, and thank you so much, Mary. This is Josh, by the way, my friend from London.'

Mary kept hold of Rosa's hand and stared into Josh's eyes. 'Hello, Josh. Look after this one, won't you?'

Before Josh had a chance to say anything, she released Rosa's hand and shuffled back up the hill.

'Blimey, one of the Cockleberry Coven, I assume?'

'Yes, that's Mary. Mad as a fruit bat, but there is something about her that I really like.'

Josh smiled. 'You fruit bats have to stick together. Anyway, what did she give you?'

Rosa opened up her hands. A little white box lay inside; she opened it to reveal a small green crystal, accompanied by a scribbled note.

Dear Rosa. This is an abundance crystal. It is called Green Aventurine and it's from the quartz family. It is also known as the Stone of Opportunity. It is considered to be the luckiest of all crystals. Good Luck today. Love from Mary and Queenie.

'Do you think she is a witch?'

'Josh, just because people are into crystals doesn't mean they are witches.'

'It's all a bit too out there for me. But very kind of her, nonetheless.'

Rosa smiled broadly as she spotted Jacob, Carlton and

Raffaele walking towards them. Jacob was hidden behind a massive bouquet of flowers and the other two were carrying platters of food.

'Happy Opening Day, my darling.' Jacob air-kissed her and handed her the flowers. 'You so need the smell of lilies to waft under everyone's noses.' He wandered into the shop as Josh showed the others through to the kitchen. 'I say, this is magnificent. Oh, and just look at these.' He picked up the Barbour raincoats. 'Well, there's your first sale already, sweetie. But let me wait and make a big scene whilst buying them later.'

'You're full of all the tricks, aren't you?'

'You've got to be down here, Rosa. This is your chance to shine. What are you wearing – not this, surely?' He pointed to her hoody and made a face.

'No. I have a bright pink dress with white poodles on and white leather ankle boots.'

Jacob laughed. 'I knew you'd pull out the stops, darling girl.'

Rosa hugged Raffaele. 'Thanks so much for doing the food, it smells amazing.'

'No problem, little one. Right – I had better get back to the kitchen. Make sure you send the crowds our way for lunch.'

At that moment her phone rang. It was Joe. 'Happy Valentine's Day,' he said.

'Aw thanks, right back at you.' She hadn't even thought about it. Mind you, she'd never bought a Valentine's card in her life before, and they weren't exactly in a relationship – yet, anyway – were they?

'Just checking all is going OK. Sorry I can't help you this morning.'

'No, it's fine, will be good to see you later though. Are you still planning to come around eleven?'

'I'm not totally sure, but the photographer, who is called

Olivia, by the way, will be with you soon: her boyfriend can drop her off at nine forty-five ready for when the doors open. Have you got a ribbon or something you can put across the door?'

'I hadn't thought of that, but yeah, I've got loads. Maybe I should have got Prince Harry and Meghan in to cut it too?'

Joe laughed. 'Then you'd have made more than the front page of the *Gazette*, that's for sure. Right, I've got to go. You will smash it, Rosa. See you later.'

'Lover boy, oh lover boy,' Josh came up behind her singing. 'Can't wait to meet him.'

Carlton had gone back to the Lobster Pot pack but was now here to say his goodbyes before leaving for Falmouth. Josh was upstairs checking on Hot, before Titch was due to take over later. 'See you then, Rosa, nice to meet you.'

'You too, and I'm so sorry for all the drama last night.'

'It's fine, I was quite happy chilling at the pub. It's been a busy week and it will be a heavy one tonight.'

Rosa smiled. 'I've been victim to many a post rugby-night hangover with Mr Smith, so I hear you.'

'Well done on the shop, by the way. I'm not sure if Josh has mentioned it, but I've fitted a few out in my time, with all the high-end latest shelving, lighting and so on, but what you've done with a small space, a screwdriver and a great eye for what works in a window, is commendable. Good job.'

'Aw, what a lovely thing to say – thanks, Carlton.' Then Rosa couldn't help herself. 'So er…what's the deal with this Lucy girl Josh has been seeing?' she asked. 'What's she like?'

'She's a nice girl – but who's he spending this weekend with, eh?' Carlton winked and patted her shoulder with his big hand.

Josh appeared. 'You off, mate? Enjoy – and I'll see you tomorrow. Just text me when you're half an hour away and I'll

211

get a cab to the station, so you don't have to come all the way down here again.'

'Nice one, mate.' Carlton looked at Rosa again. 'You take care of that hound of yours.'

'Hey, I am house-trained.' Josh smirked.

'Will do. Good luck for the match – and I've got my spare room back from tonight, so you're welcome to crash anytime.'

'I may take you up on that – when it's not so bloody cold. I thought the South-west was supposed to be warm. Right, better go.'

To the sounds of Elvis's 'Hound Dog' blaring out of her new Bose portable speaker, Rosa and Titch greeted potential customers outside the shop. The ribbon was still intact, forming a barrier through which no one could enter just yet. With Josh offering glasses of fizz or squash and trays with the wonderful canapés that Raffaele had made, there was soon a crowd of around twenty adults, six kids and five pooches milling around.

Louise, the face-painter, had set up in the little courtyard area to the back of the shop. So that everyone could see what was going on out there, Rosa had left the back door wide open.

Olivia from the *Gazette* appeared in a flurry, apologising for being a bit late and telling Rosa that Joe had also been delayed and would get here as soon as he could.

Josh handed Rosa a pair of scissors and gently pushed her forward. 'Now! Go on, everyone is waiting. Good luck.'

Titch turned the music down, causing everyone to stop talking.

Rosa blushed. 'So…um…hello, my name is Rosa Larkin and thank you all so much for coming along to meet me and see what my little Corner Shop has to offer.' She gulped. 'I will be selling predominantly pet products and pet food of all kinds,

212

with a few luxuries thrown in, as we all know how much we like to spoil our fur babies sometimes.'

Laughter ensued.

'If there is something you are after and I don't stock it, then please do let me know and I can order it in for you.' She swallowed and suddenly confidence filled her as she told them: 'This is as much your shop as it is mine. There are also gifts and trinkets to the back of the shop that the children might like, and for those of you who have brought your dogs along, please do help yourself to the doggie heart treats next to the till.' She pointed inside the shop.

'Titch. Where are you?' Titch put her hand up. 'Ah, there she is. Titch here has got ten-per-cent-off vouchers for those who make a purchase today.'

Titch started making her way around the crowd and handing them out. Sheila Hannafore, who had been standing at the back of the crowd, turned with a face like thunder and made her way back down the hill to open up the Ship.

'My wish is to make the Corner Shop an asset for the wonderful community of Cockleberry Bay, just as Ned and Dotty did before me.' Rosa cleared her throat and poised herself to cut the ribbon. 'So, I'll shut up now, just to say I hereby declare the Corner Shop in Cockleberry Bay well and truly open.'

Jacob, Raffa, Titch and Josh cheered as the crowd clapped, the ribbon fell to the ground and the small crowd slowly started filing into the shop.

CHAPTER FORTY ONE

It wasn't until she and Josh were counting the takings in the lounge, that Rosa realised Joe had never turned up. She checked her phone for messages, but the screen was blank.

Josh was making a fuss of Hot, who looked rather comical waddling around with his midriff bandage. He was already a lot livelier and had started barking at the seagulls out on the balcony once more.

'Aw. Look at you being a big, brave boy,' Josh cooed. 'Maybe me and Mummy will take you for a little w...'

'Don't you say that four-letter word out loud, Joshua Smith. He can't get too excited, but yes, I can't be doing with picking up poo from outside any more. Yuk. Makes me feel sick.'

'Good job he's not a Great Dane then, isn't it?'

Rosa looked at him sideways. 'Joe has got a Great Dane, did you know that?'

'No. I was just thinking of types of big dogs in my head. Anyway, where is lover boy? You'd have thought he could have made a bit of an effort, not only on your special day, but also Valentine's Day of all days.'

'We are not exactly dating, are we?' But Rosa couldn't deny that she felt disappointed.

Josh went to the kitchen and came back with two glasses from a leftover bottle of Prosecco. 'I want to make a toast,' he said and lifted his glass. 'To my little Rosalar, shop owner extraordinaire and a top girl. Happy Valentine's Day, chick.'

Rosa clinked glasses with him. 'Thank you – and for everything you've done to get me to this stage. I know I'm a moany bitch sometimes, but I do really appreciate it. And you can be my pretend Valentine any day.'

'Excellent. Where's Titch, by the way?' Josh asked.

'She's staying with her mum tonight. I'm quite relieved actually, as I'm too knackered to help her move her stuff.'

'What's all this about her being pregnant?'

'Crazy, isn't it? She's adamant she's keeping the baby. Good on her, because if I was in her position, I really don't think I could be as strong.'

'And does she know whose it is?'

'Well, all I know is that it isn't Lucas's.'

'What? I'm confused now.'

'She shagged Lucas and has told his mum that it's his baby, even though it's definitely not, as she used a condom.'

'What the…'

'I know, tell me about it. It gets worse.'

'Go on.'

'Sheila paid her off to have the abortion and to never mention it again.'

'Jeeze! Sheila Hannafore really is a nasty piece of work.'

Just at that moment, a text came through on her phone.

In a monotone voice, Josh quipped, 'Whoopidoo, quick, maybe that's him.'

Rosa reached for her phone and read: *So sorry, Rosa. Progress on the hit-and-run story and I couldn't get away. Hope today was successful. Will make it up to you, I promise.*

Josh saw her face fall. 'And…?'

'It's fine, he's got news on the hit-and-run, and I know how important his work is to him. I wonder what he's found out?'

'Call him, Rosa.'

'No.'

'Why not?' Josh could immediately smell a rat.

'He's made no indication of when I'm next seeing him. He can fuck off.'

'You don't mean that. For the first time since I've known you I can tell you actually like this guy.'

'Whatever.' Rosa downed her Prosecco and pulled herself together. Today was so important to her for many reasons and she wasn't going to let a man spoil it.

She jumped up from the sofa. 'Right, let's sort this money out.'

Hot plonked himself down at her feet and nuzzled them, and she gave him a heart treat that she had kept in her pocket.

Silence ensued whilst Rosa and Josh counted the takings and sorted them into plastic money bags that Jacob had kindly given Rosa that morning.

'Bloody hell.' Josh broke the silence. 'Six hundred pounds! Now if you could take that every day, you'd be laughing.'

'Oh my God, that's amazing.' Rosa juggled some of the change bags. 'Obviously it's not all profit.'

'Of course not, but for a little shop, in a small town not even in tourist season, that's fantastic. And looking at your stock earlier, a lot of it was the dog food and not luxuries that sold, so hopefully you'll get repeat business on that.'

He pointed to the money and said in a schoolmaster-ish voice: 'Now, what do you do with this on Monday morning?'

'I go and buy a designer handbag and a vat of wine, of course,' Rosa grinned.

216

Josh wagged a finger. 'Straight to the bank and into the business account.'

'You're so dull.'

'I know, but someone's got to rein you in. You don't want to be keeping loads of cash in the flat. Saying that, did you ever find that necklace?'

'No. I'm trying not to think about it. Titch did leave the back door open the other day, so if she's done that before then I do reckon an opportunist thief may have come and taken it, as I literally have looked everywhere.'

'Strange, though, that nothing else has gone missing.'

'There's nothing else here of value to take really, though, is there? I haven't even got a TV yet.'

Another text came in and Rosa hurriedly checked it. 'Oh bless, it's Jacob seeing if we are coming in for a drink.'

'Do you fancy going up there? I need to settle my bill anyway. I told him I would stay here with you tonight – guess that's OK with you?'

'Do you know what, I don't really want to leave Hot, to be honest. You go, I'll have a bath and chill for a bit.'

'OK, I won't be long. How about I pick up some fish and chips up on the way back.'

'Perfect.'

Rosa was just about to run a bath, when there was a knock on the upstairs patio door. Strange – she thought she had locked the back gate. It had to be either Titch or Josh as not many people knew they could get up the little flight of steps to the balcony in this way.

Putting her dressing gown on, she gingerly went to the glass door and did a little scream in fright at the face pressed against it.

'Lucas Hannafore, you scared the life out of me!'

'Well, let me in then.'

Rosa took in his handsome, cheeky face and was annoyed that she still felt attracted to him.

'Hear it went well today,' he said casually. 'The window looks great.'

'Thanks, but what are you doing down here in Cockleberry Bay, especially on Valentine's Day? Shouldn't you be romancing Jasmine?'

'Mother summoned me down. She tells me the police came in to see you.'

'Yes, they did, and I told the truth, sorry. I said you left here at four-thirty and I had no idea where you were heading.'

'Well, thanks for that, Rosa. That's what they said you'd said but I wanted to check. I had half-hoped you'd be loyal to me.'

'Look, Luke. I don't want to get involved. If you're guilty then why don't you just put your hands up? Jasmine won't press charges, anyway. Tell her it was a stupid accident.'

'Hmm, now that she's just caught me shagging her best friend, I'm not so sure.'

'For goodness sake, can't you just keep it in your trousers!'

'Says the girl whose knickers were off quicker than any whore's drawers.'

'That was then. I have a little more self-respect now. In fact, I'm dating somebody.'

'Really, your City boy twat? He'll be bored of this sleepy town in no time.'

'Josh is worth a hundred of you. And it's none of your business who I'm seeing.'

'Ah, got it. The guy from the *Gazette* has been sniffing around, hasn't he? Got you the gig on the radio – that must have been worth a blow job at least.'

'Get out, just get out.' Rosa pointed down the stairs.

Luke was relentless. 'And you think I'm bad blood.'

'What's that supposed to mean? You're just jealous.'

'Jealous? Don't be ridiculous.'

'Oh, just clear off, Luke. And never come back.'

'Don't worry, I'm going – but I'm so angry with you, Rosa.'

'Maybe you should ask Titch about it,' Rosa seethed.

Forming two fists with his hands in complete frustration, Luke shouted, 'It bloody wasn't me who ran that stupid bitch of an ex of mine over.'

Hot started barking wildly. Then in what seemed like seconds, Josh had bounded up the stairs, thrown the carrier bag of fish and chips on the floor, grabbed Luke by his collar and with the words 'Never, ever show your face in here again,' had dragged him down and thrown him out on the street.

Rosa crouched down to comfort a shaking Hot, whispering, 'I'm so sorry, darling boy.'

Josh went down to her level and put his arm around her.

'Keep away from him and his mother from now on, Rosa. Jacob said they were bad news, and at least we know we can trust his opinion.'

Rosa nodded and nuzzled into Josh's chest. 'Will you sleep in with me and Hot tonight?'

Too tired to even eat, they headed to the bedroom and within minutes of Rosa's head touching the pillow, she was sound asleep. Hot snored gently at their feet and with the window open Josh could hear the sea crashing on the beach. He turned his head and looked at Rosa. With her dark brown curls spread across the pillow and still wearing her pink glittery eye shadow, she looked far younger than her twenty-five years.

He thought back to a comment that Carlton had made earlier when he was saying something about Rosa not being girlfriend material. 'Love is friendship set on fire, isn't that what they say though, mate?'

Josh kissed his finger, gently placed it on the little lightning-shaped scar that he so adored, then with a deep sigh, spooned into the warmth of his pretty companion and fell into a deep sleep.

CHAPTER FORTY TWO

'Sorry I've got to leave so early, but Carlton needs to get back, as he's got a shop-fit tonight,' Josh told Rosa the next morning. He omitted to add that he had also promised Lucy a late Valentine's meal.

'It's fine. The Cockleberry Coven have actually asked me round for Sunday lunch.'

'What'll that be then – eye of newt and toe of frog, wool of bat and tongue of dog?' Josh's Shakespeare quip went right over Rosa's uneducated head.

'Euw. Stop it. I was rather hoping for roast beef and Yorkshire pudding. Now, do you want me to ring the taxi man and see if he's free?'

'Yes, please, we should have done it last night, I guess. Carlton said I need to be up at the station by ten.'

'No worries if Ralph's not free. Seb Watkins takes a fiver for some trips for extra cash as he's always up and down for work.'

Hot came running into the kitchen and jumped up at Josh's leg. 'Aw, he seems so much more himself.'

'Yes, he does, thank goodness. Jacob is going to run me up to the vet's in the morning just to check him over once more.'

'Little scamp.' Josh picked him up gently and put him over his shoulder. Hot started to lick his face vigorously.

'Er...' Josh placed him down on the kitchen floor promptly and rubbed the wet from his ear and cheek.

When Josh had gone, Rosa had a tidy-up, then went down to the shop to check on her stock levels. She smiled as she saw the half-empty baskets and now depleted row of leads on the rack. It had been such fun taking actual cash for her very own business. She was aware that it would be hard work and that every Saturday probably wouldn't be quite as busy, but at least she knew now what she had to do, and it was just a case of doing it and doing it well.

Back upstairs, thinking she'd climb back into bed for a bit before she got ready for lunch, she decided to get the letters down from their hiding place and have a read. 'Ooh, yes,' she said aloud. 'Let's see what Naughty Ned was up to.'

With Hot asleep at her feet, she unfurled the pile and began to read.

15 August 1954

My Darling T

It's been two months now since I've seen you and I really cannot bear it. They've put a new telephone box on the jetty, just below 'our place' on West Cliffs. The number is Cockleberry 7875. I will be there at 6pm this Sunday. Do promise me you will call, I have to know if you are well.

Dotty has taken a turn for the worse. Despite it being a year already since her last miscarriage and the hysterectomy, she cannot come to terms with the fact that she will never give us a family together. The doctor has been coming in daily, but we can't seem to pull her out of such a deep depression.

222

I know it seems daft, but she needs her friend. I need a friend. I know that one night we overstepped the mark, but I couldn't resist you. My love for you is so strong, T. But I have a responsibility to my wife now too. Please understand.

I hope you can find it in yourself to call me on Sunday.

Meet me where the sky touches the sea.

Your loving Ned X

Rosa was now transfixed by the real ongoing love story.

21 August 1954

Dearest Ned

I'm hoping you receive this before Sunday as I don't feel I can talk to you at the moment. The guilt and pain I feel with regard to Dotty is eating me up, and as much as I want to be in your arms, it is for her and her alone that I am going to come home for a weekend. I then will be going straight back to London as I cannot bear to be near you, but not with you.

Who would have thought that true love could be so painful? And, all the time I sit here thinking of you, I also have to think of myself and my future. There is no way you can leave Dotty when she is in this sort of state, and the repercussions will be so great if you do, that we are in a difficult situation whatever happens.

We have to end whatever this is now, Ned: it is not healthy for any of us. I can sell the cottage, move away, start again in London.

Meet me where the sky touches the sea.

Your T XX

Rosa felt exhausted just feeling the pain between the lines.

She couldn't imagine what the lovers were going through emotionally. What an awful situation to be in. She wondered why the letters were still there, but then they had been so well-hidden. Maybe Ned just got old and forgot. It was like reading a book, but she knew the ending already. In a macabre way she now wanted to know not only how the story panned out, but also how Dotty had died. From Queenie's reaction it can't have been good. She had to keep on reading.

1 Sep 1956

My Darling T

The joy of seeing your beautiful face at the weekend was almost too much to bear. And whatever you did to uplift Dotty's spirits, well, it's been like a wonder cure. I've never seen her so animated as when you left. What did you say to her?

This still does not counteract the fact of how much I still miss you. Having you so close and not being able to caress your soft skin, or kiss those rosebud lips of yours was sheer torture.

Come home, T. If Dotty can come through her depression, and I think we may be seeing the start of her recovery now, then maybe she will be able to cope with 'us' and we will have a future.

Meet me where the sky touches the sea.

Your ever-loving Ned X

Rosa checked her watch; she still had an hour before she had to be at the Coven. When Hot made a little 'feeping' sound, she leant down the bed to stroke him, then carried on reading.

5 September 1956

Dearest Ned

This is probably one of the most difficult letters I will ever have to write in my life.

You asked me what I said to Dotty. Well, I told her that I am pregnant, and that that is the reason why I'm staying in London. And it's true. How shameful am I? A baby out of wedlock – and no, Ned, it's not yours. I am thirty, after all, and I couldn't wait forever. Nobody knows me here, so they can say what they want.

Rosa's mouth fell open wide. 'I don't believe her,' she said to Hot, and continued reading.

I'm so, so sorry to break this to you in a letter. I will forever love you, Ned, but I will forever love Dotty too, and she is too good a woman to have her heart broken by the two people who love her the most.

Meet me where the sky touches the sea.

T XX

Rosa scrabbled to find the next letter, but it was just a blank bit of paper.

No. Surely that wasn't it? Bloody hell. The mystery remained.

Poor Dotty, and poor Ned. And also, poor T. It would have been hard in the 1950s to have a child out of wedlock – and nobody had ever mentioned that Ned had had a child down here, so what on earth had happened? She was sure that Seb had said Ned had died with friends around him, as he had no family. And what about T? She would have to ask Queenie now, there was just too much left unanswered.

A text message brought her back to reality. It was Joe.

Hey sexy shop owner, fancy a bite to eat later? Can be with you at 7? x

Rosa sighed. With everything that had been going on, she hadn't even thought about Joe. She replied:

Hey sexy sleuth, that sounds like a great idea! See you then x.

CHAPTER FORTY THREE

'Quick, get yourself in the warm, Rosa, it's bitterly cold out there today.' Mary shut the front door of Seaspray Cottage behind them and took Rosa's coat. A lovely log fire was burning in the kitchen. Seeing the visitor, Merlin screeched his disapproval.

'And how's poor little Hot?' Mary fussed. 'I heard about the accident.'

'Of course you did.' Rosa smiled. Not much went unreported around here. 'He's on the mend, thank goodness. Look, I don't want to be rude, but I won't stay long as I want to get back to him.'

'Queenie.' Rosa addressed the old lady who was sat in her usual chair in the kitchen. Today, her long grey hair was in beautiful ringlets; with her dark glasses she could have passed for a glamorously ageing film star. 'Great hair.'

Mary smiled. 'Yes, I thought we'd make the effort as it's Sunday and you were coming.' It was then Rosa realised that Mary's black hair was arranged in the same style.

Queenie raised her hand. 'I hear the opening was a roaring success. I just knew you would be a smart kid.'

'Not sure about that, Queenie, but I shall keep trying to be.'

'You do like roast beef, Rosa?' Mary went to stir gravy on the hob.

'I was only saying to Josh this morning that I hoped it would be just that, my favourite. Thank you so much for doing this.'

'Not at all.' Mary coughed. 'We can see how hard you have been working.'

'Ah, here.' Rosa reached into her bag. 'A lead for Merlin.' On hearing his name, the big cat hissed. 'I got green to go with his eyes. Hope you like it.'

Mary was joyous. 'Oh, that's marvellous, just marvellous.'

'How much do we owe you, duck?' Queenie piped up.

'Don't be silly, it's a gift. You two have been nothing but kind to me since I arrived here.'

'Pass me my purse, Mary.' Queenie handed Rosa a ten-pound note. 'How are you going to make a living if you are giving things away already? Now take this and put it in your kitty, with our love.'

'OK, thank you very much.'

'Now, sit down, child, and stop making the place look untidy.'

Mary dished up a scrumptious spread, which Rosa, after not having had any dinner last night or breakfast this morning, devoured in minutes.

'You were hungry, love.' Mary took her clean plate.

'I didn't even have breakfast this morning as I had found some letters hidden away a while ago – and today I felt I just had to read them.' Queenie went still as a stone. 'Anyway, I hadn't related them to the bundle of letters you saw in my tea leaves, Queenie, but this must be them.'

When the old lady remained silent, Rosa went on, 'Now, I know you said don't tittle-tattle, but well, reading between the lines, I think Ned was having an affair behind your friend Dotty's back.'

Rosa sensed that perhaps she should stop, but something was

compelling her to speak. 'It was with somebody called T. She was pregnant, but Ned didn't know the baby was his because she lied to him – pretended it was some other man's. But I guess you already knew that, as you were her friend too.' Rosa's voice grew impassioned. 'What happened, Queenie? I feel that I need to know. It really is heart-breaking to read the letters.'

Queenie suddenly banged her hand down on the table. 'Stop that talk, Rosa. I can't bear it. Poor, poor Dotty.'

'It's all right, Gran,' Mary soothed. 'Rosa, maybe you had better go. Or Gran, would you like Rosa to bring the letters to you?'

'Yesss.' The word hissed through the old lady's pinched lips like a snake.

Mary grimaced at her gran's behaviour. She asked timidly, 'Where did you find them, dear? They must have been well hidden.'

'They were. Whoever did hide them had made a secret compartment at the top of the wardrobe.'

A small smile formed on Queenie Cobb's face, which quickly disappeared as Rosa turned to look at her.

'Ned must have wanted to keep his affair secret, but was obviously too deeply in love to bring himself to throw away the letters. It's so sad. Each letter ends with "Meet me where the sky touches the sea" – whatever that means.'

'Go up to the top of West Cliffs and you will…'

'Mary! Hush up, just be quiet now.' Queenie banged on the table with her fist again. She appealed to Rosa. 'Please can you bring the letters to me? I know you are a good girl, but for the sake of Dotty's memory, I think it's only fair that the letters are left in the past where they belong now. We can put them on the fire.'

Rosa got up and went to her side, then put her hand gently on the old lady's thin, papery one. 'I will go and do it right now,' she said. 'And I'm sorry if I upset you.'

'It's all right, young Rosa.' Queenie's voice was now soft. 'Nobody can upset anyone else, I did it all by myself.'

Rosa hurried back down to the Corner Shop, put the old blue ribbon back around the letters and popped them into the Jiffy bag the flyers had come in. She gave Hot a doggie treat, then set off back up the hill again to Seaspray Cottage.

'Here they are.'

Before she'd even finished speaking, Queenie had grabbed the envelope from Rosa and thrown it straight on to the fire.

'Whilst we have been talking about difficult things,' Rosa said, and squirmed, 'I have to tell you something else.'

'Carry on, duck.' Queenie seemed fixated on the flames.

'Well, you know you mentioned a necklace when you read my tea leaves?'

'Yes,' Mary spoke up.

'I did find one. Way down the back of the old sofa in the flat.' Queenie just nodded her head slowly. 'Go on.'

'Well, I put it somewhere I thought was safe and now I can't find it. And…and I'm worried that someone might have stolen it.' Rosa blew out a long breath. 'There, I said it. I promise you, hand on heart, I didn't sell it, but I don't know how to prove that to you.'

Mary looked directly at Queenie, who nodded slowly again.

'You don't have to prove it, Rosa.'

Rosa, slightly baffled how Queenie, with such apparent bad sight and thick dark glasses, could see anything, remained silent.

Making her way to one of the kitchen drawers, Mary scrabbled around, then handed her the very same, heavy gold, engraved sapphire necklace.

Rosa was wide-eyed. 'I don't understand.'

'I found it. Outside your back gate. Maybe somebody did try

and get it, panicked and dropped it. Who knows, Rosa?'

'Oh my God, so someone has been in the flat.'

'Change the locks, dear. Maybe get an alarm now. That's all I will say to you.'

'Very well – I will. I'd been planning to buy myself a TV once I was in profit, but you're right, I should do that first. And get a new padlock for the back gate too.'

Queenie piped up, 'Good girl, Rosa, good girl. And as for the necklace, keep it.'

'But it belonged to Ned and T.'

'Neither of whom will be wearing it again,' Mary said quietly.

'Wear it on a special day, Rosa,' the old lady urged, 'and wherever you are, you can think of us and smile.'

'I suppose if Ned has no family left, then there's no harm – and it is beautiful. But what about T's family?'

'They would understand, duck.'

At that moment, Merlin jumped up onto Queenie's lap and began purring loudly. She stroked the big animal, then reaching for Mary's hand, she squeezed and shook it frantically at the same time. She looked almost ecstatic.

'I can go now,' she said, as if she was talking to herself.

Merlin let out an almighty meow and ran out of the cat flap in the back door.

Rosa mouthed, 'Go where?' to Mary, whose face had contorted so she couldn't speak.

The old lady then leant forward and took both of Rosa's hands. 'Listen to me, Rosa. Sometimes in life, if you don't know what to do: do nothing, say nothing and the answer will come to you. You are blessed.'

And with that, Queenie Cobb fell back in her chair and peacefully passed away.

CHAPTER FORTY FOUR

'Where are you, Rosa? I'm banging on your door. I can hear Hot, but there's no sign of you.'

'Oh Joe, yes, hi – I'm so sorry. I'm with Mary at Seaspray Cottage. Her gran has died, and we are waiting for the ambulance. I completely lost track of time.'

'Oh, how awful. How long do you think you'll be? I can wait for you in the pub if you like.'

'Ah, they are here now and so are the police. I'd better go, but yes, go to the Lobster Pot and I'll keep you posted. I'm going to need a drink after this.'

Mary had removed Queenie's glasses. The old lady looked very peaceful. It was as if all the lines and stresses of a long life had drained away with her soul. She also looked very familiar. Rosa had never seen a dead body before, but it didn't frighten her. It was just the shell of the magnificent person who had been housed within.

'Mary, are you sure your gran didn't leave the house at all during the past few months?'

'Well, that's what she always told me.' Mary went to the front window and opened it wide. 'We had better let her soul fly free,

Rosa. She'll no doubt be causing mischief somewhere already.'

The ambulance man and woman and policemen were thorough, respectful and informative in their duties. Rosa was slightly perturbed that one of the policemen was one of the pair who had interrogated her the other night, but he was professional and just kept to the job in hand.

As he was about to drive off with his partner, he opened his window and said, 'I am sorry for your loss, but the good news for you is that somebody has come forward to verify that you were at home at the time you said you were, on the night of the hit-and-run, that is.'

She didn't dare ask who it was, because nobody had known she was at home, apart from Luke – and it certainly wouldn't have been him ringing any sort of incident line. Before she could think of a reply, the police car had driven off.

Turning to Mary, she put an affectionate hand on her arm. 'You seem really calm, are you OK?'

'It hasn't sunk in yet, I don't think.' Mary winced as Merlin let out an almighty wail that would not stop, even on the offer of some chicken Dreamies cat treats.

'Would you like a cup of tea?' Rosa asked, and Mary nodded.

'You sit down and let me get it for you.' She put the kettle on and sorted out cups and teabags. 'I'm happy to stay with you for a bit if you want me to?'

'No, you go. You've got a date, haven't you?' Mary managed a smile.

'Kind of. It's with Joe from the *Gazette*. Don't know if you know him?'

'Not really.' Mary took a sip from the strong, sweet tea that Rosa had just placed in front of her.

'Are you sure you don't want me to stay, Mary, because you are a lot more important than a stupid man. You've had a big shock.'

'I will be fine. I probably need to be on my own for a bit. You go ahead – but Rosa?'

'Yes?'

'Take care.'

'I will,' Rosa promised. 'Right, I've got to take Hot to the vet tomorrow, but as soon as I've done that I'll come and see you.'

With a heavy heart, Rosa started to walk up to the pub. It would be lovely to see Joe, but after something so difficult happening she would rather be with someone who knew her well. In fact, the only person she wanted to speak to was Josh. She took out her phone.

'Rosalar! How it's going? Can't talk for long, sorry. Lucy surprised me when I got home. I'd said I was taking her out but she'd already cooked me a Valentine's meal. I've just popped out to get a bottle of wine.'

'She's got a key to your place then, has she?' Rosa cringed at her reaction.

'Er…no. I'm at hers. So, is everything all right?'

'No, actually. Queenie Cobb just died in front of me.'

'Shit, she was old though, wasn't she?'

'Yes, but it still wasn't very nice and I'd weirdly become very fond of her and Mary.'

Rosa could hear a woman's voice calling Josh in the background. 'You'd better go,' she said heavily.

'Yep. Sorry I can't talk properly. I'll call you tomorrow, right?'

'OK.' Rosa sighed. She didn't like playing second fiddle in any relationship, friend or otherwise.

Jacob didn't work Sunday nights, so she didn't even have the comfort of seeing his familiar face behind the bar when she arrived. Joe got up and kissed her on the cheek.

'All sorted?'

'Well, as sorted as getting someone carted off to the morgue can be, I imagine. I've never had to do anything like that before. In fact, I've never seen a dead body before.'

'At your age I doubt many people have. So, what happened?'

'Nothing dramatic; in fact, it's the way that everyone would wish to die, probably. We'd had a lovely dinner, she was sitting in her favourite chair in her lifetime home, then all of a sudden, she literally just fell back – and she was gone.' Rosa ran a hand through her curls. 'Anyway, enough of that. I'm knackered but a large glass of Merlot would be a marvellous way to end this weekend.'

'Look, I'm sorry again – about not making it to the opening.'

'So, what's the big scoop on the hit-and-run that was so important, then?'

'Well, I do know a couple of the coppers in Polhampton, and one happened to be in my local there. He said that a girl had been seen getting out of a white van and running at speed down the hill.'

'That's old news, Joe. The police insinuated that that girl could be me, although it obviously wasn't.' Rosa suddenly thought it might well have been Titch though. Yes, the two of them had different coloured hair, but their height and build were similar. But if Titch had been in the van with Lucas still, and they were driving and had hit Jasmine – surely she would have told Rosa, when she was getting things off her chest?

'What are you thinking?'

Recalling Queenie's advice, Rosa kept her thoughts to herself.

'I'm thinking that we are not detectives and should just leave this matter to the police. I reckon they will drop it soon anyway. If they haven't sussed it now, when will they?' Rosa gave a long, tired sigh. 'May I have a Joe Fox off-duty now, please?'

He lifted his beer and clinked glasses with her.

'Yes. OK. Belated Happy Valentine's, missy.'

'I don't see what all the fuss is about really, with everyone celebrating this day,' Rosa said thoughtfully. 'I see sex without love as a good form of exercise; as for love, even though I've never been in love, it looks like a lot of pain, arguing and heartache to me.'

'Blimey, ever the romantic.'

'You're the married one.' She looked at his hand and noticed he was no longer wearing his wedding ring.

He waved his left hand in the air. 'It's over. I can't do it any more. Once a cheat, always a cheat, I say. Now, what do you want to eat?'

Maybe it was because she had stared death in the face and her appetite for life had increased, because without even thinking what was coming out of her mouth, Rosa looked at the face of the man in front of her and replied, 'I want to eat you.'

Their lovemaking had been fast and furious. There had been no 'proper snogs', more like improper raw, dangerous and downright dirty sex in every room of the flat.

Finishing up under the covers in her bedroom, Rosa turned to a now red-faced but very smiley Joe, and said, 'I needed that.'

Joe cupped his hand over one of her perfectly round breasts, her nipple still very much erect. 'Who said romance was dead? Oh yes, that's right – you did.' He grinned. 'Joking aside, Rosa, you really are quite beautiful.'

She propped herself up on one elbow. 'You're not bad yourself, and if you asked I might even consider seeing you again.'

'Blimey, that would almost constitute dating in your world, wouldn't it?'

'Now, I'm not sure about going that far,' Rosa teased.

'Could we keep this quiet for a bit, though Rosa, if you don't mind? It's still early days, me being separated from Becca and…'

'I understand, but only if you can just do what you did before with your tongue again.'

'Harlot!'

'You love it! And then in the morning you can go and get me a bacon roll and coffee from Coffee, Tea or Sea – or even better, give me and a Hot a lift back to Polhampton, as we are going to see the vet. That'd be perfect!'

'Oh dear. I wasn't going to stay the night, Rosa. In fact, I need to get back. Suggs is in the house on his own: can you imagine the state of the place if I didn't give him his final walk of the evening?'

'Shit, of course. I forgot about poor old Suggs. So, does that mean you don't live with your wife any more then?'

'Like I said earlier – I can't be doing with cheaters. It's too hard to live with her, knowing what she's been up to.'

Hot was asleep on the sofa when they both appeared from the bedroom. He opened one soulful eye, then went straight back to sleep again.

'Good job he can't talk or we'd all be in trouble,' Joe commented, and picked his keys up off the arm of the sofa.

He put his arms around Rosa and looked at her.

'Thanks for the work-out – and I'm so glad everything's going well for you.'

'Pleasure.' She smiled, then added before she could stop herself: 'Maybe we can have a coffee when I come with Hot tomorrow?' Rosa inwardly cringed. When had she become so needy with a bloke before?

'Maybe. I've got to write up the new hit-and-run stuff, plus your shop article, so let's see. And don't forget you've got a shop to run now.'

Rosa put her head to her hand. 'Duh. Look at me, I've been

so used to being a free agent. I will have to see if Titch can cover me whilst I'm at the vet's.'

She walked downstairs to see Joe out.

'Don't forget to double-lock, now it's evident you have stock in here. And goodnight, sexy lady.'

'Goodnight, super sleuth.'

Back upstairs, Rosa shook out the duvet and on doing so, one of Josh's socks flew up in the air. She held it and looked at it. Yes, it had felt good having mad, bad sex with Joe, but if she was honest the feelings she had experienced when Josh had kissed her on New Year's Eve had been deeper, more intense. But Josh was far more into Lucy than he had made out, and despite Carlton's comments that he'd rather be here with her than with Lucy on Valentine's Day, anyone would help a good mate on their special day.

And why would Josh want her anyway? She wasn't that clever, not even that pretty – and definitely not that posh. He had only kissed her that night because he was drunk himself and wanted to shut her up.

As if Hot realised she needed a bit of company, he appeared in the bedroom and looked up at her with his big brown eyes.

Lifting him up on the bed, she stroked him. 'It's much simpler just loving you, isn't it, Mr Sausage?' With that, he shook his little tail and farted.

CHAPTER FORTY FIVE

Rosa stood at the front of the pretty little Cockleberry Bay church with her arm linked through Mary's. The stained-glass windows and decorative woodwork were jaw-droppingly magnificent, and it was comforting to hear the sound of gulls and the rhythm of the waves through the open door.

Queenie's wishes had been to be cremated, followed by a short blessing in the local church. Never having attended a funeral of any kind before, Rosa was relieved that the whole thing was nearly over.

Considering how old Queenie was, and with no family to mention other than Mary, the church was still half-full. Jacob and Sheila as local publicans had come to pay their respects, as had Titch, Seb Watkins and the owner of Coffee, Tea or Sea. Rosa also recognised a few people who had been at her shop opening the other day; these folks had smiled and greeted her quietly as they filed into the church.

It was time for the blessing. The goofy-teethed, balding vicar cleared his throat and began: 'We are here to celebrate the life of Teresa Rose Cobb, affectionately known as Queenie.'

As her grandmother's full name was read out, Mary, with her tear-filled eyes facing front, took Rosa's hand and held it tightly.

Sunshine poured through the windows, throwing rainbows over all present, and as Rosa clung to Mary, she felt her own battered heart fill with something that was almost like joy.

CHAPTER FORTY SIX

A few weeks passed in a flurry of stock buying, stock flying off shelves, and stocktaking. Rosa was really starting to enjoy her life as a shop owner. She loved meeting all the dogs too, and made sure it was always a completely dog-friendly environment, with dog treats aplenty and a big bowl of fresh water outside the door. To avoid Hot getting out of the shop door again, he was kept upstairs in the sitting room. A brisk early-morning walk meant he was happy to snooze until lunchtime, when Rosa closed the shop to have a snack and take him for another little trot.

Combining the pets' area with a play corner where the kids could amuse themselves too, and choose little gifts to buy with their pocket money, made it easy for their parents to take their time in selecting what they needed.

She was seeing Joe a couple of times a week now, usually on a week night as her Saturdays were the busiest shop days and he always seemed to be working towards a deadline on a Sunday. When they met, they either went for long walks on the many beaches in the area or drove to somewhere remote in one of the picturesque villages of Devon for lunch. More often than not though, they ended up in her bed at her place.

The hit-and-run trail had gone quiet, which was actually quite a relief. Even Sheila Hannafore appeared to be staying down her end of town, without incident.

Mary was doing OK on her own, but Rosa had told her she was only a text away if she needed her to help with anything.

The T-word remained an elephant in the room, and not surprisingly so. Rosa hadn't taken long to put two and two together about Teresa Cobb being 'Darling T'. Out of respect, she hadn't pushed Mary for more information – yet. Now that they were building more of a relationship of their own, the time would come, she was sure. What a complete fox Queenie must have been. Rosa would be lying though, if she said she didn't want to find out what happened to Dotty and how/whether T had brought up her child in a staunch 1950s environment. With Mary's mum dying so young too, that had made it even more tragic. So many lives had been affected by Ned and Queenie's indiscretion.

On the sunny morning of 1 April, Titch arrived to do what was now her regular Monday shift at the shop.

'Rabbits, rabbits, rabbits,' she sang, breezing in and throwing her bag down on the counter.

'Do people really say that any more?' Rosa asked, and carried on filling the till with change.

'Well, my mum still says it. I've no idea what it means. In fact, I shall ask Mr Google, whilst I'm sitting here today.'

Rosa looked at Titch's stomach. 'Still no sign of Titchy Titch then?'

'Thank goodness. I'm only thirteen weeks, even now, although it seems like an age I've been pregnant. Most women don't even tell people until this stage.'

'How's the sickness?'

'Still as bad. I have to just keep pretending I have a hangover if I shoot off to the loo at work. I've got my first scan on Friday.' She beamed at Rosa. 'I'm quite excited.'

'Are you going to find out the sex of the baby?'

'I've decided not to ask, hoping the element of surprise will take my mind off the birth, which I am already dreading, by the way.'

At that moment the door opened, causing the now familiar bell to ring.

'Seb.'

'Titch.'

Titch got up off the stool at the counter and walked swiftly into the back kitchen. Jet, Seb's black Labrador, meanwhile started sniffing up at the treats.

'Hey, Seb, how's it going?'

'Yeah, all right. Have you got any of that dog food I got last time, please? Jet loves it. It's cheaper than the Co-op too, so a win-win all round.'

'Glad I can be of service.' Rosa gave Seb his change and put the food in a bag.

'What's up with her?' He pointed to the back kitchen.

'Oh, she's fine, fine.'

'Living back with her mum, I hear.'

'Um. I think so.'

'Right, I'd better go. Say I asked after her.'

'I will, Seb.'

The lanky, ginger-bearded figure headed off. On the sound of the door closing, Titch appeared from the kitchen.

'Are you intending to tell me what's going on between you two?'

'Nothing – precisely nothing is going on. Now I'm going to

be a mother, I am keeping my distance from dirty pervs, that's all.'

'Fair enough.' Rosa grinned and Titch grinned back. 'Right, are you good with everything? There are no orders coming today but Ruth Hollis is due to pick up some sensitive cat sachets I've ordered for her, plus an engraved birthday bowl for Saatchi, her cat.'

'Cool.' Titch laid out a nail file and varnish on the counter.

'Talking of birthdays,' Rosa went on, 'it's mine on the thirteenth.' She started rearranging things in the shop window and adding new items. 'If I were to go away for a couple of days, would you mind holding the fort?'

'Why not – be glad to. Just let me know when you're certain of dates and I can work all my other jobs around it. Where are you thinking of going anyway?'

'Not sure yet.' Rosa was keeping her relationship with Joe a secret from everyone at the moment. His divorce was to be finalised soon and then he had told her that they could be out and proud. She'd alluded to a date with him to Mary way back, but the only person who knew what was going on was Josh.

Now, leaving Titch in charge, Rosa dashed upstairs to get Hot and went to meet Joe and Suggs on Cockleberry Beach. The sun on her face put roses in her cheeks; life felt good.

Joe smiled as she approached. 'Cat got the cream?' he asked.

'I'm just in a really good mood today. And this little fella and I are ready for a long walk.' Hearing the magic word, Hot starting running around her feet and barking loudly.

'I'd actually love to go up to the West Cliffs,' Rosa said above the racket. 'I've not been up there before.'

'It's quite a trek.'

'You're not in a rush, are you?'

'No, not really.'

244

'Perfect!' Rosa took Hot off his lead. Then she remembered. 'I know what I meant to ask you: do you know if there was ever a phone box in the town?'

'Thinking on it, there was someone on the local radio a few months ago who mentioned it. Said it used to be the hub of the village after the war when not many people had their own telephones. Apparently, it was near where the first ice-cream booth is – down that end of the beach.' Joe pointed. 'Why do you ask?'

'Oh, it was just something Queenie Cobb mentioned. Right, how do we find the trail to the West Cliffs?'

The walk up to the top of the cliffs was blissful in the sunshine. Joe took Rosa's hand to help her over stiles and on any rocky bits, with Hot in her arms and Suggs bounding over easily – but generally the path was clear and the view down to the ocean simply breath-taking. Spring flowers were in bloom everywhere and birds of all kinds were flying around gracefully; their tuneful sonnets reflecting their joy of being alive in this idyllic environment.

It wasn't until they reached the top flat area of the cliffs that Rosa realised what the true beauty of nature was. She had been to some great beaches with Joe and he had walked her along babbling rivers and amidst some wonderful countryside, but this view was like nothing she had ever seen in her life before.

She stared out to sea for miles and couldn't help the tears that filled her eyes. She imagined Ned and Queenie arranging their secret trysts up here. In fact, not unlike she was doing with Joe right now.

Noticing her emotion, Joe took her hand.

'It's almost as beautiful as you,' he said quietly, then kissed her gently on the lips.

'This is where the sky touches the sea, isn't it?' Rosa whispered.

'I guess you could say that about every horizon.' Joe smiled fondly. Rosa was worldly about so many things, but innocent on so many others.

Knowing that not every horizon was as special as this one, and leaving the dogs peacefully snoozing beside Joe, she walked as close to the edge as she dared and looked down. The rocks were craggy and the sea spray evident where the waves rushed against the stony edge.

She couldn't imagine what Queenie had looked like as a young woman. She should ask Mary for some photos. Nor could she imagine the pain that both Ned and Queenie had felt. To experience a love so great must have been all-consuming. And to compromise the happiness of not only a wife, but a best friend too, was almost incomprehensible. She hoped that one day, she too would feel the power of a love on this scale, or perhaps not, as the thought of losing control of herself did frighten her a little.

She was deep in thought, and still dangerously near the edge of the cliff, when Joe ran up behind her, then swiftly grabbed her in his arms and swung her around.

'Time for a siesta, I reckon.'

'Is that all you ever think about?'

'When I'm with you, yes. Is that a problem?'

CHAPTER FORTY SEVEN

After taking an urgent call, Joe had to drive off from the beach car park immediately, leaving Rosa to walk up the hill with Hot. She went straight to the Co-op to see Mary.

'Hello, Rosa. You all right, dear?'

'Yep, I left Titch in charge today. I'm just going to get a few bits and then I'll lock up when I go back.'

'Are you still looking for a telly?' Mary asked.

'Yes, I've been so busy, can't believe I still haven't got around to it. And I might as well get a second-hand one, I really don't need anything fancy.'

'That's good, because I just kept your ad running. A lady looked at it this morning, then told me her phone isn't working so she's just given me an address. It's in Polhampton. Said if you can go there tomorrow evening around seven, that would fit with her getting her kids' tea ready. How's that?'

'It's great, thanks, Mary. I'll close the shop up and get the last bus. I can just take a taxi back from there with the TV. Did she say how much it was?'

'Oh, I forgot to ask that.' Mary looked stricken.

'And did you take a name?' Mary put her hand to her head. 'No worries,' Rosa said immediately, handing her the packet of cat treats she'd brought with her for Merlin. 'You've got enough on your plate. And thank you, that's really kind.'

'Before you go, dear, you know you said to tell you if I needed anything?'

'Yes?' Rosa glanced out to see if Hot was behaving himself tied up outside.

'Would you mind maybe on Sunday stopping by to help me pack up Gran's clothes ready for the charity shop? I'm not sure I can face it on my own.'

'Of course I will.'

'I will cook you roast beef.'

'Well, it's a no-brainer then.' Rosa laughed. 'I'll let you know how I get on with the telly.'

But once she'd gone and Mary was alone, the older woman's smile vanished, to be replaced by a look of concern. Queenie would have told her to do the same...wouldn't she?

CHAPTER FORTY EIGHT

Rosa got off the bus and followed her Google maps to the address Mary had given her. It turned out to be a nice-looking new-build house on a modern estate. A pretty woman in her mid-thirties, with a long blonde ponytail, opened the door. A dog could be heard barking in a room behind her.

'Sorry. It's madness in here tonight, I can tell you.' She rubbed her very evident pregnancy bump with her left hand. 'I've got five-year-old twins waiting to be fed and a hungry teenager on his way back from college. Anyway, sorry, I'm digressing. How can I help you?'

'The TV you've got for sale? The lady who works in the Co-op in Cockleberry Bay gave me your address. Said your phone wasn't working, or of course I would have phoned you first.'

The woman looked mystified. 'Sorry, but I don't know what you are talking about. Maybe my husband would know? I can call him, if you like. He's on a deadline today, but he might pick up.'

'No, no, honestly – it must be a mistake, she must have given me the wrong address. I'm really sorry to have troubled you.'

The barking dog suddenly came running to the door.

'Suggs!' the woman cried. 'Get back.'

Rosa didn't know whether to cry or be sick. As she felt bile rising from her stomach, Queenie Cobb suddenly came into her vision. "Sometimes it's better to just say nothing." The Great Dane rushed forward and started licking her hand.

'Ooh, he likes you,' the woman said, looking surprised.

Rosa made a noise, something between a squeak and a yes.

'You'd think he'd be tired out, the number of walks he gets taken on.'

'Right, I must go.' Rosa had no idea how she managed to get her voice level. 'So, er…when's your baby due?'

'Still got a couple of months to go yet. Joe, that's my husband, is really excited, as it will be our first girl.'

Rosa felt her heart falling into her knees. 'I bet he is. Well, good luck and sorry again to have troubled you.'

She had just made her shaky exit, when a scooter pulled up at the gate. Taking off his black and silver helmet, the spotty teenager got out his phone and without looking where he was going, knocked into her slightly as he made his way up the path.

CHAPTER FORTY NINE

With neither Josh nor Titch picking up in her hour of need, Rosa turned to her old friend Jack Daniel. She had never felt so betrayed in her whole life. She had trusted in Joe; properly fallen for him – shared things with him that she normally wouldn't have shared with anyone else. And for what?

He was quite obviously happily married with a baby on the way. And with a teenage son too – so he had obviously lied about his age. What a complete and utter bastard! And what a complete and utter fool she had been!

What were the odds of her going to his house too? Imagine the scene if he'd answered the door... She had no idea how she had managed to control herself in front of his wife. Revenge was a dish best served cold on this one, and Joe Fox would be getting large portions of it.

Rosa was amazed that no one in Cockleberry had outed him to her for having a wife and kids. But then again, nobody here actually knew she'd been seeing him. She'd been so wrapped up in him, so brainwashed by him telling her not to tell anyone, that she hadn't even told Titch.

Why, oh why, did Joe have to come out with so many lies though? He could have said he had kids, it wouldn't have bothered her, but all the bullshit about his wife having had an affair and that he wasn't living with her any more...complete bloody projection, that's what it was. He was the cheater! Rosa shuddered. That poor woman.

She grabbed the spare duvet, wrapped it around her and lay on the sofa. Hot wasn't used to the sound of sobs coming out of his mistress, so at first he ran around barking, then on getting no reaction to that, he scrambled up on the sofa and dug himself in under the duvet, snuggling into her lap.

She had just sat up to pour herself another drink, when she noticed the screen on her silenced phone flashing. It was Mary. Rosa sighed. Mary never called her, but that was before she had lost Queenie – and Rosa had told her to get in touch whenever she needed to.

She greeted Mary with a slurred, 'Hello.'

'Rosa, dear, I was just taking Merlin around the block and saw that you've left the shop lights on. Is everything all right?'

'Oh, thanks, Mary. I'll go and turn them off,' Rosa said shakily, and sniffed loudly.

'Are you sure you're OK?'

The sniff metamorphosed into a huge sob. 'No, I'm not,' she wept.

'Why don't you come here for a nice hot cup of tea, love?'

'No, thanks. I'm better off alone.'

'Come on. I've just put another log on the fire.'

'No. I don't want to leave the flat.' Rosa suddenly had a vision of being twelve years old again, when her then foster-parents had informed her that, although they loved her with all their hearts, they weren't strong enough to deal with her persistent tantrums: this meant she would have to go back into care.

'Well, I'm coming to you then.'

Mary was greeted at the front door by a red, swollen-faced

little girl. 'I don't know what you were on about, Mary,' Rosa told her. 'The shop lights weren't on.'

'Oh, I could have sworn they were.'

'Drink?' Rosa offered when they got upstairs to the kitchen. 'Jack Daniel's? Wine? Beer?' She was staggering around. 'Oh, you don't, do you? Why don't you drink, Mary?'

Mary straightened her chubby frame and went to the kettle.

'Tea for both of us, I think.'

'I don't want tea.'

'Well, go and sit down then, whilst I make myself one.'

Mary handed Rosa a large glass of water, then sat down on the opposite sofa.

'You can tell me what it is if you want to, love.'

'I can't.'

'Well, I can't help you then.'

Jack Daniel had reached the sub-conscious level and there was no stopping Rosa's demons from coming out, floating on a torrent of abuse.

'Why would you think *you* could help me, Mary? You haven't even had a boyfriend before, I expect, stuck living down here with your old gran in your witchy coven.'

'You shouldn't drink when you feel sad, Rosa.'

'You sound like a bloody social worker. I shouldn't do a lot of things, Mary, but I do, and I have. Somebody once told me never to trust anyone who doesn't drink, you know.'

'Did they now?' Mary shut her eyes for a moment. 'From that little outburst, I guess this is to do with a boyfriend? So you might as well tell me, now I'm here.'

Rosa rocked to and fro, then let out a massive sob.

'I went to see the TV that was for sale in Polhampton.' She ran her hands through her hair. 'And – and well, there was no TV... but there *was* a wife.' The word *wife* came out as a whisper.

Moving to sit next to her, Mary held Rosa's hand as she howled: 'He'd told me they were splitting up, but the wife is pregnant, so they can't be, can they?'

'Have you asked him that?'

'Of course I haven't.'

'Give me your phone then.'

'What? Why?'

'Don't call him tonight when you are not in your right mind, Rosa. Come on.' Mary held out her hand. 'Let me look after it, just for tonight.'

'No!' Rosa pushed her hands angrily through her messy curls. 'I want to call him, but there's a part of me that doesn't want to know the truth, as once it's out, I know that I can never see him again, and that hurts. That hurts so much.' She began sobbing again. 'Why does everybody leave me, Mary?'

Gulping down her own emotions, Mary awkwardly crooked Rosa in her arms and began rocking her gently. Rosa was in too much of a state to resist.

'Do you think it might be a terrible mistake, Mary? Maybe his wife is the liar?'

Mary carried on her rocking motion. 'Hear these words, young Rosa. Your joy is your sorrow unmasked. The deeper the sorrow carves into your being, the more joy you can contain. Verily you are suspended like scales between your sorrow and joy. Only when you are empty are you at standstill and balance.'

'Is that some kind of spell?'

'No, Rosa. They are the words of a man called Kahlil Gibran, from a book called *The Prophet*. I know you've had a tough life, dear, but you've got room now for so much joy. People, men… will come and go, but take heart from the good ones – because although it may not seem like it at the moment, there are decent people out there. You just need to let them in.'

'A bit like Hot, I guess. He was badly treated, but look at him now.' Rosa sniffed loudly.

'Exactly. All that love you've given him, it shows. So don't *you* miss out on love for fear of being abandoned. Promise me, Rosa.'

The girl wiggled free from Mary and sat up. An idea had come into her head

'It was you! You led me to the wrong house on purpose, didn't you, Mary?'

Mary stood up. 'No, my child. I led you to the right one.'

CHAPTER FIFTY

'So, what are you going to do?' Titch was going through Rosa's wardrobe looking for baggy tops that might suit her.

'I actually don't know.'

'I'm surprised you didn't just blurt everything out to his wife. But it's not her fault she's married to a dickhead, is it?'

'No, poor cow. I can't believe it either. I was drunk, too… didn't even phone or do anything, in fact.'

'Has he contacted you today?'

'Yep, a text like he sends every day, saying *How's my favourite shop owner this morning?*'

'God, Rosa. I don't know how you haven't gone mental at him.'

'Me neither. Maybe I'm growing up or maybe it's just I'm not used to getting cheated on. Things never usually get that far.'

'We need to think of something. Something really good to get him back.' Titch pulled a blue smock-like dress out of the wardrobe. 'Ooh, this is nice.'

'I don't want him back,' Rosa said flatly.

'I don't mean that, silly. I mean we have to get back at him. How dare he treat you like that? Arsehole. But don't you worry. He won't get away with this. I shall make him pay for what he's done.'

'But how?'

'I don't know yet, Rose, but act normal for now. Say you are too busy to see him and that will give us time to hatch a plan. Now, can I borrow this dress, please? It'll be perfect to hide the bump.'

Rosa flapped her hand dismissively. 'Yes, yes, take it.'

'Have you told your Josh?'

'I need to ring him back, he left me a message this morning. I can't believe I'm not more upset. It's like I don't want to believe it's real, I suppose.'

'Did Josh know you were seeing him?'

'Er…yes, I did tell him. Sorry I didn't tell you, Titch.'

'It's OK – I knew you were seeing him, anyway. I know that look of somebody who's getting regular sex, I do.'

Rosa laughed. 'We've changed roles. Look at you being all chaste now.'

'The way my bladder is at the moment, it's a case of having to be. If somebody got within an inch of my foofoo, I'd either be sick or wee on them.'

'Nice.' Rosa started to make her bed. 'Do you know what? Even Lucas Hannafore told me that Joe was a bad 'un – and that's coming from *him*! Takes one to know one.'

'Taking of Lukey boy, have you heard from him?'

'Not since Josh kicked his arse, thank goodness.' Rosa sighed. 'I don't know what's wrong with me lately, I've always been so streetwise.'

'Your heart, that's what's wrong with you.'

'Yes, yes, you're right. It's this relationship stuff. I'm no good at it, obviously. I dropped my guard, and I won't be doing that again.'

'Good girl. My mum always says, "Follow your heart, but

don't forget to take your brain with you." About men, she has another saying: "Keep their stomachs full and their balls empty," but that's not quite so poetic, is it?'

'She's so right.'

'Yes, but I obviously didn't take heed of any of her advice!' They both laughed. 'OK, Rose. I've got to get the next bus to Polhampton as I'm cleaning there today. You need me here tomorrow though, don't you?'

'Yes, please. And Titch?'

'Yep?'

'Don't say anything to anyone about Joe, will you?'

Putting her hands on her hips, Titch faced Rosa head on. 'When are you going to trust me, Rose? It hurts, that you don't. I know I'm only young in years, but I've got your back, the same as you have mine.'

'I find it hard to trust, you know that.' Rosa looked up and away.

'Hmm. No comment.' Titch smiled.

'OK, OK. Hands up. Sorry. I trusted the slippery fox. Now come on, I've got to open the shop.' Leaving Hot upstairs, they made their way to the shop.

'Just trust the right people, eh?' Rosa nodded as Titch continued. 'And keep thinking: we will get that bastard back. Not sure how yet, but we will. See you tomorrow.'

'See you.'

Rosa made her way out to the back kitchen to put the kettle on and promptly burst into tears.

Just as she was blowing her nose, Josh called.

'Rosalar, how's it hanging?'

Rosa sniffed loudly. 'It's hanging all right.'

'Oh petal, what's the matter? You're not crying, are you?'

'You know I only cry when I peel onions. I've got a bit of a cold, that's all.'

'Aw. Well, don't work too hard. How are sales going anyway?'

'Couldn't be better. The funky dog collars are flying out of the door, and it's proved such a good idea, having the kids' trinkets. People are emailing me, putting in advanced dog-food orders, so that side of things is amazing.'

'How's lover boy?'

'Oh.' Rosa paused, then said flatly, 'He's all right.'

'Are you sure?'

Rosa felt agitation rising within her; she wasn't ready for a Josh 'I told you so'.

'Yes, Josh, I'm sure. How's Lovely Lucy?'

'She's all right too.'

'Good.' Rosa made an effort. 'You'll have to bring her down to the big bad bay so that I can meet her.'

'Er…maybe. I'd rather come down on my own, to be honest. We can have a laugh, especially as it will soon be warm enough to go on the beach. How's Hot, is he fully recovered?'

'Yes, vocal as ever. He's fine.' At that moment the little sausage barked. 'That's him, saying hello.'

'Aw. I do miss him – and no clever remarks, I miss you too. But now you're all loved up and stuff, well, I guess Mr Gazette is your number one man and us City types need to take a back seat.'

'No, Josh. My number one man has four legs and a tail.'

'Jokes! Right, I'd better get back to work. What are you doing for your birthday, by the way?'

Rosa realised that her dirty weekend away would now not be happening. God, what yarn did Joe have to spin to his poor wife, to get an overnight pass? Again, how foolish was she not to pick up on the fact that in the six weeks she'd been with him, Joe had never once stayed over?

'I've nothing planned as it happens, so why don't you come down then? Easter weekend this year, I'll have to work during some of it, but you can help me if you like? It'll be fun. And…if you do want to bring Lucy, I'm sure that Jacob and Raff will put you up, or you are very welcome to stay here, although I guess she might not want to?'

'Hmm, she has got five-star tastes, this one. Even the Lobster Pot might not be to her liking.'

The words 'stuck-up cow' flew through Rosa's mind. 'Whatever, Josh, just let me know.'

CHAPTER FIFTY ONE

Rosa stared at the ringing phone that was on the kitchen side. She had ignored Joe's texts for two days, and now the 'treat 'em mean, keep 'em keen' motto was working in full force. It was the third time he had called that morning. Bracing herself, she picked it up and answered it.

'Joe.'

'Oh, you are alive, then? I had visions of you with your feet sticking out from under crates of dog food that had fallen on you.'

'Well, you didn't come to find me or I could still be lying there with Hot starting to eat my toes for sausages.'

'Ha! Aw, I've missed you, sexy one. How are you doing?'

'I'm fine, just been ultra-busy. I've got a new line of leads in and have been creating an ad to put in the *Gazette* as it goes.'

'Well, how about I get it put in for free, for you?'

'That's kind and also slightly strange. You never do deals on that blasted paper, I hear.'

'For you, Rosa. I would do anything. I was going to pop in later, if that's OK? I've got some flowers for you that have been sitting in my car for two days.'

Rosa gulped down a 'Yeah, right.' And replaced it with, 'Anyone would think you've got a guilty conscience, Mr Fox. Free ads? Flowers?'

Joe tutted. 'Don't be daft. I've missed you, that's all. And you're the one not picking up your phone.'

'Been busy running around with all the boys in the bay, you know me.' Rosa now had an 'if looks could kill' type of face on. 'Look, I can't see you today, Joe. I'm really up against it and have promised Jacob a couple of shifts this week as his sister and Brad are away.'

'Well, maybe I can come in and see you there sometime?'

'Not a good idea. I'll be in the kitchen, helping Raff. I'll call you, I promise.'

'Smells like you don't want to see me.' Joe sounded downhearted.

'No, just smells of Rosa's busy...see what I did there?'

'You'll go far,' Joe acknowledged.

'See you, Joe.' Then when the call had closed, she added: 'And you'll go to hell.'

CHAPTER FIFTY TWO

Josh sat at his desk and Googled the Corner Shop, Cockleberry Bay. He was so proud of Rosa. From being someone who had no regard for herself or where she was going, she had completely turned her life around. Whoever had put their trust in her and left her the shop must have known what they were doing. They had lifted not only her spirits but had given her joie de vivre and a focus. Jacob was a good bloke too; he had created the website for her and with her – just a simple DIY one, but it looked great, and the fact that Rosa was now advertising phone and email orders on there was fantastic.

He had meant to ask her if she'd got any further clues on who had left her the shop, as he was sure that the Cockleberry gossip train must know something. He also wanted an update on the hit-and-run, which he guessed had been put to rest now. Everything pointed to Lucas: it had to have been him.

Josh was slightly concerned because Rosa had sounded a bit down on the phone. He wondered if something was wrong. But surely, if things weren't going well with her fella, she would have told him. Maybe she just needed to see a familiar face. He would surprise her. Go down on her birthday weekend. He had been spending a lot more time with Lucy lately and knew she wouldn't be best pleased if he said she was going to see Rosa, especially at Easter. But he could just tell her that he was doing something rugby-related with Carlton. Yes, that's what he would do. She'd understand.

He picked up the phone to call Jacob. He would book a special birthday meal for Rosa at the Lobster Pot and include Jacob and Raff. Get them to bake a cake. Make it a birthday to remember.

CHAPTER FIFTY THREE

The delicious smell of roast dinner cooking greeted Rosa as Mary opened the door to Seaspray Cottage.

'Hello, come in, come in.'

At the sight of a visitor, Merlin screeched and flew between Rosa's legs, nearly knocking her off-balance in his bid to escape. Mary did her lopsided walk straight through to the kitchen and did a quick check of the oven.

'Thanks for coming, Rosa. Hopefully, it won't take too long to go through Gran's things, but…well, I didn't fancy doing it on my own.'

'It's fine, Mary, I'm happy to help.'

'How are you feeling after the other night?'

'A bit better, I think.'

'Have you spoken to him?'

'Yes, but only to stop him constantly calling and to tell him I'm too busy to see him at the moment. Titch and I are hatching a plan to ensure he gets his comeuppance.'

'Oh.' Mary opened a cupboard and reached for the gravy granules. 'Are you sure that's the right thing to do?'

'Probably not, but why should he get away with it? Little shit.'

'Right,' Mary said, looking at her watch: 'we've got forty-five minutes to get some stuff sorted before I put the Yorkshires in.'

Queenie Cobb's bedroom was every bit how Rosa had imagined it to be. Dark, with dream catchers and crystals on every available space. It wasn't dusty though, Mary obviously kept a tight ship where cleaning was concerned. There was a magnificent throw on the old mahogany sleigh bed; it was navy-blue and covered in white stars and moons.

Rosa gasped when she saw it. 'I bloody love that throw!'

'Well, have it then.'

'Are you sure – you might want it?'

'I have one already. I want to make this room clean and clear now. I'm even going to sell the bed. I want just the big rocking chair in here, so I can sit and read. It's too damn draughty in that kitchen, even with the fire going.'

Between them, the two women had soon made two piles: one for the charity shop and one for the rubbish bin. They handled the clothes with reverence.

'I can manage the rest, dear, the shoes and the other bits and bobs, but thank you so much for your help. I'm glad that Gran was cremated in her favourite long, amethyst velvet dress and daisy-patterned shawl.'

Mary coughed and became a little breathless. She reached for an inhaler from her apron pocket.

'I didn't know you used an inhaler.'

'Yes, love. My breathing's not so good today. I don't think Gran going has helped me, quite frankly.'

Rosa detected tears forming in Mary's eyes.

'She loved you, Mary. I could tell, even with her brusque ways.'

'She resented me too, Rosa. She never ever got over Maria dying, you see.'

'Maria?'

266

'My mum. Gran named me after her. My mum was so beautiful, Rosa. She was only twenty when she died. And she died whilst she was having me, you see. She lost so much blood, there was nothing they could do to save her.'

'Oh my God, that's so sad! So, Maria was Ned and Queenie's baby then?'

Mary began folding the throw agitatedly.

'I can't speak about it, Rosa. I know she's not here, but Gran would go mad if I did.' At that moment, the bedside light flashed on and off.

'Did you see that?' Rosa took a step back.

'Yes.' Mary did a little laugh. 'Didn't think it would take her long. That's her for sure.'

'Do you believe in ghosts then, Mary?'

'I believe in the power of the spirit, Rosa. Never be afraid. It is a magical thing.'

'It's great to think we could all come back and annoy those who had hurt us and comfort those whom we loved. I would like to come back as a dog, but only if I could have an owner like me,' Rosa said light-heartedly.

Mary's chuckle turned into another cough. She put her hand on Rosa as if to steady herself. 'And me, a cat. Although not quite as mentally disturbed as Merlin, I'd hope.'

'I'd like to ask just one more question. It will be the last now, I promise.'

Mary put her hands on her hips and stretched up to take in some more air. 'Go on.'

'After reading those letters, I have to know what happened to Dotty.'

Mary's attitude suddenly changed. 'No more questions, Rosa.' She reached for her inhaler and took another massive puff. 'In Queenie's memory, no more questions, I beg of you.' Her face was etched with pain now. 'I must get back to the dinner. I'll call you when it's ready.'

Pausing for a moment, then huffing and puffing, she seemed to change her mind. Pulling a letter from her apron pocket, she said huskily, 'I found this earlier. I was told that she had had an accident.' She stifled a sob and headed down the steep old stairs as quickly as her big frame would allow her.

To My Ned

By the time you read this letter I will be at our place – you know, the one where the sky touches the sea. I often wonder if you took HER there too. At least the view will be amazing when I jump.

Did you really think I was that blind that I could not see what was going on between you and T? And did she really think that we would both believe her story that it wasn't your baby inside of her?

Rosa put her hand over her mouth.

I love you, Ned. You are a good man and have been a perfect husband, but my inner torment of not being able to give you what you so badly crave is like white noise in my head that just won't go away.

Goodbye, Ned, and be happy with your new little family.

Yours forever, Dorothea X

Rosa was motionless. The exact place where she had looked over the edge when she was at West Cliffs with Joe could have been the spot where Dotty jumped. The poor woman. And poor Mary. She even felt sorry for Ned and Queenie. What an awful ending for everybody who had held so much love for Dotty, despite the tragic love triangle.

So, Ned had been Mary's grandfather all along. Mary had lived virtually opposite him and she didn't even know it. No wonder she was in such a state. But Queenie knew – so why not tell her poor granddaughter? With no mum in her life – or dad that Rosa knew of either – Mary had had no male influence in her life.

As Rosa went slowly down the stairs to eat the roast dinner with Mary, she thought to herself how Queenie Cobb had died with many secrets and even more unanswered questions. The biggest one now being: Who *had* left Rosa the Corner Shop in Cockleberry Bay? And why? *Why*?

CHAPTER FIFTY FOUR

'Rosa, come quick, it's the motorbike that knocked into Hot, I'm sure. Look, there's a black and silver helmet hanging from it.'

Rosa came out of the front of the shop to see the bike parked just up the road a little. A sudden realisation hit her. She opened her mouth to call Titch inside, but it was too late.

'Hey – you!' Rosa stood at the door and cringed as her errant friend continued her onslaught. 'Make a habit of hurting poor innocent animals then riding off, do you?'

In her horror, Rosa dropped the bag of one-pound coins she was holding and started chasing them as they started their descent down the hill.

The teenager noticed her. 'Oh, it's you,' he said spitefully.

'Pardon?' His likeness to Joe made Rosa feel suddenly angry. She was about to say something further about Hot, when the lad spoke up.

'Keep away from my dad, bitch, or that mutt of yours will get more than a kick next time.' He then pulled the helmet over his long scraggy locks, started the bike and zoomed off up the hill. Titch sat Rosa down in the back kitchen and got her a cup of strong tea.

'I know it's been a shock. He's obviously seen you with Joe

somewhere, but he doesn't know anything for definite, I'm sure.'

'I'm not even bothered about that. I just can't believe that a human being would want to harm my Hot.'

'Chip off the old block – isn't that what they say?' Titch put the milk away. 'In fact, I'm glad Joe Fox is staying married. You can do so much better than a scumbag like him.'

'I agree. But after what's just happened, it's made me realise that I need to see him squirm. Guess what, Titch – I've just had an idea of exactly how I can do that.'

Joe smiled broadly as Rosa approached him in the car park. He turned off the radio in his Jeep and jumped down to greet her with a hard kiss on the lips.

'Long time no see, and you are looking hot, hot, hot. Talking of Hot, where is he?'

'I'm doing a radio interview, Joe. He's best left at home, I think, don't you?' It took all of Rosa's strength not to weaken and say exactly what she was thinking.

'Thanks for including me in the *Gazette* piece too,' he said smugly. 'I was quite impressed you got in there all by yourself.'

'Girl Power and all that, Joe. I'm quite capable of picking up a phone. And I knew that old Barry Savage would be gushing at the thought of me revealing who the mystery benefactor was, of the Corner Shop.'

'Wow! Rosa, why didn't you tell me? I could have had the scoop for the *Gazette* before it went live on radio.'

Rosa shrugged her shoulders at Joe as the smart, bespectacled woman appeared with her clipboard as before. They followed her through to the studio, with Rosa ignoring Joe's questions about who it was who had left the shop to her.

The radio jingle boomed out of the speakers around the studio: *South Cliffs Radio – two four eight to two four nine FM*

– Barry Savage.

Rosa quaked inwardly as she sat opposite the pompous DJ, who was wearing the same ill-fitting three-piece suit as last time. Barry motioned for the two of them to put their headphones on, and giving a wide, false grin, which made him look like Mr Toad going 'Parp Parp' in his motor car, made ready to go live.

'Welcome to my Saturday guest slot, where we have not one, but two wonderful peeps to talk to us this morning. A big hello again to Rosa Larkin, the owner of the Corner Shop in Cockleberry Bay.'

'Er…hi.' Rosa took a slurp of water to aid her drying mouth.

'Welcome to you, Rosa, and also to our housewives' favourite, Joe Fox, editor of the one and only *South Cliffs Gazette*.' Barry winked at Joe. Rosa felt sick; maybe he was dipping his wick elsewhere too.

'So, Rosa, how's it all going?'

'It's going great, thanks, Barry. The locals appear to have a penchant for dressing their dogs in designer coats and tutus.'

Barry guffawed. 'How very London.'

'We are starting to get a lot of visitors down now the weather is improving, so yes, it is a mixture of tourists and locals popping in.'

'Now for those of you who were listening before, the story goes that Rosa was left the shop by a mystery benefactor. Are you any the wiser as to who that might have been?'

'Actually, Barry, yes I am.' Barry put his thumb up. 'But I'm here today to tell your lovely listeners about my ordering service. The Dogalot wet and dry food has proved such a hit, that if people want to email me in advance I can get their orders in the next day. Which is a win, both for myself and my customers alike, as they get a fast service and I don't have to store as much bulk product.'

'Great, great. Thanks for that, Rosa. Now about...'

Rosa butted in. 'The email address links directly through to my website, which your producer said she would put up on your website at the end of this show.'

'Thanks, yeah, fab, yeah, and so to Joe. Listeners, we've come up with the idea of learning about a day in the life of a newspaper editor. The ins and outs, what makes him tick. How does he fit a family in with so many time pressures? But before that, let's go to a song. Let's sing it loud and proud for "Paper Roses" by the one and only Marie Osmond.'

Barry took off his headphones and said to Rosa: 'Brilliant, what you did there creating the suspense about the benefactor. Let's do a big reveal at the end, as agreed.'

'Oh yes, there is going to be a big reveal, Barry, I can assure you.'

'So, who is it?' Joe couldn't help himself. 'You can tell us now, surely.'

'You'll have to wait.' Rosa took a slurp of her water.

'Loving the idea of this slot – good work, Rosa. You all ready to go straight after this, Joe?'

'Yes, he's ready.' Rosa grinned and squeezed Joe's hand.

Joe made a questioning expression, but not wanting to lose face or credence in front of Barry Savage, he kept his mouth shut.

'Fabulous. Great questions you suggested, by the way, young lady. You should think about this reporting lark yourself, maybe?'

Joe dug his finger into Rosa's left thigh, causing her to squirm and let out a little squeak. The producer glared at them both.

'So that was "Paper Roses", now to a real-life newspaper editor. So, Joe Fox, welcome to South Cliffs Today radio.'

'Hi. Thanks for having me.' Rosa loved the fact that Joe was visibly ill at ease and fidgeting.

'So, tell us, how long have you worked for the *Gazette* and what, in your opinion, makes a good reporter stroke editor, Joe?'

'I've been there five years now, for my sins.' He laughed. 'Well, I would say to those of you who are starting out: just write, write and write some more. The more you hone your craft, the better you will become.'

'But to get a good story out of somebody, how do you do that?' Barry was browsing the questions list and nodding.

'I think...erm...a mixture of empathy, plus knowledge of the facts you have already.'

'Nice, nice.' Barry Savage nodded his head sagely. 'And obviously you need to be able to cover both sides of a contentious issue, that's right, isn't it?'

'Yes, yes, of course.'

'Not many of those down here though, I guess?'

'A few. The Christmas hit-and-run is still causing interest.'

'Oh yes, nasty business. So, what is the word on the street on that, so to speak?' Barry laughed at his own useless quip.

'To be honest, unless some new information turns up soon, I think it will become a cold case.'

'A cold case. Do our listeners know what that is?'

'Oh, sorry – a cold case is an unsolved criminal investigation which remains open pending discovery of new evidence. Actually, there is something new I need to report.'

'Go on, Joe, we all want to know.'

'There is a reward being offered by the *Gazette* for any further information about what happened on that night.'

'Now you're talking, Joe. How much?'

'That I can't disclose yet, but I will get a number and put it up on your website.' Joe was making it up as he went along.

But with the *Gazette* figures falling of late, he knew this would create a buzz, especially if he set the reward high enough.

'Brilliant!' Barry was now animated. 'So, all of you out there, if you know anything, however small, get on the phone to the *Gazette*. Good stuff, Joe. So now a bit about you. Let's recap. What sort of person do you think it takes to be a reporter?'

The words 'a complete cheating arsehole' went through Rosa's mind.

'Dedicated, hard-working, good at research, the ability to think outside the box.'

'Yes, all of those Joe, and you must work long hours?'

'Yes, I do work silly hours.'

'My researcher tells me that not only do you have a Great Dane and three sons, you have a baby girl on the way. How do you go about fitting all that in too?'

Rosa could see the colour draining from Joe's face, so she chipped in, with a voice calm as the spring tide. 'Wow, Joe, yes – how do you fit all that in? I have trouble finding time for just my dog Hot, now that the shop is so busy.'

Joe shut his eyes momentarily, opened them, then inhaled deeply.

Barry mouthed, 'Are you OK?' as Joe made the 'cut' sign across his throat.

'And it's time for traffic and travel with Yvonne Greggs. Make sure you stay listening to see just how Joe manages to fit everything in, with such a large family commitment.'

Joe took off his headphones. 'So sorry, Barry. I suddenly feel unwell. I must have got that bug doing the rounds – I'm going to have to go.' And he hotfooted it out of the studio.

Rosa took her headphones off too, saying solicitously, 'Best check he's OK.'

'OK, OK, no worries. Although do come back very soon,

both of you,' Barry shouted as Rosa ran out in pursuit, before remembering that he still hadn't had the answer to the mystery of the Cockleberry Bay Corner Shop bequest.

Joe rushed to his Jeep, got in and turned the engine on. Rosa quickly followed and jumped into the passenger seat.

Joe took a long drink from a bottle of water. His hands were shaking. 'I can't believe you just did that to me,' he hissed.

Rosa's mouth was wide open in amazement. 'You can't believe that I just did that to you? Oh, I am sorry if I embarrassed you, Joe.'

'Hear me out, Rosa, I can explain.'

'Yes, you can.' The anger in Rosa's voice was now evident. 'You can explain right now.'

'OK, OK, I have got a wife, as you know.'

'Yes, a wife, a nasty teenage boy, five-year-old twins, a dog and another baby girl on the way.' Rosa put on a funny voice. '"Oh Rosa, poor me, my wife is a cheat and I'm leaving her. Oh Rosa, I have no children." You're a fucking liar, Joseph Fox.'

'How do you know all this about me?'

'It doesn't matter how I found out, Joe, but now I want to know the truth. I've already done my grieving for you, but I need to hear it from your lips, then I can move on.'

'OK, OK. She has cheated on me, I don't want to be with her. We don't even like each other. Rarely talk to each other. We are just staying together for the baby. I don't even know if it's mine.'

At that moment, his phone rang through the hands-free in the Jeep, and Rosa saw the words WIFEY flash up on screen.

'Answer it,' she said through gritted teeth. 'Answer it now!'

'No.' Joe was angry now too. He went to cut the call, but Rosa grabbed his phone and pressed the answer button.

She recognised Becca's voice from the other night. 'Darling, it's me, I was listening in. Are you OK? I told you not to have one of last night's leftover cream cakes for breakfast but you wouldn't listen. Are you on your way home?'

'Yes, yes. I can't talk, I feel too shit. See you soon.'

'Love you. And, don't forget…' Joe cut the call.

Rosa tried to stop herself from crying. One lone tear started to run down over her little scar. 'Really sounds as if you don't like each other, doesn't it?'

'I'm so sorry, Rosa.' Joe went to wipe her tear with a finger.

'Get off me! I can't believe you. You used me.' Her voice began to crack. 'And – and…I liked you.' She jumped down from the Jeep and started walking briskly towards the bus stop.

Joe drove along slowly next to her, saying, 'I can give you a lift.'

'I don't want anything from you ever again.'

'Are you going to tell my wife?'

Rosa stopped walking. 'Give me some credit, you creep. I don't want to embarrass myself and she's welcome to you. But what I will tell you is that your eldest son knows something about us, as he was the one who hurt Hot – deliberately, or so he said. It was him on the motorbike that night. Nasty piece of work he is too. Like father, like son. A chip off the old block.'

'God, no!' Joe put his hand to his forehead.

'God, yes. But I'm sure you can think of some lie to tell him too, eh? Goodbye, Joe.'

'What about getting coverage for the shop in the paper? I will need to see you about that,' he floundered.

'I'm not sure which part of "Goodbye, Joe" you didn't understand.' Rosa held her head high and carried on walking away.

CHAPTER FIFTY FIVE

Holding Hot on his lead outside, Rosa popped her head round the door of the Co-op. She was surprised to see that Mary wasn't behind the till, since she generally worked there on a Friday evening. The lights were on in Seaspray Cottage, however, so Rosa made a mental note to call her later to check she was OK.

Finding out that Dotty had taken her own life had clearly deeply affected poor Mary – that, and the dramatic death of Queenie. Rosa had deliberately left her alone after their last meeting, giving her time to think everything through and start to come to terms with the shock of her bereavement and the recent revelations. Rosa didn't trust herself not to keep pestering her with more questions, so she was keeping away. Once things had calmed down a bit, she would talk to Mary again. But since Mary had not been privy to all the facts regarding Ned and Dotty, maybe she wouldn't be able to enlighten her anyway.

When she pushed open the door to the Lobster Pot, Jacob hastened over and gave her a massive hug. 'Happy Birthday, Princess Rosa,' he said, and did a twirl.

'Thank you – but how did you know that?'

'It's the duty of a publican to know everything.' He crouched down and tickled under Hot's crinkled chin. 'I expect you want to go up and see your mates, don't you?'

Hot started barking and running around them both as Raffaele appeared from behind the bar. 'Ciao, Rosa.' He kissed her on both cheeks. 'I hear you have a birthday.'

Rosa smiled happily. 'You hear right.'

'Hang on, let me put him upstairs with Pongo and Ugs.' He swept Hot up in his muscly arms and took him through the bar. Reappearing minutes later, he handed Rosa a beautifully wrapped present.

'Happy Birthday, bella.'

'Aw, that's so sweet of you.'

Alyson popped a bottle of champagne open behind the bar.

'Cheers.' They all toasted Rosa with a glass of bubbles.

'Twenty-six, eh?' Jacob sighed.

'And never been kissed,' Rosa added, grinning.

'By more than ten men at a time. Dirty slut!'

Rosa beamed at him. 'Only you could get away with that, Jacob – and maybe Josh.'

She felt a bit low mentioning Josh; she had hoped he might come down, but when she had spoken to him last week he said he had had to change his plans. Probably because of Juicy Lucy and it being Easter weekend, she thought, and she hadn't questioned him further.

'Right, I have to rip this present open, I can't ever wait.'

Rosa pulled the pink sparkly paper apart to reveal a beautiful little tartan coat for Hot and an equally beautiful sweater dress for her, which was bright green with a white dachshund print.

'I didn't think you'd appreciate a Barbour one, far too poncey for both of you,' Jacob told her and Raffa nodded.

'Exactly, but how did you sneak in and buy that for Hot without me knowing?'

'Titch is obviously getting better at keeping secrets.' Jacob refilled their glasses. 'We did ask if she wanted to stay for a glass of champagne earlier, but she said she was feeling knackered after her shift and might come down a bit later.'

'I bloody love this dress, thank you SO much.' Rosa held it up against her. 'And I can definitely see Hot wiggling down to the beach in his little number.'

'I loved the poodle outfit you wore for your launch, so when I saw this in a boutique in London when I popped up last week, I knew it was made for you.'

'It goes with your eyes,' Raffaele added. He checked a text that had come in on his phone and winked secretly at Jacob.

'Right, are you ready to eat?' Jacob ushered them through to the restaurant area and sat Rosa with her back to the bar. They had put a pink birthday balloon on her chair.

As they all sat down, Alyson cranked up the music to Altered Images' 'Happy Birthday'.

Engrossed in conversation, Rosa was completely unprepared for somebody putting their hands over her eyes and kissing her right ear.

On hearing the word 'Rosalar' she let out a little scream of delight and jumped up.

'Josh? Oh my God! I'm so pleased to see you – you lying toad.'

'I couldn't not come down for your birthday, could I?'

Jacob and Raffaele got up and shook his hand. Raffa signalled to Alyson to bring Josh a beer.

'Are you on your own?' Rosa asked, suddenly anxious.

'I am tonight – I had to do a bit of negotiating. I'm meeting Lucy at Polhampton station tomorrow.'

'Excellent. I get you all to myself and then get to meet the new bird too. '

'Have you booked anywhere for tomorrow night?' Jacob enquired.

'No, I thought we could stay here, if you have room.'

'Oh Josh, it's Easter weekend, we're fully booked,' Jacob told him. 'I can try the Ship for you.'

'I don't mean to be rude, but I'd rather sleep on the beach, thanks, Jacob.'

'The Streatham Hotel in your neck of the woods may have something?' Rosa asked Jacob and Raffaele.

Raffa grimaced and shook his head.

Rosa shrugged. 'She'll have to rough it for the night, then. You two can have my bed, I'll sleep in the office.'

'Just give me that beer. I'll worry about it tomorrow.' Josh drank a third of his lager down in one go. 'I'm so pleased I can relax now – bloody Friday traffic.' He then asked casually: 'No lover boy tonight, then?'

He saw the look of horror on the faces of his hosts. Rosa had relayed the whole sorry tale to them both.

'What? What have I said?'

'He's a cheating bastard. I don't want to talk about it today.'

'Aw.' Josh squeezed Rosa's hand. 'Forget him.' He lifted the champagne glass Jacob had just handed him. 'I propose a toast: to Rosa, for being the best shop-owner in Cockleberry Bay and a generally top lass all round.'

Rosa felt that tingly sensation that she was starting to get used to since she'd moved down here.

'To Rosa,' Jacob and Raffa echoed.

'You really are a joy to be around and we really appreciated you helping us out when I damaged my foot,' Jacob told her, smacking his lips as he drank.

Josh smiled. 'Look at you with all the boys loving the Rosalar.'

'It's Hot they love, really.'

'Oh my God – I forgot our little Hot. Where is he – and how is the little fella?'

'Fully recovered now, thank goodness. He's upstairs with the pugs.' Rosa didn't dare tell Josh just yet about Joe's son having been the one who hurt him, especially after his previous reaction to Lucas Hannafore. 'I'll go and get him when we leave. It's too busy in here now, he'll cause havoc.'

Two very happy hours later, with Hot safely on his lead and with hugs and goodbyes all round, Rosa and Josh made their way arm in arm back to the shop.

'What a lovely evening – thanks for organising it. And that cake the boys made,' Rosa sighed. 'That was bloody delicious.'

'Yes, I had a great time too. They are good friends to you.'

Rosa noticed that Seaspray Cottage was now in complete darkness. 'Bugger.'

'What's up?'

'I meant to call in on Mary, as she wasn't at work. I've been keeping an eye out for her since Queenie died.'

'I expect she's got plenty of spirits to keep her company in the Coven.'

'Oh, bless her, don't. Ned was a dark horse – I've got so much to tell you but I'm still none the wiser as to who left me this place and why.'

They went round the back so as not to make the shop bell ring when they entered. Rosa hiccupped as she reached for her starfish keyring. 'Thank God we didn't hit the tequila, I'm drunk already.'

'We can hit it now.' Josh steadied her as she lost her balance. 'Whoa, tiger. Shit!'

'What?'

'You really need to get a security light outside this back door, Rosa. I've just stubbed my toe on something.'

Josh shone the torch from his phone to the ground to see Hot sniffing at a black binbag.

'What is it?'

'Let's get in first and get some lights on.'

After closing and locking the door against the chilly spring night, she pulled the bag away to reveal an oblong white box with a green bow stuck on it. It was heavy.

On rather gingerly removing the lid, they both let out a massive 'Awww!' For there, looking up at them, was a life-size bronze sculpture of Hot. Hanging from his left ear was a little present bag. Rosa reached out and wonderingly opened it: inside was a green square ring box. She looked questioningly at Josh.

'It's not from me!'

The diamond and sapphire ring, set in white gold, was the most beautiful piece of jewellery Rosa had ever seen in her life. The diamonds were so sparkly they sent shafts of light around the room. There was a crumpled-up note in the bottom of the little box.

'Go on, quickly – read it,' Josh urged.

'Oh my God.'

'What is it, Rosa?'

'This is too spooky. Listen.' Rosa began to read the note which was printed in capitals. *'DON'T QUESTION THIS GIFT, FOR YOUR HEART IT WILL LIFT. I WILL REMAIN BY YOUR SIDE, HOWEVER HIGH THE TIDE. HAPPY BIRTHDAY, DEAR ROSA xx.'*

'And that's it?'

'You're missing the point, Josh. The wording is virtually the same as the letter that I got with the documents for the shop. Which means,' she added excitedly, 'that whoever has left me this place is probably not dead – because they wouldn't have known about Hot, would they? It's hurting my head, Josh, I don't understand.'

'I'm too pissed to deliberate over your mystery benefactor tonight,' Josh said truthfully. He yawned. 'Come on, let's go up – and don't lose that ring, it probably came from Tiffany's or something.'

'You'd better not show Lucy, she'll want one as big.'

Josh followed Rosa upstairs with the heavy statue in his hand. 'I'm not marrying her, Rosa.'

Rosa made a funny little noise. 'It's been a few months now though, hasn't it? And she's around your age, right? She'll be getting broody soon, will want you to put a ring on it – you wait and see.' Rosa waved her wedding finger in the air and started to do Beyonce-type dance moves.

'Oh, shut up, Rosalar and pour me a drink, wench. I need to get your present out of my car, as well.'

Deliberating who could be bothered to go downstairs to get Rosa's birthday gift, they sat outside on the balcony with blankets over their legs, Hot sitting beside them companionably in the moonlight, and a nightcap of JD & Coke in their hands. The soft sound of the sea created a hushed and magical atmosphere.

'Look at us, like an old married couple.' Rosa swung her hand over and put it inside Josh's.

Josh squeezed. 'I'm sorry about Joe.'

'I'm not. It's a good lesson, not to let my guard down. They say love is blind. I can't believe I was so stupid.'

'Did you love him?'

'The L word – I don't know, Josh.' She looked right at him. 'But whatever it means, I do feel something when I'm with…'

'Get the fuck off me!' The female voice carried in the still night air. 'I mean it.'

Then a man's voice. 'Are you really so cheap that you'd grass me for a poxy reward of a thousand quid? You were there too, remember.'

'It's the only thing I will get you behind bars for, I know that now.'

'You're just a dirty little slag.'

They then heard a thud and a man running down the road at the back of the shop. The girl was now sobbing loudly.

Josh jumped up. Hot started barking furiously.

'I'm going down.' Josh vaulted over the little gate in the balcony, leapt down the spiral steps and out through the back gate, where leaning against his car he found a shaking Titch. Blood was running down her face, her dress was torn, and her right knee grazed.

Swinging her up into his arms, Josh carried her upstairs and laid her gently on the sofa. Noticing her little pregnancy bump, he had a pained expression on his face.

'What happened? Who did this?' Rosa demanded.

Titch looked up. 'I'm so tired,' she said – and with that she promptly fell asleep.

'We can't leave her like this, covered in blood,' Rosa fretted.

'She's knackered, poor lass.' Josh put two blankets on top of her, tucking her in and covering Hot as he did so too. The little dog had settled by her side, and was watching over her. 'We can sort her out in the morning. She's living with her mum now, isn't she?'

Rosa nodded as Josh continued. 'Do you think we should text her mum to let her know that Titch is here?'

'How can you think of things like this, even when you're drunk? You're so sweet, Joshua Smith.' Rosa rested her wobbly head on his chest. 'That man's voice was familiar, but I can't think who it was.'

'Come on, Rosalar, bedtime for birthday girls. Everything will seem clearer in the morning.'

Rosa dragged her legs like a little girl and groaned, 'Carry

285

me to bed.'

Josh laughed. 'You're like a little kid sometimes.'

'I've never been one of those.' Rosa made her own way to her bedroom, stripped off to her underwear and got into bed. She patted the pillow next to her. 'Come in with me tonight, Josh. I could do with a cuddle. I've missed you.'

Josh smiled down at her. 'All right, but no funny business. Keep your hands to yourself.'

'Oh yeah, I forgot. You're a married man now.'

'Shut up about that,' Josh joked and pinned her down with her arms above her head.

'No funny business, you said.' Rosa, squirming around, brushed his lips with hers by accident. Josh needed no further invitation; with his lips stuck right on hers and his tongue firmly in, they were suddenly kissing as if the world was about to end.

'Get down there,' Josh panted, gently pushing Rosa's head down under the covers towards his now very hard cock.

'It's *my* bloody birthday,' Rosa objected, causing them both to roll about laughing. 'And, no. Lucy is coming tomorrow and after what I've just been through, I've realised Rosa Larkin is far too big to be a bit on the side.'

Josh sat up, did a slow hand clap and exclaimed, 'At last!' And, then without even thinking about it, the words, 'I bloody love you, Rosa Larkin,' flew out of his mouth.

At that moment, Hot came charging in and managed to leap on top of them both on the bed, making them collapse with laughter. 'If it's not one of you, it's the other,' Rosa giggled, and made a fuss of her trusty hound.

'Now, you get on your own bed, Mr Sausage, and Josh – just hold me and go to sleep, you big hunk of rugby love.'

CHAPTER FIFTY SIX

Titch awoke to the sound of somebody knocking on the upstairs balcony door. Disorientated and whimpering with pain from her damaged knee, she put her hand to her face and felt the blood that had dried on to her now very sore cheek.

With half-open eyes, she managed to crawl off the sofa, nearly tripping over a barking Hot, who had come scampering in to see what was going on, and unlocked the French windows. She was nearly bowled over by a tall girl, dressed in smart jeans, a red V-neck jumper and a black puffa jacket. Blonde curls flowed down her back, as if she'd just stepped out of a Mayfair salon.

'Hi, I'm Lucy,' the stranger said. 'Can't you shut that dog up? Happy Birthday for yesterday – and oh shit, what have you done to your face? And where's Josh got to?'

Before Titch could open her mouth to speak, Lucy had already made her way through the flat, inspecting the empty spare bedroom, the kitchen and finally walking unannounced into Rosa's bedroom. On discovery of the sleeping pair, she stood for a moment taking in the scene then pulled the cover off them and threw a glass of water from the bedside table all over Josh's face.

'What the fuck?' Josh sat straight up. Then on seeing Lucy, he groaned and tried to explain. 'Oh my God, Lucy, this is so not what it looks like, I promise you.'

Rosa, too hungover to actually care about another woman's jealousy attack, offered her hand. 'Hi Lucy, and Josh is right, we literally just crashed out in here because,' she gestured out to the lounge, 'Titch, my friend, needed to stay over. Josh would have been on the sofa, otherwise.'

'So, *you* are Rosa. I knew it all along.'

Josh, pulling his jeans on quickly, went to hug Lucy.

'Get off me!'

'Knew what all along, Lucy? Don't be ridiculous. Rosa and I are friends. Yes, this doesn't look good, I agree, but you can see that we both have underwear on. She's like my sister. And what are you doing here anyway?'

'I came down last night, I had a feeling I couldn't trust you.'

At this point, Titch came limping into the bedroom. 'Lucy, they are not shagging,' she said wearily, 'so can we please all have a nice cup of tea, then I need to get home.'

'Josh, we are leaving now.' Lucy flicked her hair back over her shoulders in dramatic fashion. 'And if you *dare* to say otherwise, then...'

Rosa dragged on her dressing gown and went to put the kettle on.

'Then what, Lucy?' she said. 'You really are overreacting here.'

'Maybe you won't think I'm overreacting, when I tell you...I tell you...that I'm pregnant!'

'Snap,' Titch said under her breath as a saucer slipped through Rosa's fingers and smashed into a million pieces all over the kitchen floor.

CHAPTER FIFTY SEVEN

'What's happening?' Rosa clasped her cup of tea in both hands and sat on the sofa. 'Ooh, I feel so rough.'

Titch had rallied round, swept up the glass and put some bacon under the grill. 'They've both gone.'

'I can't believe she's pregnant,' Rosa sighed. 'I also can't see Josh with her. But I know what he's like, he will have to marry her now.'

'Oh, Rose. You can still be mates.'

'It won't be the same. I think I love him, Titch. But then, it doesn't feel the way love is supposed to feel like.' Rosa took a slurp of tea. 'Oh, I can't explain.'

'My mum says that sometimes the heart sees what's invisible to the eye.'

'Your mum and her observations.'

'I know – great, aren't they? But going back to me for a minute, after last night, I'm glad I'm still pregnant. Well, I think I'm glad I am, anyway.' Titch put her hand over her little bump. 'Let me sort these bacon sarnies and I will tell you all about it.'

Rosa munched her toasted sandwich hungrily. Between mouthfuls she said to Titch: 'To be honest, I can't really remember much about last night. Just that we heard voices arguing and then Josh galloped off to your rescue.'

'It's big, Rose.' Titch looked solemn. 'What I'm going to tell you is really big.'

'Be gentle with me, Titch. I am so hungover.'

'I don't care, I want you to know this. You know somebody accused you of running down the hill, the night of the hit and run?'

'Yes.'

'Well, it was me.' Titch lowered her eyes and looked ashamed. 'Shit! Oh, OK.'

'I can't believe that I'm telling you this. I know I can trust you, it's just that it's so awful – disgusting. I'm ashamed.'

Seeing tears welling in the girl's eyes, Rosa moved to sit next to her and took her hand.

Titch went on shakily: 'So, Lucas comes out of your place, he's a bit drunk after your Prosecco, I'm wearing a little skirt, he's in the mood and likes what he sees, I've always fancied him, so we jump in his van and shag. All pretty straightforward, all pretty slut-like, but…it gets worse.'

'It's fine, go on.' Rosa squeezed her hand.

'Seb comes by me in his van and pulls over. He must have seen us jumping out of Lucas's van, I reckon, I don't know. Anyway, I can tell he's stoned, maybe a bit pissed – it was Christmas, after all, and everyone drinks and drives around here. He tells me that Sheila Hannafore has paid him a tenner to go and get Lucas's girlfriend.'

'Go and get, as in pick up, or run her over?' Rosa was only half-serious, but she knew Sheila disliked Jasmine.

'Shit, Rosa, don't say that! I didn't even think of that. So, he offers me a lift up the hill back to Mum's. But he drives right past Mum's road and starts to put his hand up my skirt. I struggle and push him off, but he carries on, calling me names

290

and saying that I'm always after it. We reach the top of the hill by the garage, and I don't know if you know it, but there's a car park there when you can go off and walk through the woods.'

'Fuck. I think I know what's coming.'

'He raped me, Rosa.' Titch now had tears flowing down her face. 'He hurt me so badly. Afterwards, he insisted on dropping me home, even though I just wanted to run away from him – couldn't bear the sight of him. But then, as we were driving down the hill, in the headlights I suddenly saw this girl's face.' Titch shuddered, and for a moment she couldn't speak. 'I heard a massive *clonk* – and then Seb told me to get out and run. I should have stayed and helped, but I was scared and in a state. And he'd gone screeching off downhill at top speed.'

'Fuck. So I'm guessing Sheila Hannafore doesn't know he's guilty?'

'My mate Gully, who works in a car-sales place in Ulchester, he said she paid for the new red van that Seb's driving these days, as the other was crushed soon after white paint was found on a bumper. So, make of that what you will, but she must know.'

'Fuck.'

'Rosa, can you please try and say something other than fuck?'

'So, what happened last night then?'

'I was going to let it lie about the rape, especially when I found out I was pregnant – by Seb presumably, since I'd used a condom with Lucas. The last thing I would want my child to know is that he or she was a product of something so violent and awful. Can you just imagine?'

'At least they'd know where they came from, I guess… unlike me.'

'Sorry, Rose, I didn't think…'

'It's fine. Ignore me being such a self-pitying bitch, I'm just upset this has happened to you, Titch.'

'I can deal with it, but it's been eating me up lately as I thought, what if Seb went and did it to somebody else? Somebody even younger, more vulnerable? I would never forgive myself. So, in my head I decided, if I can't go through with reporting him for the rape as it's probably too late now, at least I can get him put away for the hit-and-run.'

Titch's voice wobbled. 'I left an anonymous message on the *Gazette* answerphone and somebody there must have told Seb! I know that because he phoned me last night, accusing me. I denied it, of course, but he kept saying he wanted to speak to me in person. He was kicking off so badly and I didn't want him coming into Mum's and causing a fuss, so I arranged to meet him at the back of the shop. I figured I'd be safe and could come to you if he started on me – which he did.' She rubbed her hurt knee and looked tearful.

'Blimey. Titch, you should have told me before. I really can't believe you are having his baby. Would he have done this to you if he'd known you were pregnant?'

He doesn't know I'm pregnant – and he will never know it's his,' the girl said fiercely. 'even if he or she turns out to have ginger hair.' She smiled through her tears. Then: 'I can't get rid of this little soul, not now, it's too late. And I love him or her already.' She sniffed. 'We all need someone to love, Rosa.'

Rosa wanted to cry. She hugged Titch tightly. 'Yes, you're right, we do.'

The younger girl exhaled loudly. 'I think all of this just has to be put to rest now, just like the suicides of Dotty Myers and my brother. What was it that Joe said on the radio? Closed cases, wasn't it?'

'Did you know about Dotty killing herself then?' Rosa asked. 'Surely that was many years ago.'

'You know what this town is like. We're all the cast in its very own soap opera.'

'So, would Mary have known that – about Dotty's suicide?'

'She'd certainly have heard the rumours. After all, her gran was Dotty's best friend. Why do you ask?'

'It doesn't matter.'

'Right, I'm going to take myself home and have a long bath. If the *Gazette* or the police contact me, I'll just say that it wasn't me who called. I rang from a phone box anyway, so they won't be able to trace my mobile.'

'But that means he's getting away with everything – with running Jasmine over, with rape, which has a hefty penalty by law, and with beating you up last night too! He should be locked up!' Rosa's blood boiled.

'It's fine, Rose,' Titch said, and this time she was comforting Rosa. 'A boomerang always returns to the person who throws it. Karma will get him in the end.'

'Did your mum say that too?'

'Yes, she did.'

They both laughed, and it was a release.

'Take care, Titch, and I'm here if you need me,' Rosa told her. 'Any time.'

'Likewise. Don't stress too much about Josh, either. He's a big boy. He'll do the right thing.'

Rosa bit her lip. The knowledge of just that was what was troubling her.

CHAPTER FIFTY EIGHT

The delivery man waved through the window as Rosa was coming down the stairs to open the shop.

'Rosa Larkin?'

'Yep, that's me.'

'I'll have to park up the road a bit as the back alley's blocked.' He was back in minutes, carrying a massive flat box, wrapped in sausage-dog paper and adorned with a big red bow.

'Birthday girl, I assume?' he grinned.

'It was recently, thank you. Do I need to sign?'

'No, that's all right. Can you manage, love, it's a bit heavy?'

'Yes, thanks, I'll be all right.'

Rosa put it down, quickly locked the front door, then carried the parcel very carefully upstairs. Hot was running around in and out of the wrapping paper as she ripped it off and threw it on the floor. She was delighted to see that it was a shiny new HD television, a perfect size for her living room. Half-hoping to find a note from Joe, gushing with apology, she scrabbled through the paper on the floor and saw a pink envelope addressed to *Rosalar* in black ink. Ah. She smiled as she opened it.

Birthday girl!! In all the commotion, I drove off and forgot to give you this. What a bloody mess. Will call you soon, promise. Cuddles for Hot. Slap on the arse for you. Your Joshx

Rosa held the card to her heart. 'My Josh.'

She went to the kitchen to get a knife to open the box, then cursed in pain, as it was her turn to stub her toe on the bronze sausage dog that had been mysteriously left on her doorstep, the night of her birthday.

With everything that had been going on, she had completely forgotten about the beautiful sculpture. Hurrying into the bedroom, she went to her bedside table drawer and pulled out the ring with its crumpled note. Thank heavens *that* was still safely there. Holding out her hand, she admired the sparkle of the stones as it sat snugly on her fourth finger. It was as if it had been made to measure. She picked up the note and read aloud the words in capital letters.

DON'T QUESTION THIS GIFT, FOR YOUR HEART IT WILL LIFT. I WILL REMAIN BY YOUR SIDE, HOWEVER HIGH THE TIDE. HAPPY BIRTHDAY, DEAR ROSA

The shop had been Ned and Dotty's for so many years, there just *had* to be a connection. It was time for Mary Cobb to spill some of those magic beans of hers.

The TV set-up would just have to wait until later. Rosa was carrying the box downstairs to put in the recycling when she heard the key turn in the front door lock and Titch was shouting her name in panic.

'I'm here, I'm here!' Rosa called back. 'Are you all right?'

'I am, but they've just carted Mary off in an ambulance from the Co-op; she had an oxygen mask on her face and everything.

295

Blue lights and sirens too. I'm surprised you didn't hear something.'

Rosa was stricken. 'Titch, are you busy?' she asked. 'Can you manage the shop for me for a while and keep an eye on Hot?'

'Just go, girl. I'm on it.'

Rosa waved Jacob off, who had given her a lift, then headed straight to the A&E Department of Ulchester General. A friendly-faced receptionist greeted her.

'I'm here for Mary Cobb,' Rosa said, flustered.

'Are you family?'

Rosa started to garble. 'Er…no, I'm a friend, but she's just lost her gran, and she's got a cat called Merlin, and I need to know if she's going to be all right, and whether the cat needs feeding or not, and…'

'Right. OK, calm down, love. Miss Cobb is in Resuscitation at the moment, but I will make sure somebody lets you know as soon as we have some news for you. Take a seat, and there's a coffee machine in the corridor.'

'Thank you so much.'

Rosa went and sat down. Resuscitation? She'd watched enough medical shows to know that it was serious then. She couldn't settle, so went outside and phoned Josh. The call went straight to message without even ringing. She texted Titch to say she could be a while, then went back inside and started flicking through the pages of magazines she'd never think of picking up normally. She was halfway through an article about growing your own chillies, in *Gardening Times*, when somebody called her name.

A tall, bald consultant ushered her to a room to the side of the reception desk.

'Hi, Rosa. You're Mary's friend, aren't you?'

'Yes, she doesn't have any family of her own, I don't think.'

'Well, the good news is, she's out of the woods.' Rosa breathed a sigh of relief as the doctor continued: 'She has a condition called COPD – Chronic Obstructive Pulmonary Disease – and it was a nasty attack this time. A respiratory tract infection set it off.'

'It's serious then?' Rosa had never heard of this COPD, but she knew that Mary coughed most of the time.

'Like today, it can turn nasty. We recommend "rescue drugs" to be on hand ready for an attack, but Mary obviously didn't have these at home. We have stabilised her breathing and started her on steroids and antibiotics. We will also increase the dose on her inhaler before she goes.'

'OK, thanks so much. What causes this condition?'

'In Mary's case, years of smoking. Those warnings on the cigarette packets aren't gruesome without good cause, you know.'

Rosa raised her eyes to the ceiling. 'That's awful.'

'That's reality. We do need to keep an eye on her for tonight, but she can go home in the morning. She will need a bit of nursing if you can manage to keep an eye on her.'

'Can I see her now?'

'She is very tired and will be for a few hours, so please don't stay long.'

Rosa was given the name of the ward and was directed to a private room off a corridor. A drip was feeding clear liquid through a canula into Mary's hand and she was being fed oxygen through her nose. Her head was turned to the side and in her deep slumber a small trail of dribble had run from her mouth. Rosa went to her side and gently wiped her mouth with a tissue. She then sat down next to her and held her free hand.

She felt Mary squeeze it slightly, then saw her half-open her eyes and glance at the ring, which Rosa hadn't had time to take off her finger.

'Rosa?' She managed a little smile.

'Ssh. You need to sleep.'

'Queenie was beckoning me, but it isn't my time – not yet, is it, Rosa?' Mary whispered.

Rosa bit her lip. 'No, Mary, not yet.'

Mary shut her eyes again and her breathing became deeper. Letting go of her hand, Rosa stood up, careful not to disturb the sick woman. Poor Mary. She wasn't even that old, but it seemed life had aged her before her time.

Once outside, vowing to never touch another cigarette or even have another puff of a joint again in her life, Rosa sucked in a massive breath of fresh air and went to get the bus back to Cockleberry Bay. If she was lucky, there was one due in twenty minutes.

After a full text update from Rosa on the bus, Titch was waiting in the Corner Shop's downstairs kitchen with hot cups of tea and bourbon biscuits.

'You're a good 'un, you are,' Rosa sighed gratefully. 'Thanks for holding the fort – has it been busy?'

Titch shoved down two biscuits in as many minutes. 'Trust me to get cravings for something unhealthy.' She spat biscuit crumbs as she added: 'A lot of visitors have been passing through on their Easter holidays, so the shop bell has been ringing constantly. I do wish Hot wouldn't bark each time.' She grinned. 'Oh, and cue for a drum roll, please.'

Rosa bashed her hands on the counter. 'Not the Versace tie?' she said disbelievingly. 'But the price was exorbitant!'

'Yes! What's more, I thought the dogs' heads on it were hideous – but some city slicker will be prancing around wearing that in the office on Monday.'

'Hilarious! That's Jacob for you – he insisted someone would love it and he was right. But great, that can go towards my washing-machine fund.' Rosa opened the till and handed Titch a twenty-pound note. 'And that's towards the Titchy Titch Fund. I'll do your wages as normal at the end of the week, but I really appreciate you stepping in today.'

'Thanks, Rosa – are you sure?'

Rosa thought back to all the awful bosses she had encountered during her shaky employment history. 'Course I'm sure. The Titchy Titch Fund needs filling too. Now get up the hill to Mumma Whittaker and rest those little legs of yours.'

Titch was just going out of the door when Rosa called her back. 'Would you do me a massive favour, so I don't have to go out again? I forgot to get a door key off Mary. Can you just take this bowl of crunchies and put it outside the back door of Seaspray for Merlin, please? He'll be all right with that until tomorrow.'

At the end of a busy afternoon, Rosa shut the door behind her last customer, locked it and turned the sign to Closed, then made her way slowly up the stairs. Hot was sleeping in his bed in the front room. He opened one eye and then with a little yap of a hello, closed it again. Suddenly feeling completely drained from the day's events, Rosa went to the kitchen to pour herself a glass of wine.

She tried Josh and was surprised that her call went straight through to answerphone again. He hadn't even replied to her earlier text thanking him for the TV and telling him about Mary; it wasn't like him at all. Maybe he was just busy at work or had his phone on silent, so he didn't have to suffer the wrath or hormones of Juicy Lucy?

Drink in hand, she flopped down onto the sofa. The TV sat opposite her, all ready to be set up, but she didn't even have the energy for that. Try as she might, she couldn't get the vision out of her mind of poor Mary lying in that hospital bed, all alone. They were similar in the fact they had both lost a mother, albeit in very different circumstances, but that was where the line was drawn. But for some reason which Rosa couldn't put her finger on, she was very fond of Mary Cobb, with her quirky ways and spiritual doings.

Growing up without a mother's love had made Rosa resilient, independent and somewhat streetwise in one way, but it had also made her reckless and insecure. But those were the cards she had been dealt. Now, thanks to the miraculous inheritance of the Corner Shop in Cockleberry Bay, and the gifts that had come with it, her life had been transformed.

There and then, Rosa vowed to find out who was responsible. Once Mary was better, her quest would begin – in earnest.

CHAPTER FIFTY NINE

It was a sleepy Rosa who woke from a restless slumber to find Hot lying right down the side of her with his bum in her face and his tail tickling her.

'Oi, Mr Sausage, no wonder I don't sleep.' Her adorable mutt turned himself around, licked her cheek, then shut his eyes again. She admired his crinkly neck, and soft black whiskers for a moment whilst inhaling his heavenly dog scent and his less heavenly dog breath, then checked her phone: nothing still from Josh, but there was a text from Mary.

It's Mary. Rosa loved the way she always started her texts with that. *I'm alive* (smiley face) *and I'm getting a lift back with a practice nurse from Polhampton. I forgot Merlin!* (horrified face).

But I didn't (smiley face), Rosa replied immediately.

(picture of wings) *You are an angel.*

I know. Text me when you're back.

Rosa stretched and yawned. 'Right, come on boy, let's get down that beach and have a walk. It looks like it's going to be a beautiful day.' On hearing the magic 'w' word, Hot was whiffling around, waiting for his lead and harness to go on, after his mistress had thrown on some clothes and cleaned her teeth.

After all the cold winter walks they had taken together, it

was a joy, Rosa thought happily, strolling on the beach with the sun on her face, and not having to wear a coat. Hot barked in delight as he mingled with all the other dogs out this morning. The sea was still and calm, and even the seagulls didn't seem to be crying as loudly as usual. The horizon was so straight it looked like it had been cut with scissors. It wouldn't be long before it would be possible to sunbathe, and even swim.

Despite the peaceful outlook, every time that Rosa looked out to sea now, she couldn't help but think of Ned's letters to T – and also of the distressing image of Dotty jumping to her death from West Cliffs, the very place where Ned and Queenie had found such love. Poor Dotty. What on earth must have been going through her mind as she made that final walk up to the edge?

Rosa still found it hard to believe that T was Queenie. She still hadn't seen any photos of them when they were young, but she doubted, with all the secrecy surrounding the affair, that there would be any of Ned and T together.

Easter had definitely brought many visitors to Cockleberry Bay. If she was honest, Rosa preferred the solitude of the bay out of season. However, low season didn't sell Versace ties and pay the rent, so she would just have to embrace it – and it was actually quite nice to meet new people.

She tried to call Josh again, but met with the same response. Maybe he had gone on a work trip overseas, but she was sure he would have mentioned it. If she hadn't heard from him by this evening, Rosa decided she would call his office. She knew he was probably going through hell at home, but surely a friend was what he needed right now? She didn't want to believe that Lucy was pregnant; nor did she want Josh to settle for someone who wasn't right for him. The truth was, she could not bear for him not to be in her life, not to be in her heart.

She was just picking up a ball that Hot had dropped at her feet when she noticed commotion going on, up at the Ship. Holidaymakers looked on to as two police cars screeched into the car park of the old pub. The unmissable hair and teeth of Sheila Hannafore were then in full view as she was escorted out of the front door and into one of the waiting cars.

The arrest of the wily old publican was enough of a shock for Rosa, without then seeing Seb shooting down the outside fire escape at speed and making a run towards the beach. A policeman who had been sitting in one of the cars spotted him and leapt out in hot pursuit. Rosa just managed to jump out of the way as the breathless officer trod on Seb's shoelace, causing the scruffy redhead to go flying over on to the sand.

Another uniformed policeman had now caught up and restrained Seb by cuffing his hands behind his back.

'Sebastian Watkins, I'm arresting you on suspicion of the hit-and-run incident in which Miss Jasmine Simmonds was hurt, on the evening of twenty-third December last year. You do not have to say anything, but it may harm your defence if you do not mention, when questioned, something which you later rely on in court. Anything you do say may be taken in evidence. Do you understand?'

Seb shook his head, as the policeman then shouted: 'Do you understand, Watkins?'

'Yes, now get me off this bloody beach.' Seb snarled at Rosa: 'And what are you fucking staring at?'

'Nothing, nothing at all,' she said calmly. 'I thought I just saw a boomerang, that's all.'

CHAPTER SIXTY

Rosa put Hot on his lead and on her way back up the hill, she phoned Titch. 'You can breathe again, darling girl, as it looks like Madame Hannafore and Wanker Watkins will be getting their comeuppance – and soon.'

She was just relaying what had happened, when she heard a call waiting in the background. 'Titch, sorry to be so rude, but I'm going to buzz you back. I need to talk to Josh.'

But it wasn't Josh. 'Rosa, it's Lucy,' said an imperious voice. 'Josh thinks it's for the best he doesn't come down and see you again.'

'You what? I think he'd be man enough to tell me that himself, Lucy. And I don't believe it anyway. Put him on.' But Lucy hung up.

Rosa was now steaming with anger. She immediately phoned Josh's mobile, which went straight through to answerphone again. She tried phoning his office but got his answerphone on that too. Why did nobody pick up their sodding landlines any more?

Titch managed to pacify her slightly by saying she knew it had nothing to do with Josh as their friendship was as strong as an ox – although she did think it was a bit odd that he wasn't taking calls from her. 'Look, go and see Mary,' the girl suggested, 'then call me and we will hatch a plan.'

The door to Seaspray Cottage was on the latch when Rosa arrived. Mary told her to come straight in and shut the door behind her. Rosa jumped, as she was expecting her to be up in bed and not in Queenie's rocking chair in the kitchen.

Rosa smiled at her. 'Hey, how are you feeling?'

'As if I've had the air sucked out of me. But so much better than I was, dear.'

'I thought you just had asthma?'

'It's a little bit worse than that, but I'll manage. I should have had the right drugs here ready as I felt an attack coming on, but somehow I wasn't in the right frame of mind. I was all over the place. I have them all now, so it's panic over.' She looked at Rosa's hand and said, 'Do you like it?'

'Yes, it's lovely. We need to talk, don't we, Mary?'

'After what just happened to me, yes, we do, Rosa. I have been kept in the dark far too often and for far too long, and I don't want the same for you.'

Mary coughed and Rosa could see she was trembling. 'Get us a nice cup of tea, dear,' Mary said, 'and come and sit down with me.'

The tea was brought, along with a couple of ginger biscuits for Mary to nibble on, and after a little while she was less shaky and ready to talk.

'I was a new-born baby when Gran became my mum. That's why she resented me at times. She was fifty, felt too old to bring up a young kid like me, but she didn't have a choice. And every time she looked into my green eyes, she felt that she was looking into the eyes of her dear, lost daughter. She even chose my name, Mary, to be like my mother's – Maria.'

'Did you know your father?'

'Yes, but when he got in his car to drive home from the hospital, the night my mum died, he had a blow-out in his car which led to a fatal accident. Well, that's what Gran told me anyway. Perhaps he didn't want to live, even though he now had a baby daughter – me.' Mary's lips quivered and she took a puff on her inhaler.

'Oh my God, it gets worse.' Rosa put a hand over her mouth in horror. 'But what about Ned? He must have helped. He was Maria's dad, after all, right? Tell me the truth, Mary, please.'

'Yes, I did know that Ned was my grandad, but Gran didn't want anyone to know that, as she was so ashamed of the affair. Queenie only gave me crumbs of information, but what I could gather is that after Dotty's death, she went through a dark period of grieving, afflicted by feelings of guilt and regret. Being pregnant as well must have been just terrible for her.' Mary looked at Rosa. 'Until I found her suicide note the other day, you see, I didn't realise Dotty had taken her own life. I thought it was an accident. No wonder Gran had been in such a state.'

Mary took another sup of tea then put her cup down. She turned to Rosa. 'When I got older, I did used to talk to Grandad Ned; we spent many happy hours together, up on your little outside balcony. Gran carried on telling Ned that she didn't love him any more and that Maria wasn't his child until the day he died. But he didn't believe her. He knew, all right. Maria was the spit of him. He did everything in his power to be with Queenie, but she wouldn't have it, so he would help in different ways. Practical ways, so she'd never want for money or repairs on this house.'

Mary concluded quietly, 'They never had any other lovers, they just had their own special relationship. It was probably better than most conventional ones, in fact, as they both loved each other to the core. Queenie just couldn't allow herself to

306

love him openly, thanks to her guilt, even after the Cockleberry rumour mill had died its own death.'

'That's sad.'

'Not really, because in a way they were still together; they just didn't share a bed.'

'But sad for Maria, not knowing her dad was Ned, don't you think?'

'He told me he treated my mother just like he would a daughter anyway, they loved each other, but when she died he said it was like a rocket blowing up both his and Queenie's lives. But neither of them could give up or run away, as they had me to look after. Grandad Ned said I saved their souls. And, yes, fundamentally Queenie forever struggled without Maria, but I know deep down she loved me too.' Mary's voice cracked.

Rosa put her hand on hers. 'She loved you fiercely, Mary. I could tell.'

'Really?'

'Yes. Truly, madly, deeply. I struggle to understand the feeling myself, but when I see it, I know it.'

Mary's eyes were full of tears. 'Ned left you the shop, Rosa,' she said.

Rosa could feel a lump rising in her throat.

'It was me who came into your flat – I kept the keys, you see. I tried to find the letters before you did. I can't believe he hid them so well, but Queenie knew they'd be there. I also took the necklace.'

'And what about the ring and the bronze statue? Was that you too?'

'The statue of Hot was from Queenie and me, for your birthday, dear. We've been looking out for you, Rosa.'

'The hit-and-run alibi? Sending me to Joe's house?'

Mary nodded. 'All of it. Queenie didn't have eye problems,

she wore the dark glasses in the house to make pretend her sight was bad, and the black scarf when she was out of it, so that people would not notice her. She wanted to be your ears and eyes when you arrived down here, so you wouldn't be afraid.'

Tears were now running down Rosa's face. 'Tell me the rest, I have to know.'

'I don't drink because I am an alcoholic, Rosa. Gran was hard to live with, as I've explained, and I didn't have a mother's love. I just used to be a barfly in the Ship. So, one night, after a massive drunken row, about nothing in particular, I took some money out of the teapot where Queenie used to hide it, packed a small bag, then got on the train and went to live in London. Can you imagine how naïve I was? But I was twenty years old and always drunk, so I didn't see danger – or if I did then, I would probably have welcomed it, to help dull the pain. I didn't give a damn. All I cared about was where my next drink was coming from.'

Mary rocked back in her chair. Rosa blew her nose and carried on listening intently.

'There were many drunken nights and many men. But one morning when I woke up in a bed in somebody's bedsit, in what turned out to be Clapham, I was bleeding and sore between my legs. I was also so hungover I couldn't move. I knew if I reported it, it would never stand up in court, as I didn't even remember who the man was or if actually we'd had consenting sex. I also knew that I couldn't put Queenie through anything else. She'd suffered enough.'

Mary heaved a sigh as she thought back on her life. 'I didn't even tell her or Ned that I was pregnant. I had the baby and got myself on benefits and in council accommodation. And even though I cut right down on alcohol through my pregnancy, and didn't even fancy smoking, once I had the baby I started doing both, just like I'd done before. The health visitor had alerted social services: I was being monitored and I knew that.'

Mary took Rosa by the hands, her face contorted. 'But one night, I got so drunk that I dropped my baby and she knocked her beautiful little face on the edge of the kitchen cupboard.' The woman was now in floods of tears. 'It was only a little knock, just enough to make her cheek bleed, just enough to form a scar in the shape of a perfect little lightning bolt.'

CHAPTER SIXTY ONE

Rosa knew people were staring at her tear-ravaged face when she got on the train at Exeter, but she didn't care. She sneaked into a first-class compartment and placed Hot on the seat next to her in his basket.

Hours passed; she did not notice. Approaching London, the guy in the seat opposite gently nudged her arm. 'We're at Paddington, love.'

Rosa came to her senses with a jump, hurrying with Hot to the outside of the station as she could tell he was dying for a pee. She stared around her and took several deep breaths of the dirty London air, feeling overwhelmed by the noise and traffic after her months in Cockleberry Bay.

As soon as she had received confirmation that Mary Cobb was her mother, and had learned the circumstances of her conception, birth and early upbringing, Rosa just couldn't cope with the tidal wave of feelings. She needed to get away, to try to absorb this revelation, and most urgently of all, she needed to share the news with the most important person in her life: Josh.

It was so bittersweet; her own birth mother was alive and well and she had become friends with her! It seemed so surreal. And how had Mary and Queenie traced her? There were still questions to be asked, but maybe now she knew enough. And even though part of the story was hard to bear, when Rosa thought of her lonely, motherless childhood, eventually, when the time was right, her mother and great-grandmother had come to find her, to put things right, the way they saw it.

It all made sense now, the reason why they hadn't wanted her to sell the Corner Shop; it was a massive part of everyone's life and they saw her inheriting it as mending some of the wrongs of the past. If Queenie hadn't died, Rosa knew that Mary would have been forbidden to tell her the truth. But life doesn't work like that, it's all written. Rosa had to know who her mum was, she deserved that ultimate peace, so she could now carry on and live a happy and fulfilled life.

Ethel Beanacre's head bobbed up from nowhere as Rosa knocked on Josh's door.

'Here, duck, where have you been all this long time, eh? And what are you doing here now?' Hot started barking as their nosy ex-neighbour lowered her voice and carried on, 'Your bloke has got hisself a fancy piece.' The old lady screwed up her face. 'Blonde tart, shrieks worse than you ever did when she's drunk.'

'Is that so? Oh well, I'll just have to take my chances,' Rosa replied politely, thinking, who needs the BBC when we've got you, eh, Ethel? She had lifted her hand to knock again, when Lucy opened the door. She immediately went to shut it in Rosa's face.

'What the fuck? *Josh!*' Rosa shouted.

On hearing her voice, Josh came running to the door. Rosa threw herself into his arms, sobbing. Hot still on his lead, jumped up at both of them.

'Mary…Mary,' she wept, and couldn't say any more.

Josh led her inside, away from Ethel's inquisitive gaze. 'It's OK, Rosa, I'm here now. What's happened?'

Just feeling the warmth of Josh's hug and hearing his soothing voice made her feel safe and cared for.

'M-m-m-Mary is my m-m-mum.'

'Oh Rosa.' He squeezed her tighter.

'Ned was her grandad, Queenie's lover. He left her the shop to leave to me. Ned was my great-grandad, Josh.'

'Look, come through and sit down,' Josh said tenderly. 'Lucy, put the kettle on.'

'Yes, Lucy put the kettle on,' Rosa spat. She turned to Josh. 'What's all this about you not wanting to come and see me again down in Devon?'

Josh frowned. 'I don't know what you are talking about.'

'I haven't been able to call you either. I've tried loads of times and it goes straight to voicemail. I've texted you too.'

'Here.' Lucy went to grab his phone.

'No.' Rosa was swifter. She picked it up. 'Let me.' She looked at it for a moment and then said: 'So you blocked my number on Josh's phone, did you?'

Josh looked at Lucy in disbelief. 'Did you?'

'I thought it was women who were supposed to want a bit of rough?' Lucy said spitefully and flounced towards the door.

'What did you say?' Josh stood up.

'Well, she's not exactly smooth around the edges, is she? And with no parents or family to mention either, what sort of moral code will she have?'

Rosa stood up. 'I'll have you know, my mother is worth ten of you – and do you know what? Maybe I haven't got long blonde hair, false nails, false eyelashes, bits of filler in my lips OR false tits. But what I have got is a heart. And when you strip all of that other shit down, isn't that what we are made of, really?

Everybody's heart looks the same, Lucy, it's just some are colder than others.'

Lucy stood open-mouthed.

'And how's the pregnancy going?' Rosa demanded.

'Er...I think I'd better...'

'There is no pregnancy, is there?' Rosa challenged her.

'Lucy?' Pale-faced, Josh went over to her and stared right into her eyes.

'I didn't want to lose you...to her.' Lucy could hardly speak for anger.

'So, you told me a blatant lie? About something that major?' Josh was outraged. 'I've been worried sick about this. About what we should do, moving forward – and it's all been a complete and utter sham. Get out, you horrible person. Collect your things another time, but for now, just leave my house and get out of my sight.'

Her face ugly with rage and chagrin, Lucy grabbed her coat and handbag and without looking at either of them, went out and slammed the door behind her as hard as she possibly could.

Josh was visibly shaking. 'If she was a bloke, I kid you not, I would have decked her.' He looked at Rosa. 'How did you know she wasn't pregnant?'

'I didn't for sure, but you can't kid a kidder. And after what she did, having the cheek to phone me to say you didn't want to see me again, well, I knew she was up to something.'

Hot nuzzled into Josh's legs.

'Aw, look, he's missed you.'

Josh reached down to pick the dachshund up and rub his face in his smooth coat, then put his other arm around Rosa.

'And God, I've missed you – so much. I didn't realise she'd blocked your number. I just thought you were busy, and I've been so wrapped up in working out what to do for the best with her…' Josh hung his head and Hot licked his nose. Not knowing whether to laugh or cry, Josh managed to say, 'I'm sorry, Rosa. So very sorry.'

'You're forgiven – this once.'

A moment passed, then: 'Josh?'

'Rosalar?' Josh put Hot down on the floor, then turned to Rosa and took both her hands in his.

She moved slightly away from him, but kept hold of his hands. 'I'm not good at this relationship lark,' she told him, 'but I do know one thing.'

'Which is?'

'My world is a brighter place when you are in it. You make me laugh, you see things in me that other people don't. You believe in me. You bring me furniture when I need it – and the TV's great, thanks. You are just bloody brilliant and if I knew what this love thing was supposed to feel like, well then, I think… I think, Joshua Smith, that I love you. Whatever that means.'

Josh let go of her, walked across the room and with his back to her, ran his hands through his hair.

'I get it, if you don't feel the same way.' Rosa was on a roll now. 'But I had to say it. I can't bear to see you with another woman. I know one hundred per cent, that I want to be with you.'

Josh, with eyes brimming, turned around. 'Not many people can drive this six-foot-two rugger bugger to tears, Rosa Larkin. Now, come here, you.'

He pulled her towards him, bent down and gave her the most toe-curling kiss she had ever experienced in her life.

When they eventually broke free, breathless, Josh kissed the tip of Rosa's nose.

Then, trying not to be distracted by the sight and clattering sounds of Hot, who was stretched up on his short back legs

314

and rummaging beneath the kitchen-bin lid to try and get at a slice of last night's pizza, Josh just managed to say: 'And for the record – and whatever it means, I think I love you too,' before they both burst out laughing.

EPILOGUE

They picked a sunny September Saturday for the wedding. Just a simple unconventional affair. A short service at the church in Cockleberry Bay and a small reception at the Lobster Pot.

Mary had lost weight, and as mother of the bride she wore a beautiful new dress, green to match her eyes. Now that her health had improved, she would be able to walk Rosa down the aisle, her back straight and her head held high with pride. And Hot was a splendid sight in his little doggy bow-tie, fresh off the shelves of the Corner Shop. The vicar kept a slightly nervous eye on him as the sausage dog sniffed at the pews.

Josh stood at the altar, looking more handsome than ever before, and Titch, bless her, having nearly reached her due date, appeared about ready to pop, her mum supportively by her side. Jacob, Raffaele and the in-laws all gazed on, their hankies at the ready.

And Rosa? Well, Rosa just looked happy.

Standing at the church door in a dazzling pool of sunlight, waiting for the right moment to walk down the aisle, she placed the gold pendant necklace into Mary's hands.

'"Wear it on a special day and think of me", wasn't that what Queenie said? I bet she saw today in those tea leaves, you know.'

'You can count on that,' Mary said with a fond smile, fastening the necklace around her daughter's neck. 'And I just love the fact that her ring is your engagement ring now too.'

Rosa rested her head on Mary's shoulder for a moment, saying dreamily, 'To Queenie, Ned, Maria and Dotty. Let's hope they are all having a party – where the sky touches the sea.'

Hearing the first resounding chords of the organ playing The Wedding March, Mary said hastily, 'I'll second that, my love, but please, just answer one question. Who do you think you'll pass the shop on to?'

'Let's get me married first, eh, Mother?' Rosa placed a hand over her slightly rounded belly. 'Then we'll see…'

ENJOYED THIS BOOK?
READ THE SEQUEL

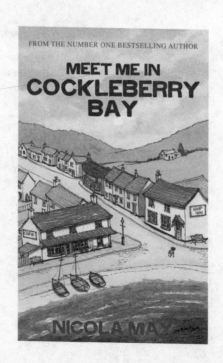

MEET ME IN COCKLEBERRY BAY

The cast of the runaway bestseller *The Corner Shop in Cockleberry Bay* is back – including Rosa, Josh, Mary, Jacob, Sheila, new mum Titch and, last but by no means least, Hot, the adorable dachshund.

Newly wed, and with her inherited corner shop successfully up and running, Rosa Smith seems to have all that anyone could wish for. But the course of true love never did run smooth and Rosa's suspicions that her husband is having an affair have dire consequences. Reaching rock bottom before she can climb back up to the top, fragile Rosa is forced to face her fears, addiction and jealousy head on.

With a selection of meddling locals still at large, a mystery fire and Titch's frantic search for the real father of her sick baby, the second book in this enchanting series takes us on a further unpredictable journey.

BY THE SAME AUTHOR

Working It Out
Star Fish
The School Gates
Christmas Spirit
Better Together
Let Love Win
The SW19 Club
Love Me Tinder

The School Gates won Best Author Read at the Festival of Romance in 2012, as did *Christmas Spirit* in 2014.

Nicola May likes to write about love, life and friendship in a realistic way, describing her novels as 'chicklit with a kick'. She lives near Ascot racecourse with her black-and-white rescue cat, Stan. Her hobbies include watching films that involve a lot of swooning, crabbing in South Devon, eating flapjacks – and, naturally, enjoying a flutter on the horses.

Find out more about the author at **www.nicolamay.com**. She is also on Twitter **@nicolamay1**, Instagram as **author_nicola** and has her own Facebook Book Page.